Praise for *Love Orange*

'Imagine Richard Yates becoming fascinated by Donald Antrim before writing *Revolutionary Road* and you'll have some idea of *Love Orange*. At turns funny, discomfiting, and darkly harrowing, Randall's debut is real life inscribed upon the page. The classic American family of countless TV dramas and comedies is here fractured against the hard fulcrum of the current age. One of the most satisfying novels you will read this year. This book rules'

Christian Kiefer, author of *Phantoms*

'In *Love Orange* we see the American nuclear family in meltdown, a phenomenon Natasha Randall describes with wisdom, wit, and a lot of heart. I enjoyed every minute of it'

Chris Power, author of *Mothers*

'As an acclaimed translator of Russian novels, Natasha Randall has a fine-tuned sense of the absurd, and a wonderfully original way of seeing the world. A stunningly accurate portrayal of American society, shining with vivid dialogue and observation'

Chloe Aridjis, author of *Sea Monsters*

'[T]he first novel by this acclaimed translator is an exuberant, comic, irresistibly dark examination of contemporary anxieties'

Vanity Fair

D1382417

Natasha Randall is a writer and translator, living in London. Her writing and critical work has appeared in the *Times Literary Supplement*, the *Los Angeles Times Book Review*, *BookForum*, the *New York Times* and many others. *Love Orange* is her first novel.

LOVE ORANGE

Natasha Randall

riverrun

First published in Great Britain in 2020 by riverrun
This paperback edition published in Great Britain in 2021 by

riverrun

An imprint of

Quercus Editions Limited
Carmelite House
50 Victoria Embankment
London EC4Y 0DZ

An Hachette UK company

A CIP catalogue record for this book is available
from the British Library

PB 978 1 52940 460 9
EBOOK 978 1 52940 458 6

10 9 8 7 6 5 4 3 2 1

Typeset by CC Book Production
Printed and bound in Great Britain by Clays Ltd, Elcograf S.p.A.

For Antonia

CHAPTER I

JENNY TINKLEY COULDN'T SEE any criminals on the streets of Bentonville – she really couldn't see anyone at all. There were big, square cars shifting here and pausing there, obeying the traffic lights that dangled above the wide streets. 'No criminals. No drug dealers, not like in the city,' the realtor had been telling her, with one hand lifted off the steering wheel, fluttering her fingers at the gentle population of vehicles beyond the windscreen. A small russet bird caught Jenny's attention as it landed on the sidewalk nearby. It looked up, and checked some diagonals before directing its little eye straight at her, a tiny black point contracting and expanding. When the bird darted off, Jenny thought it had perhaps been trying to deliver a caution to her.

Inside the car, an air freshener swung from the rear-view mirror between them, and Jenny supposed from its shape, it was some kind of berry, though it looked more like a mashed brain or a fleshy skin growth. The spreading odour of its tinny chemistry turned her stomach.

Jenny opened her window quietly sucking in some air, as they idled at a stop sign. The sharp-faced realtor, whose voice had been droning in vicious harmony with the engine's hum, interrupted her sales pitch to say that Jenny really didn't need to open the window, that 'the air inside the car is conditioned, honey'. And the woman pressed the button by her side to close her passenger's window. With that, she pointed at a large sign positioned in front of a gift shop – interchangeable black lettering demanded: REMEMBER THAT WRAPPING MAKES IT A GIFT. THANK YOU.

Where were all the people? Jenny's gaze was pulled to the brick edge of the drive-thru coffee place. There was something moving there. As they glided towards a stop sign, Jenny could see around to the other side of the building where some teenagers had gathered by the Dazzlebucks. They looked like a flock of cockatoos: fluffy white females leaning against a wall, stuffed into tight jeans, brandishing bright fingernails. The males bobbed and weaved before them with parachutes for trousers and swirling patterns shaved into their hair. The realtor glanced over at Jenny, leaning forward a little, looking into Jenny's face.

'What I want to know is, how do their denim jeans not fall right off? Are there safety pins? . . . I never understood that. A lack of belts. Maybe that's what it is. People aren't buying belts anymore.'

'Heh,' Jenny smiled.

'They've been causing a little trouble recently, those young people, I'll tell you,' said the realtor. 'I mean, this town has so little trouble that even the ti-ni-est little events feel like a big deal.' She showed Jenny a pinch with her fingers and huffed a deep laugh.

'Well, anyway,' she began again. Jenny thought that the realtor seemed to be enjoying herself now, eyes dancing, lips curling, as she checked her rear-view mirror, veering way off the script for the house she was trying to sell to the Tinkleys. 'Apparently, they all downloaded an app. You know, an app? Well, it was an app for the weejee. You know the weejee? It's supernatural.'

Jenny looked at the woman, confused but nodding. 'Like a Ouija board?'

'Right. That's it. Exactly,' and she started chuckling. 'They scared the jeebies out of theirselves, had to call Father Brian at St Peter's in the middle of the night and get him over with holy water, they were so freaked out.'

Jenny laughed and shook her head. 'Oh goodness.'

'Yeah, well, regular priests don't do exorcisms, so all he really did was to tell them to delete the app and go to bed. But someone told me they're all still worried that they're going to disappear when a satanic fog rolls into Bentonville on the twenty-eighth of August.'

Jenny couldn't think of anything to say.

'Teenagers,' the realtor said, flapping a hand. 'Gotta love 'em.'

THEY COASTED ALONG MAIN Street in the realtor's large, wide car, rolling past strip malls and gas stations. 'There are drive-thrus in Bentonville for just about anything you might need,' the realtor told her. Jenny could see that for herself; you could buy coffee, tacos or noodles, you could withdraw cash. 'You can even fill a prescription without getting out of your car,' the realtor beamed.

'Watch,' said the woman as she pulled into Bentonville Pharmacy's drive-thru lane. An electronic jingle sounded as they drove over a bump at the back of the pharmacy. The silver-haired pharmacist looked up from his wad of prescriptions and opened the sliding drive-thru window: 'How can I help?' It wasn't a cheery phrase; he said it with gravity. Jenny recognised in him the wisdom of pharmacists. He had to lean out of his window to hear them. She could just about see his clean chin and the collar of his blue lab-coat.

'Got any magic pills to make us rich today, Doc?' The realtor looked back at Jenny and winked. 'If only, right?' Jenny could see that the realtor had a lot of long teeth, and that there was a piece of pink gum clenched between them on one side.

Mr Salton had the keys to the house, the realtor explained. 'I'm not here to get my crazy pills,' she said, shrieking a laugh into the air between them, throwing the gearstick into PARK.

As the realtor and the pharmacist exchanged greetings, Jenny looked at Mr Salton's dry knuckles, his clean fingers lightly holding a prescription pad. She tried to imagine the worst pharmaceutical problems that Mr Salton had brought to him by the people of Bentonville but all she could come up with was haemorrhoids and foot fungus. Maybe pinworms, someone's kids must have pinworms, she thought. Some of those teenagers probably had chlamydia or HPV. Jenny kind of wished that Mr Salton was showing her around town instead of this mouthy realtor.

'Hope you like Maple Drive,' the man chimed, hunching over, trying to see past the realtor into the car. 'It's a cul-de-sac . . .' Jenny and the realtor nodded at him as they rolled away. Jenny raised her hand in a half-wave. He was turning to the next car as it pulled up to his window. The realtor pressed the brakes before turning onto the street and held up the keys, half looking towards her passenger and jingling them at Jenny's face: 'He's your neighbour,' she said.

HANK, JENNY'S HUSBAND, WAS standing on the lawn, studying the window frames of the house when they arrived. The price hadn't yet been agreed.

'The house is Arts and Crafts with a Contemporary Twist, as I'm sure you will see,' said the woman, grappling with the doorknob and twisting the key in the lock. 'And that means . . .' The door swept open. 'That means quality.' As they entered, Jenny could see there was a lot of wood-like panelling inside. 'Some of it is actually wood,' the realtor boasted. 'And the parts that aren't – well, it's just more hygienic, isn't it?'

'Needs some work,' said Hank.

'No, sir, it doesn't,' she countered. 'It's brand new, everything made to order . . . Take a look around, Mrs Tinkley,' the realtor announced at her.

Hank gave Jenny a look that warned her not to be too enthusiastic. The realtor turned on the ceiling fan. 'Nice fan,' Jenny said, and peered up the stairs. A brown cuckoo clock looking down from the top of the stairs was ticking but told the wrong time. Jenny hoped the cuckoo would pop out while they were there – she'd never actually seen one before; she'd thought they were just in cartoons.

'Mrs T?' the realtor was calling to her from a room off the kitchen.

Jenny went towards the voice, and came upon the realtor opening the washing machine in the utility room. She felt a streak of disappointment down the centre of her chest.

'I know you'll appreciate this,' the woman said, looking inside the drum. 'It's the quietest machine on the market,' she said. 'The spin cycle is silent,' she whispered.

Jenny walked up to the machine and looked inside. It was a shiny chamber and there was a lone grey sock pressed up into the corner of the cylinder. Jenny let out a short chuckle-grunt. 'Stuck in a drum.'

The realtor looked into the machine again. 'Stock-what? Hah, a sock! Now how did that get there?' She rolled her eyes and smiled a row of teeth and gum.

Jenny's gullet was tight and her voice was thin. 'I hate that the spin cycle is silent.' She turned away and walked out of the little laundry room.

The realtor paused, and then her painted lips spread into a smile again: 'Oh, I get it, you don't like doing the laundry. I hear ya, sister,' she said, and followed her out.

AFTER COMPLAINING ABOUT THE lack of natural light in the dining room and the angle of the staircase, Hank got a pretty good deal from the realtor and the Tinkleys moved into the house on Maple Drive several weeks later, on 1st April 2014, with two young boys, and a pet goldfish. They would have so much more room than they did in the city. And it would be safer here for the kids, who were just seven and twelve years old and had been growing up too fast in the thrumming cynicism of Philadelphia. The first thing that Jenny did was to stick glow-in-the-dark stars onto the ceilings of the boys' rooms. She put scented candles in the master bedroom. She bought some easy-care cacti from the local superstore to punctuate the windowsills.

In those early weeks, Jenny thought the house smelled a little like adhesive, and a little like car oil. Hank said that car oil did not smell like that and that it was probably off-gassing from the new carpets. But it did seem that the house had been glued together in places. The skirting boards were plastic and didn't quite fit against the wall. The kitchen cupboards had some kind of veneer, with tiny upturned edges already threatening to peel away. Everything was dark brown, and though the consistency of this was pleasing, the colour made it all look heavy – which was odd since the exact opposite was true.

Hank Tinkley surveyed the house over and over again those first few days, opening closets, examining the plumbing, testing the hinges of things. The third night, in the dark, as they lay in bed, smelling and listening to their new house, he declared that he would make their Contemporary Arts and Crafts house into a 'smart house'.

'Arts, Crafts and . . . Technology,' he said.

Hank told Jenny how the house would work, how much better

7

their lives would be. The temperature would be regulated, and lights would switch on at a clap. The fridge would know to make more ice in the summertime. You could regulate the heating from your smartphone. The house would recognise your voice.

'Whose voice? . . . My voice?' Jenny asked.

Hank persevered with his technological explanations in the dark but she only heard snippets: 'Protocols . . . Network controller . . . Domotics . . .' She knew the answer. The thing, the house-being, might recognise her voice, but her words would be like pinballs in an arcade game, buffeted by the grammar of the machine.

'There is a hierarchy of devices . . .'

She would have to learn a new set of prompts just to do what she had already been doing: the feeding, the washing, the noticing, the containing.

'Some controllers initiate messages, and some are only "slave devices", which means they just carry and respond to messages.'

'I carry and respond to messages,' Jenny said into the dark bedroom.

'Oh, come on, Jen, this is supposed to lighten the load – can you just get on board here?'

Jenny tipped her head backwards on the pillow and reached for air with her lungs, her nostrils flaring slightly, and then she held her breath, hoping to inflate herself a little bit from inside. Her ribs, the bars of bone that kept her heart in place, pinched and resisted.

'Yeah, honey, I know what you mean,' she said, releasing her breath and turning over to face him. 'The washing machine has a silent spin,' she offered.

CHAPTER 2

LUKE TINKLEY ENTERED THE kitchen from the basement. The basement was the only place in the house that Hank hadn't managed to make 'smart' in the year since they moved there, and Luke, who was eight years old, had created his playroom there.

'We need to think in geological time, which is not normal time,' said Luke, as he released a handful of white rock samples onto the tablecloth. Jenny mustered a faint smile and turned back to the screen of her tablet, where she was looking at pictures of celebrities who had aged badly. Luke slid onto a chair at the kitchen table next to her.

'You . . . are the bones of dead insects smashed together,' he said to the rocks, blowing dust from them.

She smiled again as she read. A ding from the microwave, and an electronic female voice: 'It is the third of April, two thousand and fifteen. The time is six eighteen p.m.. Dinner is ready.'

The voice was caring and earnest, and low and calm.

9

Hank entered and harrumphed into his chair, putting both palms on the plaid tablecloth.

'Home, tell Jesse to come to the kitchen. He has to exit his game,' Hank said.

'Contacting Jesse,' the house-voice confirmed.

'Luke, clean up the rocks. The water is ready,' Hank said.

Luke gave a big blink of acknowledgement, swept the rocks into his open palm and pushed them into a pocket.

The water-drinking before dinner was something that Hank invented after going to a mindfulness workshop the year before. It had been part of his job training as a health-products sales associate. He had a different job now at a company called FINDASERVE but that didn't matter: you're usually thirsty when you're hungry, he told the family.

'Yes. I'm coming.' They heard Jesse's high voice from the dotted panel of the speaker. But his voice had recently started breaking and he was always striving for the deeper register. 'I'm just logging off,' he growled.

THEY BREATHED LOUDLY WHILE they were sipping their water. Sipping promoted the absorption of *prana*, Hank told them. Plus the point of the water and the breathing was that it would concentrate your mind for the meal and therefore you would not overeat. And, he told them, everyone knows overeating causes cancer. Hank was the loudest breather since he had mastered *ujai* breathing. Jesse sounded more like he was imitating someone snoring. Jenny was quieter than everyone, but she seemed to be getting some benefit from it since her eyes were closed through most of the water course. Luke took a little zephyr breath between sips, but only when he remembered.

Jesse took a final gulp, and Luke did the same, adding a little smacking sound and an 'ahh'. Hank looked at them askance. He knew they didn't understand the importance of hydration. But it was for their own good, one day they'd see.

'So, kids, lentil casserole for dinner. Does that sound good?' Jenny said, and both she and Hank got up to bring the casserole and plates to the table. At Hank's instigation, the Tinkleys had been flirting with vegetarianism for several months now, although Hank couldn't resist the occasional hotdog, and Jenny couldn't really think up many appetising meals that didn't involve meat. She did, however, sometimes suggest that they become dairy-free. 'I know what it's like to produce milk from your own body, and it's harder than it looks,' she told the family, but they didn't really hear her. 'It's like draining a mother of her marrow. And they do it with a machine.'

At the kitchen counter, Hank lifted the casserole, sniffed it, grimaced and put it down again.

'Fuck's sake, Hank, you haven't even tasted it,' Jenny said softly while their backs were turned from the table.

Hank flashed her an inkling of a winning smile. 'Alright, Jen.'

Back at the table, he launched into the children.

'So, what's for homework this weekend, Luke?' Hank pitched a forkful of casserole into his mouth.

'It's about math.' His young voice was sonorous and high.

'And how's that going for ya?' Hank was chomping his noodles as he spoke.

'Okay.'

'You don't sound too convinced there. Need some help?'

'Well, I'm not sure you can. Can help, I mean. It's a conundrum I have.'

'Oh well, I can certainly try . . .' Hank set his fork face-down on the lip of his plate.

'Ok-aay, you asked for it . . .' Luke pushed half of his casserole pile to the edge of his plate in gentle, arcing fork-sweeps. With his fork, he pointed to the food. 'When you want to add something or take away something, are you counting the numbers or the spaces in between them?'

His brother mouthed a snide *What're you talking about?* at which Luke glared and continued:

'From zero to one is the stuff inside one. Like you take a round hole called zero and you can make it into one orange.'

Hank gave him a look that said *I'm taking you seriously, son.* 'Well . . .'

'I mean, it's hard to know. Like, is two at the end of the second part of stuff? . . . They make you feel like two starts after the number two. You have to remember number names but you're supposed to forget that they are talking about places. Places where the numbers are. Or maybe I'm just crazy.'

Jenny slid a flattened hand down the table in his direction and

patted the tablecloth. 'You're not crazy, baby. Don't ever say that.'
She patted it again.

'You need to stop biting your nails, Jen,' said Hank, looking at
Jenny's dry hand as he got up to leave the table. He held the back
of his chair: 'Luke, numbers count stuff, okay? It's how you know
how much stuff you have.' Hank raised a finger and pointed at each
family member in turn, starting with himself. 'One, two, three, four.'

'So you're saying that Mom is renamed "four" and the air between
us is like a vacuum,' Luke said.

'Hah, you got me. Okay, what about this?' Hank raised his finger
again and started again with himself. 'First, Second, Third, Fourth.'

ON FRIDAYS, GRANDMA AND Grandpa called in on Skype. The
screen showed them from the waist up, sitting side by side, with
hands in their laps. Jesse tried to tell them that they were not having
their picture taken, that they could move around during a phone
call. Hank once had to tell them to adjust the view-cam, though he
didn't say it was because you could see up Grandma's dress to the
tops of her roll-up stockings. At that, Grandpa had to adjust the
masking tape he used to trace lines in their front room around the
viewable area of the Skype call. Neither grandparent would move
outside the masking tape while the session was active. It was okay,
Jesse explained, if one of them needed to go to the bathroom or get
some coffee while they were live.

But Grandpa said, 'It's alright, I like it here. In the tape. It's good.'

Grandpa would ask, 'You got good neighbours there? They good people? You keep an eye out though,' he said. 'I hear that people are tapping into those wires and listening in on folks. They had it on the news.'

'Oh, I wouldn't worry, Grandpa, we have very nice neighbours,' said Luke.

'And those people, I'll tell you, will never tell you what they're thinking, but they sure want to find out what you're thinking.'

'Hm-m.'

'And how much money you have too. Don't tell them that.'

When Grandpa started with his lecturing on all the people out there that are out to get you, the Tinkleys drifted off one by one with weak promises that they'd be 'back in a minute'. Hank could barely stand the sound of his father's voice. It was often just Luke left talking to them. He asked Grandma why she called the refrigerator a 'frigidaire'. He also asked her why they put plastic coverings on their sofas. After a while, he would force Grandpa to say things that he'd rather not.

'Don't you think Grandma looks beautiful in her blue dress today, Grandpa?'

'Well, sure, it's a nice dress.'

'Aren't you lucky that you married Grandma? She's such a good cooker of meatloaf and lasagne.'

'Yes. Grandma is a good cook ... Your mother cook lasagne, Luke?'

'Yeah, I guess so,' he answered. 'Sometimes the fridge tells her recipes and she tries to make them.'

'The frigidaire knows recipes?'

'Yeah, it tells you what you can cook from what you have in the fridge. It's mostly stir-fry stuff. Like tofu stir-fry. With, like, broccoli.'

'Well, isn't that something. A thinking fridge. That recommends tofu.'

As much as he might chat with them on Skype, Jenny was aware that Luke hated visiting his grandparents. He didn't say it, he might not have had the words for it, but she knew it was something to do with that generation's affinity for synthetic materials. You walked up their front path on a clear plastic mat that covered the paving stones, a sheet of clear plastic was moulded to the tabletops, furniture was plastic coated too, or sticky with some kind of vinyl. The carpet had a polyester sheen, their Christmas trees were never real. Luke would get a funny feeling in his stomach, and be offered a bright blue popsicle.

'A bright blue popsicle!' he would say, shrinking away. 'What flavour is bright blue anyway – cornflower?'

IN HIS BASEMENT PLAYROOM, Luke liked to line things up. Along one wall, there was a stack of paper, a pile of wood-chips, a bucket of water and a small section of tree trunk, all in a row. It was the paper process. Another wall had a pile of wild cotton, a mound of cotton balls, a picture of a spinning wheel, a spool, some thread, an embroidery frame, some knitting needles and a bolt of fabric. The fabric process. Two library stacks jutted out from under the basement stairs, which contained the multi-tiered processes for making plastics and smelting metals. A Dunlop poster on the wall explained how rubber comes from gum trees. This was Luke's archive.

'I swear he's spectral, or whatever they call it,' Hank said to Jenny as he sat down to watch TV after dinner. 'Did you see? He lined up a bunch of rocks.' Jenny looked around to make sure the boys weren't within earshot.

'Shit, Hank, he's not autistic. Just leave him alone.' And then: 'Mrs Paxton says he's fine, just a curious eight-year-old.'

'Well, if you and Mrs Paxton are so effing sure about that, then get him tested, why don't you? Then we'll see who's on what spectrum.'

She was standing by the sofa, looking at Hank, who was looking at the TV. 'Okay, fine. I'll get him tested. So you can back off.' And she turned away and walked out of the room to the sound of canned sitcom laughter from the TV.

Jenny went to the kitchen and stood in front of the smart-home panel on the kitchen wall.

'Home, how can you tell if your child is autistic?'

The panel glowed pink, and a female voice replied: 'Here's what I found. A test for autistic traits.'

Here goes, she thought. I'll take the test for him – save him the embarrassment.

'Number one. I prefer to do things with others rather than on my own. Agree? Don't agree? Not sure?'

'Don't agree,' said Jenny. The house-voice dropped a techno-burp before starting again.

'Number two. I often notice small sounds when others do not. Agree?'

'Agree,' Jenny whispered. She didn't want to interrupt the 'home being'.

'Number three. I frequently get so absorbed in one thing that I lose sight of other things. Agree?'

'Agree,' Jenny mouthed.

'Number four. I would rather go to a library than to a party. Agree?'

'Yes.'

'Number five,' the house-voice said.

'Home, no more, please,' Jenny said. 'Thank you.'

Yikes, Jenny thought, that did not go too well. She could see where this was heading. Maybe she wasn't getting her son's answers right.

She trotted over to the basement door.

'Luke, honey?' she asked down the stairs.

'Yeah?'

'Just a quick question, honey – just an easy one . . . Um, would you say that you often notice details that other people don't notice? I mean, would you say that is true? You know, in an easy kind of a way . . .'

He came to the bottom of the stairs and looked up at her. He had a small shovel in one hand and a glove on the other.

'Mom, you had a haircut and it looks a little weird.'

She paused.

'Oh, okay.' She wondered whether to ask him again, or to try another question. 'Okay, honey, I see. You are really very good at noticing . . . That's all I needed to know. Thanks, sweetie – you're so helpful!'

She closed the door gently; she didn't want to disturb him. He needed time in his basement room to unwind. She hoped that he might be a scientist when he grew up. But yikes, she thought, leaning her head against the door. Yikes.

CHAPTER 3

HANK DID YOGA ON Saturday mornings. It was an online class, in real time, with Leslie, in California. The rest of the family were reminded of his class when the smell of incense slithered up the stairs in the early morning. At that smoke signal, everyone was supposed to be quiet. Hank, on the other hand, turned the volume up on the yoga class so that the whole house hummed with sacred orders.

'Let your thoughts dance across the screen of your mind . . . Release your shopping lists . . . Become aware of your third eye.'

The boys were still in their beds. Their Saturday morning ritual was to repeat these chantings to each other with zombie faces.

'My third eye is blinking!' Luke said to his brother, sitting up in his bed, his eyes rolling upwards.

'I could poke you in your third eye.' Jesse was still waking up.

Luke waited. The voice from downstairs continued: 'Find your tension triggers and release them.'

'Kapow,' said Jesse from under his blanket, and Luke giggled.

'Jesse, Jesse, who am I?' Luke said, and hung his head with a sorrowful expression. 'Ruff-ruff.'

Jesse's head emerged from his pillows, looking up – 'Ha ha. Down, dog!' – and fell back to the bedding.

When the singing part started, the boys joined in, careful to keep within the music's beginnings and endings. They both sat bolt upright and howled:

'Ommmm! Ommmm! Shanti. Shanti. Shanti-hee-*ee*.'

The last syllable they belted out, in a higher pitch, with some operatic waverings. And then quickly shut up, falling back onto their beds and guffawing into their pillows.

DOWNSTAIRS, HANK OPENED HIS eyes and looked up. The sound system rarely echoed so roundly. He took air into his flaring nostrils and turned his attention back to the screen. Leslie, with her beautiful limbs, with her nice clean feet and articulate toes, was starting the sun salutations. He would try to keep up. Sometimes he rested in his own modified child's pose – looking up from the supplicant pose, hands supporting his chin. She said they could. There were lots of modified poses for those who needed them. Hank wasn't very flexible, it was true; he couldn't touch his toes. But Leslie was flexible, he thought, both in body and mind.

Hank tried to empty his brain. At his most successful moments, he was still dogged by random words that pinged into his headspace. Vaginas. Grapefruit. Escrow. In the warrior poses, Hank could feel powerful, but then, sometimes, suddenly, he would become spittingly furious. He experienced surges of rage, tinged with humiliation. But he wouldn't give up. Sometimes he did emit tears during those internet yoga classes. He wasn't sure where they came from. According to Leslie, people stored emotions in their hips, so maybe it was that.

Why can't men wear yoga pants? Hank was thinking during one of his modified rests. There were just a few things that women could do that Hank wished he could – like wear yoga pants. Once, he tried some ballooning palazzo pants that were apparently for yogis. Some major yogis were men, after all. But why did they only have rust and olive colours to choose from? He found some dark purple ones, bought them, wore them once and threw them out – he felt like a genie released from a bottle. So he settled for latex running shorts under plain white shorts. That way, he wouldn't shine his jewels at anyone during Downward-Facing Dog in a studio class.

Okay, so he didn't look like a yogi, but that was probably because he had Viking blood. He found that out by sending off a sample – a swab of his inner cheek – to a DNA identification company. '*Who Are You?*' their ads shouted. And he was sure that it would be gratifying to know. 'Sixty-eight per cent Viking' was the result, which would explain his light blond hair. He thought it might also explain why he felt sometimes that justice needed to be upheld. A beard would probably have suited him, but these days it was too hipster to grow a beard and Hank didn't want to make that particular statement. Plus he didn't grow facial hair very easily.

Hank looked at his big hands and gnarly knuckles and wondered if the fact that he moisturised them was heresy. What kind of Viking was he anyway? He didn't have all that rugged a look. If anything, he was a little bit pretty. He knew that. He'd been teased about it by boys and men. They'd called him a 'dumb blonde' and sometimes a 'bimbo'. Women liked him though, and told him he looked like Rob Lowe, with his long eyelashes and pink cheeks. But sixty-eight per cent was a lot of DNA – why weren't his shoulders more broad? He needed more jaw and more nose, and a larger brow. He'd watched the first two seasons of the HBO series just last year and seen that Vikings were humongous men.

Hank wondered if he was what they called a 'metrosexual', but then, there was nothing sexual about his grooming. He wanted to look good – what was wrong with that? Hank's grooming was a private matter. It had all started as a twenty-year-old when his nose was littered with blocked pores and he asked his sister what to do. Face masks, facials, scrubs, she told him. These days, behind the closed doors of his bathroom, he would sometimes use a face mask. Sunday nights, Hank would sit on the toilet lid for the required ten minutes of mask time, crossing his legs and looking at his nails. It was also a good time to address his toenails, as the creamy gel was hardening on his face. Soon he couldn't move his jaw, couldn't frown. He wondered if this was what Botox felt like. Men do get Botox. He was sure some of the guys at the gym had it – the ones that looked immovable, steely. It made you look more masculine.

He was in Child's Pose when Leslie mentioned something about feeling reborn after the *Savasana* Corpse Pose. 'We roll onto our right sides because it mimics the process of birth,' she was saying. Wrapped in his curled body, Hank's thoughts wandered to those Chilean miners that were trapped a few years back. He had been watching TV with Jenny when the miners were finally rescued after weeks underground. 'They are experiencing a kind of rebirth,' the President of Chile said as the news cameras focused on the blackened men appearing one by one from the rescue shaft. The miners were pulled up and out in a tiny elevator, wearing the sunglasses they had been given to allow their eyes to adjust to the glare of the 'surface conditions'.

'I'd be too claustrophobic to be a miner,' said Hank. He took a sip off the top of the beer he'd just poured. They were both facing the TV screen, looking into the faces of the miners. Would they be able to see the trauma or wisdom that came from that mine? But their sunglasses were a perfect foil – they gave the miners the privacy they might have needed in this time of being born again, in the process of their salvation. The men were smiling, they were breathing, calling up to God and collapsing to their knees.

'I cannot believe it, that guy with the girlfriend and the wife,' Jenny offered. One of the trapped miners had an apparently unresolved love triangle above ground – a mistress and a wife who were vying for ownership of the unfolding tragedy. When the desperate family members of the miners had all gathered at Camp Hope by the borehole to the miners' refuge, the girlfriend had been turned away. It wasn't clear where the wife was – but they knew that when her miner-husband sent his dirty clothes up the borehole to be washed, she kept the clothes without washing them. He had hoped they would reach the girlfriend, apparently. The wife wanted some revenge, for him to sweat it out, naked.

'Jeez, you wonder how they all had so much tooth decay when they came up – I mean, it wasn't like they had a lot to eat down there.' Hank changed the subject.

'But they had cookies, remember? They shared cookies.' Jenny reminded him. 'And I guess they didn't brush their teeth . . . or maybe it was the lack of sunlight, of vitamin D.'

'After two months? Nah. I just think that the last thing they were thinking about was dental hygiene.'

'Yeah,' she said. 'Can you imagine the heat? The total claustro-phobia? The panic attacks . . .'

Hank turned the TV down and turned to Jenny, putting his arm around her and drawing her to himself. 'Well, how about a little mining over here, eh?' And he buried his nose in her neck. She relaxed and they lay back. But the miners were still coming out of the ground and Jenny looked at the screen over Hank's advances. 'Not here,' she whispered. 'They're still coming out of the earth!' she said sweetly, nodding at the screen.

JENNY STAYED QUIET ON Saturday mornings during Hank's online yoga class. 'Welcome to *your* time,' Leslie intoned. 'Yes,' said Jenny quietly, placing noise-cancelling headphones over her ears. The house-voice had informed her already that the quality of her sleep had been 'poor', that she had awoken twenty-six times during the night. She turned over and tried to go back to sleep. It was so luxurious to sleep in a bed by yourself. She sent one leg right across the bed diagonally and pulled all the pillows around her, settling into the position she liked best – the recovery position. But sleep didn't resume and she opened her eyes to look at the bedroom curtains. Why were they so sunbleached already? she thought. But clean, they were clean, at least. The sun cleans things with its light. Water and light – these were cleansing elements with their waves that gently stroke at things. You bathe in sun and water. Perhaps she should have a bath.

As the taps were running, it annoyed Jenny that having a bath was an act of rebellion in her household. Hank didn't believe that baths counted as bathing – since you soaked in your own filth. 'Basically you redistribute the different dirts around your body. Just think about it. That is *not* becoming clean,' he intoned. But the house could not detect between someone having a bath or a shower, and Jenny simply wanted a bath; she wanted to soak in a different medium. Air was too fizzy, too tingly – sometimes it seemed to her that she could feel molecules and photons hitting her skin. One day, she thought, she'd fill the bathtub with warm almond milk and have the most luxurious Cleopatran soak. Hank would be horrified, but he didn't have to know.

It was healthy for spouses to have secrets, Jenny reminded herself as she reached up to the upper bathroom cabinets looking for something fragrant to put in her bathwater. Her grandmother had once warned her knowingly that marital secrets were inevitable.

And lately, she had seen her point: little secrets were the pins of resistance. With secrets, you could escape the reflection you were trapped within – the picture of the person your spouse thinks you to be. Jenny liked baths and Hank didn't have to know about it. Nor did he have to know about her crush on Barack Obama. (How she admired his integrity!)

Hank also didn't know about her correspondence with John, Inmate 6587 at Flainton Correctional Facility. It started as an outreach initiative she joined at the local church – and she had mentioned it to Hank at the time, but he had never asked about it and so he didn't know she had been corresponding with John for nine months now, sharing light news, health worries and occasionally warmer, sometimes darker feelings. She sent him cookies every month, and if there was a nice correctional officer on duty sometimes he actually received them. John was so grateful for her letters, and his humility was breathtaking at times. He told her that he kept two pieces of paper, one in each pocket. One said: *I am nothing.* The other said: *I am everything.* The tone of his letters was sometimes a little strange, wooden maybe, until she realised that he was often quoting from the Buddha. John was a rookie Buddhist.

She went to retrieve his latest letter from her bedside-table drawer and perched on the edge of the bath to read it again.

Dear Jenny,
You ask good questions, Jenny, you're a curious person. The sound of incarceration, that's a nice way of putting it. There

is nothing that I can do to keep the noise out I even have ear plugs I even tape bunches of tissue paper over my ears and I wear a hat over that and it probably looks real stupid. I lie on my bunk, and if I don't block up my ears, all I can hear is banging, because people bang here. It's not rhythm, its not tribal or primal or anything. This noise – it's like being inside a broken clock. Guys rap at the bars on their beds, and they knuckle-punch at the steel on their doors. In my meditation practice I try to block it, or just hear the clangs and the clacks, and I think to myself energy is energy. But it's hard to forget that people are angry here. Pent up.

I should probably tell you I have moved cells so that you can put the right address on your envelopes. (it's still just as loud here though) I am now in Unit 5238, Block C3. Some new inmates have come in. I was just glad I got a new guy because I didn't want to be put in with a cell warrior. The last guy was sharpening pens all day and trying to boil up some foul-smelling alcohol and I wasn't going to get any sleep. There's been trouble in the cells so I have to stay in my cell for a week and we're not allowed to the vending machines or the exercise yard, and they've taken away our stuff but I borrowed a pen and some paper from a friend to write this. Anyway the whole block is on lockdown because someone stabbed a guy in the neck yesterday. I guess you might of sent cookies but I don't think packages are getting through right now. They are supposed to check and make sure the mail gets to the right prisoner but when you change cells sometimes they just drop the packages in with someone else. Right now the guy I'm in a cell with cries all the time, someone said he got attacked on his first day and I guess he has some medical issues now. A guy got burned by someone else with an iron last week too, and they didn't even take him to medical. Supposedly the guy burned him because in the morning he got too close when they were standing in line for food. People bust up here over the smallest things. You don't even want to look at people or they can say you looked at them wrong and go at you.

Keep writing to me, Jenny. Long is the night to him who is awake.

Peace,

John

She sat on the edge of the bathtub, and for the hundredth time she felt awash with guilt. What was this intimacy she had struck up with a convict? They told each other things. Nothing too concrete; she was careful to use a post office box for their correspondence. She didn't know anything much about John's life before prison, that was true. At first, they had written to each other with light descriptions of their lives – Jenny told him about the patients at the plastic-surgery clinic where she worked part-time, and John replied with the canteen menu and a record of how often the inmates were counted and checked – but, some letters later, they began to share their private horrors. John told her how the prison educators tried to make them get in touch with their rage by howling and roaring in group sessions. He said the shrieking had given him tinnitus. Sometimes he felt like he was spinning. Meanwhile, Jenny told him that she was tired, very tired, and that she felt like she was spinning too. 'My washing machine has a silent spin,' she once wrote to him, but later erased it. 'Do you ever feel like you're invisible?' she asked him instead.

A tenderness, an unnecessary kindness, developed through their exchange. The convict and the housewife, the rough and the smooth – each with its own damnation. It was something about the thunder and lightning of his life, and the marshmallow numbness of her own. Her new Bentonville life was so fat with ease, she told herself. 'I have no reason really to complain,' she told him. 'I'm really very lucky.' John's life, on the other hand, was a savage hermitage.

It had started by accident, almost. Father Brian had suggested the correspondence with prisoners after he read the parable about the goats and the sheep, and Jenny realised that she wanted to be a sheep, so she signed up. That is, wasn't it the sheep who help the wretched, and thereby gain their places in heaven – while the selfish goats go to hell? Well, whichever was the good one, she wanted to be one of them. It wasn't that she was such a good Christian – she was good, just not that kind of good – but most of all, she just wanted to ward off trouble. If she was good, then maybe other people would be good to her too.

John's prisoner profile listed his crime as 'voluntary manslaughter' but Jenny had never asked him about that; it seemed like a very personal question. Of course she could ask him, but she felt she didn't want him to have to explain himself to her that way. The court already convicted him; she didn't need to do that. John had told her he was a good person who had made bad choices, and that one of his bad choices was that someone else was imprisoned as an accessory to his crime. He felt very guilty about it. The whole thing was a big mistake, he said. He hadn't yet really told her in broad detail about his other bad choices, but now Jenny was in her forties she felt she knew about bad choices.

Bad choices. What a phrase. It's the kind of phrase she carefully used with her children. She could hear herself saying: 'You're not a *bad* boy, but biting is *bad* behaviour.' Her own bad choices were more protracted. She made long and slow bad choices. The kind you could regret only with decades of hindsight. For example, it was only now that she knew, she really knew, that she had made a mess of her twenties. Again and again she had found herself out of her depth, but was so caught up in the manic pursuit of life that she hadn't realised how totally vulnerable she had been. She had dated horrible jerks who had STDs and coke problems and who left her stranded in far-away nightclubs in the middle of the night. She once accepted a drink from a stranger and was sure she'd been roofied when she woke up on a sofa in a place she didn't recognise. She had lost her deposit on apartments to unscrupulous landlords whose telephone numbers never picked up. She had been shouted at by her bosses in ways she shouldn't have accepted. One particularly vicious female boss even said into her horrified, tear-welling eyes,

'Ah, it's a pity that women cry so easily.' She had been to hypnotists and acupuncturists to gain the courage needed to forge ahead after these small brutalities.

'But did I ever really make any choices?' she wrote to John a few months back. 'I mean, I feel like most things just happened *to* me. I didn't really do them.' He didn't seem to understand her and responded that 'even going along with things is a choice'.

'O-ba-ma . . .' she mouthed, noting through the earphones just how much of her voice she could hear passing through her nose. She stirred the cloudy, oily bath with her hand. She hoped Obama was the man she thought he was. He was wise – and how few, how very few wise people there were these days. She couldn't think of any at all. Maybe Ellen DeGeneres – her wisdom was sewn into her humour. The Ellen that was projected into the world was kind and good. She cheered people on, she made them laugh, she gave them TVs. That will be her legacy. Like Obama – who read a lot of good books and spoke the kindest words. And when he danced with his wife, Jenny watched them avidly, the wide and tender take of their embrace, and Jenny imagined how that felt.

Jenny had memorised one of his lines: 'If you're walking down the right path and you're willing to keep walking, eventually you'll make progress.' She had written it to John in a letter, and he had replied expressing doubts about right paths – the thing is, he said, there are no wrong paths, just unhappy ones. This is what the Buddha says, he told her.

Paths, thought Jenny, slipping into her eucalyptus bath – was hers the right path? It seemed like a stupid word to apply to herself. The word applied to heroes. Along with 'quests' and 'journeys'. But Jenny wasn't on a path. She had removed her headphones temporarily to get into the bathtub and she could again hear the yoga mantras through the floor, saying: 'The past and the future are here and now.' Yes, she thought, not a path, more like a lonely treadmill.

Maybe Obama was talking about purpose. Jenny had one glaring purpose these days – to mother her children. It was nice to have a purpose, a crucial purpose. But 'purpose' wasn't quite the right word. Motherhood was weighty. A vicious tenderness, coloured by the colossal horror that her children might die. And freedom – what exactly did that mean anymore? You couldn't ever escape the state of motherhood – whether you were with your children and tending to them, or whether you were away from them. It didn't matter: because they existed. They existed as though your very own beating heart was out in the world, walking around, vulnerable to the vagaries of street and forest. And so you are never free of them. You're locked in your own love. It was stupid to think of motherhood as a prison but that was how it felt, and Jenny really hoped that John would understand that without her having to spell it out. He was sent to prison, and they pushed him through a door and locked him in there. But Jenny felt like that dumb frog from the apocryphal story, the one that gets boiled: for so long she felt her life warming up nicely – she got a job, got a car, got a very handsome boyfriend, the handsome boyfriend proposed, she went part-time, and they started a family – but, soon, when it was already too late, she realised that she was trapped in a boiling role that would skin her of her ripening self.

She wondered: at the Pearly Gates (or whichever threshold awaited), what would she have to say for herself? She hated the epithets on gravestones, they were so confining. A gravesite of identity: *Mother, Sister, Daughter*, they said. It would be better to put down what people could have been – without the restraints they had suffered. Like: *Mary, quite contrary, she should have planted millions of trees*. Or: *Little Bo-Peep, she might have clothed the whole town with her excellent knitwear*.

Here lies Jenny, she thought, *mother of two, wife to one, daughter, sister, niece*. She was a sheep, not a goat. Or a frog who thought it was taking a bath.

CHAPTER 4

ON SUNDAYS, THE TINKLEYS took another dose of spirit-
uality and went to church. 'The family who prays together
stays together,' Jesse chanted from the back seat. Luke joined in with
a righteous grimace: 'And shaaaaaring is caaaaaaring.' The ride to
church was short, but it was too far to walk in the shoes they all
wore for the weekly occasion. The boys had brushed their hair in
the low mirror by the front door, pulling it forward and then spiking
the front. Jesse even used hair gel. Luke wouldn't because he didn't
like the way it hardened on his scalp. They were dressed up in their
Sunday clothes, which they didn't dislike. In fact, the neatness of the
clothes was calming – and Luke was allowed to wear the very soft
white cotton/linen-mix shirt that he liked so much. It had uneven
fibres and a visible pattern of warp and weft.

The church was a building with angular bumps along its roof-
spine and a steeple at the fore. It looked as though the architect had
been inspired by that little song that children play with their clasped

34

fingers: Here's the church (knuckles), here's the steeple (forefingers), open the doors (thumbs) and see all the people (fingers)! And inside, the scheme was blond wood – the pews, the columns, the altar. Everything was fitted and immovable – and everything was curved. There are no corners in God's house, Father Brian had once said from his swirly soft-serve pulpit.

The Tinkleys entered the church, where greetings swooped at them like a Mexican wave. They headed for their usual pew, about two-thirds up the aisle. Once you gained your pew, the greetings subsided somewhat. Jenny fussed with her boys' coats to avoid having to volley any more hellos. When the organ music started, people were allowed to zone out, settle down.

Jenny spent a lot of the church service trying to get comfortable – the pews were so hard. She wasn't really a believer but she wanted the boys to experience some goodness. They needed a dose of this, she thought, sitting there. She knew she was outsourcing some parenting here, but the church could teach them about doing the right thing that she sometimes felt just too exhausted to go into. She didn't believe much in God these days, and as she sat watching the clergy's vestments swinging at the altar, she created a graph in her head. When you're young you can surge into belief in God – you're looking to make sense of the world and its behaviours. You believe because you have to trust what you're told, your parents hold the truths. So to start off with, the trajectory is steep. But with each really bad experience, you might have some of that belief eroded away and the line evens out until it starts to falter. How can God kill children? Why do some suffer the privations of war while others merely lament their gluten intolerance? Female genital mutilation? Justice is patchy in this world. And God's plan makes no sense . . . And then, Jenny concluded, you get old and the belief line on the graph rises again because the stakes are against you, so you better believe in something because you're going to be taken soon from this world, and it's hard to face a void. Jenny was on her way down the belief line, and she was pretty sure that her downward trend hadn't finished its run.

Father Brian was experimenting with technological advance: he was trialling new cellular technology methods for his services. God needed a presence in cyberspace too. He had started his experiment a few months prior with the 'Peace be with you' part of the service. That is, instead of shaking hands with the people around you, you could simply point your cellphone at the people around you and and ping the words via WhatsApp. The church was silent and everyone was looking down at their phones. Some people sent shouty messages -PEACE BE WITH YOU!- and others littered them with emojis. The kids enjoyed this part of the service, and Jesse and Luke quietly pretended to shoot people with their phones, making *peece-peece* sounds like BB gunshots. Luke whispered to Jenny: 'Did you know that Bluetooth was the name of a Danish king called Harald Bluetooth in the tenth century?'

Jenny typed her Peace in italics, hoping not to catch anyone's eye. Hank sent out his peace message a little reluctantly – he just wrote Peace from Hank. Phones were supposed to be on silent but lots of them around the church started pinging wildly. How many weird sounds there were: barking, sighing, train hoots, snippets of hip-hop. The congregation chuckled and the children guffawed.

Father Brian knew not to expect everyone to remember to silence their phones. But it was important that the WhatsApp peace precede the next use of mobile data: the confession. At the point in the liturgy where silent confession was offered to the Lord, again the congregation looked down into their phones. They quickly typed out their weekly sin and texted it to a special cellphone the priest reserved for confession. 'It will focus our minds,' Father Brian said. 'It will make us truly think of what we regret . . . And it will send a message, literally, to God.' The cellphone was kept on the altar in a glass box and it lit up as all the messages were fired at it from the churchgoers. Sometimes, especially in the early days, there were some accidental mass confessions – using the 'peace' WhatsApp instead of the confession text-messaging and spreading sins committed from phone to phone. Someone admitted to lying to their boss, another owned up to drinking milk from the carton. Jenny suspected that people were only reporting their minor sins. No one was going to confess to infidelity or shoplifting over the ether.

So they confessed. For whatever it was worth, Jenny confessed to old sins, episodes of mother-fury that had spewed torrents of shame forever afterwards. She typed **I squeezed my toddler's arm once when I was really angry and it left a bruise. I'm really sorry.** She looked down at Luke's hovering thumbs; he seemed unsure of what to type.

Jesse and Hank were very quick about it, either because there was a lot or a little to report, Jenny thought.

When it came time for Communion, the Tinkleys filed down the pew and up the aisle. They waited, they knelt, and they crossed themselves in various configurations. The bread, the transubstantiated body of Jesus, was a difficult metaphor for Luke. The other Tinkleys just went along with it and ate the wafer. But Luke had one particular reservation that he asked Jenny about quietly when they were walking back to their seats: why were they eating Jesus's body? Wasn't that cannibalism? Jenny wasn't sure how to explain that.

'They could have just transubstantiated Jesus's hand into a glove and then placed it on each person's head to wash the sins off.' He slid along the pew.

'Yes, I guess they could have. Well, these things were thought up a long time ago and I suppose they thought it was a little like the Last Supper with the bread and the wine.'

But she wasn't convinced. Was the church thing a little gruesome? It certainly did seem strange to be placed for an hour in front of a bloody and crucified corpse. Cannibalism and torture, she thought. Maybe it wasn't such a dose of goodness after all.

She consoled herself that at least her children liked to go out for sushi after church – and that not all kids liked sushi so maybe she'd done something right.

CHAPTER 5

THE FISH TANKS IN the Sushi Palace were flashing with tropical species.

'Can we sit next to the see-through fish?' Luke asked the waiter.

'He means the tank over there,' Jenny said, pointing deep into the thicket of chairs and tables.

'He's eight,' Jesse told the waiter.

'Yes, of course,' the waiter said, and led them along a winding path to the table. 'I'm your waiter and my name is Torio.' And just before he bowed, Luke tugged on Torio's uniform. Hank and Jenny became alert, both looking at their younger son.

'Torio, what does your name mean?' he asked.

'Sorry? I didn't hear you.'

'Your name – Torio – does it mean something?'

'Oh yes – it is the tail of the bird. I am the tail of the bird. Toh-ri-oh.' And Torio gently flapped his straight fingers in the air, smiling.

'Oh, well, that's a relief – I though you said Oreo!' said Hank, laughing, winking and opening his menu. 'Come on, Luke, what'll it be? A little yellowfin tuna? How about some *uni*?'

'Eww-ni!' said Jesse, and the boys tittered. Torio left them to look at the menu.

'Hey, Torio!' Hank called after the waiter, pronouncing his name like the cookie. 'I have a question for you.'

The waiter came up behind Hank so he could see the dish at which Hank was pointing.

'What's . . . that?' said Hank, jabbing at a picture on the front of the menu.

'Oh, oh . . . that is . . . that is . . . *omakase*,' Torio replied. And he nodded, adding, 'Yes.'

'So, uh, what is it?' Hank asked.

'*Omakase*. It means "trust".'

'Is that some kind of fish?'

'No. No. Trust. Trust the chef,' Torio explained.

'Truss the shelf?'

'No, Dad – trust the chef!' Jesse and Luke reprimanded Hank in unison.

'Oh, I get it. Okay. Sorry, Torio.' He handed his menu to the waiter. 'That's what I'll have then. Trust the chef . . . I trust the chef.' Hank seemed a little proud of himself.

Torio took the menu and hesitated, then acquiesced. He looked up at the others to see if they were ready too.

'I don't even know the chef,' said Luke. 'So I'll have an eel roll.'

'Same.' said Jesse.

'Uh, the salmon and avocado for me, please,' Jenny said, handing over the last menu. 'And lots of extra rice. We like rice.' She smiled.

The Tinkleys' sushi lunch was often a time for a family ethical discussion. Hank would riff on the sermon and Jenny would adjust his arguments. After he gave his menu to Torio, Luke started fiddling with his chopsticks.

'Oh no!' He slapped his forehead. 'Oh noooo,' he whined, looking up.

'What's wrong, honey?' asked Jenny.

'Oh no. Oh . . . it doesn't matter.' He was now looking at his lap.

'Did you forget something?' Jenny probed.

'No . . . no . . . it's just . . . I made a mistake.'

'That's okay, everyone makes mistakes, buddy,' said Hank. 'What was it? Can we right it for you?'

'No . . .' And Luke pulled out his phone and opened the messaging app. 'I want to unsend a message – can you do that?'

Jesse grabbed Luke's phone and a scuffle broke out. Hank and Jenny stood up to separate the boys while Jesse mocked his younger brother. 'You sent a dirty message to a girl!'

'No, I did not!' said Luke and, turning to his parents, 'I didn't!'

'Okay, okay, calm down, you two.' Jenny gave Luke back his phone.

'I just made the wrong confession.'

'I knew it!' said Jesse. 'I confess that I do weird things in the basement, ha ha ha ha . . .' Jesse laughed while his parents pointed their disapproval at him.

'No. Shut up,' said Luke. 'It's that . . . I wasn't sure what to say, so I confessed to all of the sins – and I just remembered that I didn't murder anyone. And I didn't covet my neighbour's wife!' Luke was distraught.

'Oh Jeez, Luke,' said Hank. 'They don't really read those messages, and anyway, God knows you didn't do those things.'

Luke was somewhat appeased. 'I just want to take it back.'

'So send another message to say you didn't mean it,' Jenny offered. And so he did. The sushi lunch could proceed.

They didn't speak for a few minutes. The restaurant was filling up with new diners. It was a quiet place, probably thanks to the rice-paper partitions that were variously placed around the tables, and the low ceiling that was also lined with some kind of textured material. No music. The waiters wore simple black clothes – but the waitresses were trussed up as geishas. Well, American geishas maybe. They didn't paint their faces white and their cheeks with round red spots. They did wear red lipstick and kimonos though, and, most notably, they clip-clopped around in wooden flip-flops worn with white socks. They wore their hair up and twisted into swirls, and it looked a little painful. They were the ones that brought food to the tables – the male waiters took orders. It seemed to Jenny that the geishas didn't speak, or weren't allowed to.

'So if God knows everything, and is everywhere, in everything, does God see everything we do?' Jesse asked Hank.

'Yes, he does. And that's why he knows about Luke's sins, no matter what he confesses.'

'So we're supposed to believe that when you go to heaven, you can see down to all the things that living people are doing? Like, Grandpa Harrison could see us now?' Grandpa Harrison was Jenny's father, who had died last year of an aneurysm.

Hank looked at Jenny, unsure how far to take this discussion. She replied with a gesture that said *Be my guest*.

'Even though he is ashes now?' Luke said.

'Yeah, they're all up there, looking down on us, wishing they were about to have some *kamakaze*,' Hank joked.

'Like, all the time though? They watch *everything* you do?' Jesse persisted.

'There is nothing that they are seeing that they haven't done themselves at some point. Or worse,' Hank reassured Jesse. He whispered, 'Even those Japanese cartoons you've been watching – you know, the ones with those girls and their big . . .' and made a quick gesture that would translate to the word 'jugs' if spoken aloud, and then winked.

Jenny looked horrified. She shot him a look and burst out in a hissed whisper, 'Hank? Is this really the time and place?' She was speaking in half-code, referring to a conversation they had earlier in the week upon discovering Jesse's internet search history. After the many searches for 'minecraft' and 'gun shooting', a long stream of searches blared at them: Henti. Henty. Hentay. Hentai. And after that, the pages Jesse had opened: 'Hentai Booby Adventure' and 'Hentai Pussy Power'. The next search was 'how to avoid doing homework', which was kind of a relief.

'I'm just saying!' Hank rebuffed her. 'Jesse, you're thirteen, and there is not anything wrong with looking at girls. Girls are beautiful! Girls are great! But only nice girls – you know what I mean?'

Jesse sat there blushing and staring at Hank, possibly furious. 'I. Do. Not. Know . . . what you are talking about.'

Jenny jumped in to shift the whole situation elsewhere. 'Oh my goodness, I love Japanese cartoons. When I was a little girl I was crazy about Hello Kitty. The Japanese are *so* good at cute things . . . And there's Studio Ghibli too. What's your favourite cartoon, Luke?'

'Uh.' Luke looked as though he wasn't sure whether he was missing a big opportunity for a sibling put-down, but he followed his mother into a less charged discussion. 'Uh, I like Chinese cartoons.' He shot a look at Jesse.

Jesse countered, 'What? Oh no, that is *not* true, Luke, you like Power Rangers and you *really* like those old-fashioned cartoons about the Jetsons and you also *always* watch cartoons about cats. But actually you don't even love cartoons at all. So you don't know what you're talking about.' Jesse was challenging Luke, but Luke looked at Jesse and over to his mother.

'Yeah, well, cartoons are stupid. And at least I don't have to confess about that!' Luke returned.

'Yeah, you only confess about murdering people.' Jesse rolled his eyes.

At this point, the fake geisha was placing the sushi dishes on the table, directed by Hank, and Jesse excused himself to go to the bathroom.

'Thank you, thanks . . . thank you.' Jenny was trying to compensate in some way for the woman's servitude. When the geisha had delivered it all, she bowed and left. Jenny nodded back, as a sort of head-bow, and then turned on Hank.

'The Japanese-cartoon discussion is not a family discussion. That was something to take care of in a smaller conversation,' she said sternly to him.

'Oh, come on,' he dismissed her, looking into his plate. 'Hey, Luke, any idea what this is?' he said, pointing one chopstick at his plate. It was piled high with swirls of carved root vegetables and dotted with all kinds of fish eggs and slivers of gleaming fish. 'It's very pretty . . . I sure wish I knew what it was so I could eat it!'

Luke peered over at his father's dish. 'Just put soy sauce on it, it'll be okay,' he offered. '*Shoyu*,' he whispered, passing the bottle.

'What was that, Luke?' Hank said quietly to his son. 'What was that you whispered?'

'Hank, leave him alone,' said Jenny.

'Oh, nothing, it's Japanese,' Luke replied.

'Yeah, right, you speak Japanese,' Jesse said, as he sat back down in his seat.

'*Shoyu* means soy sauce. It's written on the bottle,' Luke said without looking up at anyone, pushing a lump of boiled rice into his mouth.

CHAPTER 6

LATER THAT SUNDAY NIGHT, Luke was trying to interest Hank in the subject of words.

'Hey, Dad, do you know Viking words?'

'What's that, Luke?' Hank asked. Hank's attention had been sucked into his smartphone, and Luke was going to have to try harder to pull him out of it.

'Dad . . . Dad . . . Dad . . .'

And finally: 'Dad!'

'Yes, son.' He put his phone down, gave it one last glance, turned it over and then looked at Luke. Another quick glance at the screen and he put it down more decisively. 'Where's Jesse?'

'On the computer.'

'That kid's addicted,' Hank said, and was about to turn back to his phone.

'Dad.' Luke poked his father once. 'Do you know that we speak Viking?'

'Is that right? Tell me more, buddy.'

'Okay. Words that came from the Vikings are . . .' And Luke began listing them: 'Anger. Crash. Bang. Ruthless. Slaughter. Ransack. Husband. Blunder.'

Jenny walked into the kitchen as Luke's list was tailing off.

'Husband-blunder?' she asked them.

'Yeah,' Hank was quick to retort. 'Sound familiar? I told you I was a Viking.'

They smirked at each other. Luke was still pursuing his last point.

'But don't you see, Dad? The words are all very fierce.' He turned to Jenny. 'They're Viking words.'

'Well, if I'm sixty-eight per cent Viking, then you are half that, which is . . . thirty-four. Luke, you're thirty-four per cent Viking-isn't that cool?' Hank looked over at Jenny, who was opening kitchen cupboards. 'And your mother, well, her people came from England, so they're good at, uh, manners.' He pretended to sip from a teacup with his pinkie raised.

Jenny didn't rise to it.

The smart-home panel on the wall lit up and the house-voice spoke: 'The milk is past its expiry date. Would you like me to order milk?'

'No, Home, thank you,' Jenny said, swiping a hand towards it. 'I will get the milk when I'm good and ready.'

The panel went dark.

'Hey, Luke, want to make cookies with me?' she said.

Jenny helped Luke to jump up and sit on the kitchen island. This was always how they baked together. He sat by the mixing bowl and she handed him the ingredients. He measured out the quantities.

'The baking soda reacts with the flour. Or the sugar. I forget,' he said quietly.

Jenny shrugged. It always amazed Luke that grown-ups just walked through the world using things that they didn't even understand. Like telephones. And electricity. And don't even try to ask them where the internet actually is – they really don't know. They can only mumble something about servers.

Luke made notes on his hand to remind himself about the things he needed to look up. He sometimes had writing up and down his arms. His mother seemed worried about this, as though he were hurting himself. But pens don't hurt and ink wasn't really all that poisonous. He just wanted to make sure to solve some mysteries each day. Luke's main objective was to crack the plastics. He had never met an adult who knew where different plastics came from. And the internet knew too much to be helpful.

Luke had stopped stirring, holding the wooden spoon upright in the cookie goop. He was looking at the kitchen, his eyes moving from object to object. Jenny watched him, waiting – Luke was itemising.

'Hey, Luke, how's that dough coming along?' she asked.

He didn't answer immediately; he finished the line of vision he was following.

'Twenty-seven,' he said.

'Hm?' she proffered.

48

He looked at her: 'Twenty-seven plastic things in this room, and I'm not even finished.'

Jenny watched him quietly. And then, as if awakening: 'Oh yes, I see! . . . And are they carbon-based or silicon-based?' She was looking for nuts in the cupboard.

'Mom . . . there are a lot of different plastics here,' he chided her. 'And the sad thing is that we will probably never know how they got from the earth to our kitchen.'

'Is that sad?' she turned to ask. Her face looked love-worried.

'Yeah, it's sad. Because somewhere, someone dug a hole. Or someone drove a tractor that dug the hole. And they took the petroleum out of the hole and put it into a truck and drove it somewhere else. Or an airplane. Or a ship. And they took it to a factory . . .' He paused to figure out the next bit.

'And then they heated it, or they mixed it up with something, and then . . . Then they put it in a mould, or they poured it in a mould, and it hardened. And *then* . . .' He took a big breath to continue. 'And *then*, they put it in a box and sent it, in trucks and ships and airplanes to all the people in their kitchens.'

Jenny had stood there listening, sock-footed on her chequerboard linoleum floor, a bag of crushed nuts in her hand. Luke had stopped talking and was stirring the cookie mixture again.

'And that could be sad?' she said.

'It's sad because . . . You just don't get it.' He shook his head. 'It's sad because our toaster probably just wants to go back to the hole it came from, but it will never, ever, *ever* be able to turn

49

itself back into its first shape. You can't change plastic back. It's a one-way system.'

Jenny tilted her head and put a hand up to her heart.

'Oh, Luke, yes, that's a sad story,' she offered quietly. 'And you can only hope that they feel like they're doing something useful here instead of just sitting in a hole and getting all muddy.'

He smiled and she smiled.

'And what do you think *that* is going to turn into?' She pointed at the cookie dough with her own wooden spoon.

'Cookies!' And she took the bowl from him, trading it for a baking tray lined with wax paper.

'Now we have to wait for it to . . . chill out.' And she wrapped the cookie dough in cling film and popped it into the fridge.

'How many cookies can I eat?' asked Luke, turning his head up to his mother's face as she washed his hands in the kitchen sink.

'Oh, you can have one – but these cookies are for someone else. Someone who doesn't ever get cookies, so they need them,' she said.

'Who doesn't get cookies?' Luke said, eyes bulging with the question.

'Unfortunates,' Jenny replied.

The two looked up, through the window, to the street outside. The evening was still, it was a chilly Sunday night in their cul-de-sac. The neighbours all had their mini street lamps lit at the end of their driveways. Windows were flashing with the coloured light of the various screens inside. You could see what everyone was doing because nobody closed their blinds. Blinds were more for decoration. The Tinkleys lived at the bulbous dead-end of Maple Drive where cars could turn around before heading back out to the archipelago of cul-de-sacs in Bentonville. Mostly, things were quiet. As they waited for the cookie dough to cool and harden, Luke and Jenny could see the neighbour next door shouting for his dog, standing in his driveway in a T-shirt and sweatpants. 'Jen-n-nny!! Get in here!' he shouted, and Jenny looked at Luke, closed her eyes, lifted her chin and gave out a little '*Ruff!*'. (She hoped that through their laughter Luke didn't hear the neighbour spit out a short curse: 'Shit.') The neighbour's dog had her name, and this caused regular mirth in the Tinkley household.

Luke watched the cul-de-sac from their kitchen window while the dough sat in the fridge. There were beautiful things about this place. He liked the cedar chips that surrounded every tree and shrub. They weren't from local cedar trees but they were a material the trees might recognise at least. They approximated a forest floor, and that was a kind concession to the plants. Bugs could even live among them, little beetles furrowed and fumbled there.

And you could play a lot of basketball in Maple Drive. If you were a bionic man who could jump far and high, you might even dribble with huge leaps from driveway to driveway and slam-dunk again and again and again. Every garage had a basketball hoop, whether there were boys or girls in the house. People rarely played basketball though – except if some kid was trying to get on the school team, or there was a dad challenging a small boy to 'pick up'.

Recently, Luke had had a revelation about lawns. For a long time, he had accepted them as a feature of his native landscape, but he had finally understood that they were outdoor carpets. Well, that people treated them that way. If you tried not to think of grass as flooring, then you could see that it was the gentlest of plants – each blade so slender and striving. There were older blades, and then a thicket of youngsters below them. The blades weren't competing exactly, there was enough room for everybody, but you had to twist and turn to find your place among the crowd. You could think of grass like hair – that might be more right. But you shouldn't trample all over it, and you shouldn't actually chop it with the razorblades of a lawnmower. Grass wanted to grow tall so it could tell you the direction of the wind.

Hank had told Luke and Jesse that his Great-Uncle Rudolph had invented astroturf in the sixties. This was exciting – a real inventor in the family. The only other thing they knew about Uncle Rudolph was that he had twinkly eyes and he drove a motorcycle with a sidecar. Jesse said that they should be rich if Uncle Rudolph invented astroturf, and Hank only answered, 'Well, it doesn't always work out that way . . .' In his basement, Luke kept a sample of astroturf on his desk – he admired it. He was proud of his astroturf ancestor as he felt that astroturf was a very good idea actually – it exposed the purpose of lawns. It was a mockery to lay huge rolls of grass turf over bare earth like you would lay a linoleum floor – snipping at the edges and throwing away the offcuts. Astroturf was honest that way. For a polymer, that is.

What wasn't honest was the information that if you rub two sticks together you can make fire. Luke had tried this so many times that he had suffered splinters and blisters. Next Christmas, he was going to ask for a flint, which would make fire-making easier, or so he hoped.

CHAPTER 7

THE SCHOOL WEEK BEGAN and Jenny went to the post office to check for mail, just as she did every morning. It was like going fishing – casting at the persistent hope that something will come up on your hook.

Dear Jenny,

I just realised there are no doorknobs here. Like none. It's like I just saw this fact for the first time, weird how that happens when you just see something you never really saw before. No doorknobs. Last night I just felt like opening a door, not getting out or anything, just opening up a plain old door. And I saw that there is nothing here to hold on to.

Some of my friends left this week. Guys leave, finish up their time and then they say they are never coming back. But I've been here only a year and some, and I've seen guys back after just a few months. I like to try to tell them to start again, make it good and they swear they are never coming back. Usually they just do the same thing that got them locked up in the first place and boom they are here again. They don't see the bigger picture, how much they have to change their shape, so they can fit into the world in a different way. They don't see that.

They think I'm old here – I'm only 48 but that still makes me an OG, an old guy. In fact it's really not a bad thing though because the young guys spend all their time fighting with each other. They leave the OGs alone, and even sometimes try to get fatherly advice from people like me. I don't have much but I usually tell them to just cool it.

I just read your letter again and I'm confused about your talking house. Why would you want your house to tell you the weather when you can just open your front door and see it for yourself? They got cameras here too and people watching us. Who is watching you?

Bless you.

From, John

PS. They been telling us to go to church services here with all kinds of clappers and freaks but there is no actual regular Christian priest. I grew up a regular Christian, you know what I mean? It would be nice to talk to someone normal from time to time. It's another reason why I enjoy your letters so much, Jenny.

Back at her kitchen table, Jenny replied:

Dear John,

Thanks for your letter. I was wondering what your cell looks like? Can you tell me about it? I'd like to picture you there.

My house witnesses everything I do. It is even watching me right now, I guess. It knows what room I'm in, it knows the contents of my fridge, it even listens to what I'm saying. Sometimes the voice of the house makes weird noises but I'm learning to ignore them. They're like burps. Or like those snippets of truckers' conversations you can hear on a CB. I used to talk to myself a little now and then, you know, when you accidentally speak your thoughts aloud, but I've learned not to do that anymore. Just in case.

I used to try to talk to the house, you know, ask it questions. It didn't know where it came from. It didn't even know where it was – it just said 'here'. When I asked it what it believed, or what mattered to it, the only thing it could say was: 'I am not a person, Mrs Tinkley.' I thought that was a little rude so I haven't talked to it ever since. What's the point?

I was thinking about it, your postscript note. In all serious-ness, I can actually give you the number our church uses for confession. We're regular protestants too. Well, episcopalians anyway. Maybe that would kind of help since you don't have a priest there? We use it in church to send messages with our confessions to it. Our priest says it is like 'a direct line to

God' . . . It's a new technology trial for the church and seems to be successful.

It can't hurt, right?

Jenny gave him the number for the God-phone and signed off just as the phone rang.

Jenny's mother called at supposedly convenient times. 'Hi, oh good, I'm glad I caught you . . .' Her mother usually started with this phrase, and Jenny vaguely winced each time. She looked around for a task she could do while her mother was on the phone. The house plants needed watering.

'I'm on my way to the bedding store and wondered if you needed any sheets.'

'Uh, no, I've got plenty of sheets, that's okay,' Jenny replied. She felt she should add something so that didn't seem unfriendly. 'But, if you see some nice hand towels . . . if you see some, that would be good.'

Jenny wondered if there was going to be something wrong with her request for hand towels. She tried quickly to divert the conversation.

'How is Mary?' Jenny asked. Mary was her mother's sister, who lived in a retirement community in Oregon. Mary was prone to provoking Jenny's mother with well-placed barbs.

'Well, we talked on Sunday and she was antigonising me, pressing my buttons, and she ended up singing "Row, row, row your boat" so I hung up on her.'

Jenny's mother was the queen of the non sequitur – and Jenny knew not to ask for clarification. Her mother would just resort to her hot temper. So Jenny rode the metaphors and took in as much as she could in order to answer. But 'antigonising' – that was a beauty. Of the two Greek sisters, Antigone and Ismene, her mother was not Antigone, wild, strong and rebellious. She was an Ismene – abiding to the laws of men, taking her place as a submissive female. At least, Jenny had learned that much in college.

'I talked to your sister last week and she is so negative. I just wish they would be more, I don't know . . . positive. I mean, aren't you happy that you are married and have children? Why wouldn't you be?'

Jenny was unsure of what to say. Her habit was to reflect her mother, not have her own mind on matters. This was purely because any opposition caused a hyperbolic reaction in her mother, and it just wasn't worth it. 'Oh yeah,' she offered, filling her small watering can again at the sink.

'Imagine the alternative – I mean, being a single woman is no fun, I can tell you.'

'Oh . . . yeah,' said Jenny again.

'Are you in the bathroom?' Her mother sounded annoyed. 'I can hear tinkling.'

'No, no – I'm in the kitchen, watering plants.' She was quick to explain herself.

'Can't you ever just do one thing at a time? I mean, it's not like I call you every day.'

'Okay, sorry – I just noticed the fern was wilting, and before I forget, I wanted to revive it a little.' Jenny tried to sound upbeat.

'I remember what it's like – to be a young mother. It's a busy time. Nobody said it wasn't.'

Jenny wondered how her mother could call her a 'young mother' at the age of forty-one.

The house-voice piped up: 'The dryer cycle has finished.'

Jenny's mother was confused. 'Who's that there? Is someone there with you?'

'No, Mom, it's just my robot alter-ego telling me to she has finished drying the laundry.'

'What are you talking about?'

'Didn't I tell you that Hank made this into a smart house? Didn't I tell you that?' Jenny was walking towards the beeps coming from the laundry room now.

'A what house? An art house? What kind of house is an art house? You're making art now?'

'No, Mom, we're not making art. Anyway, look, I have to go, I have to get the boys early from school today because we're going to the dentist,' Jenny lied. Why had she lied? She wanted some time to herself before the children returned from school.

SOMETIMES, WHEN SHE WAS alone like this, Jenny played with the 'smart' house. 'Turn on Beyoncé!' she shouted, and the speakers obliged. 'Volume up!' she barked. 'Voluu-u-u-me d-oooo-wwn!'

she bellowed. She went into the living room and, as long as she was carrying her phone, the lights would switch on automatically. So she jumped into the room, and leapt out again – prancing at the threshold to see how much confusion the house could take. But the fun never lasted because she soon started feeling that the smart house was rigged and that she was being preyed upon. Didn't Hank set up some kind of high-tech alarm system that tracked movement through the house? Did it sense body heat or something? There were little devices in the ceiling corners – they might be cameras. At these moments, Jenny would feel like she was on some reality TV show, and then start to behave as normally as she possibly could. She would often do some cleaning. Folding the laundry always looked distinctly innocent – though apparently, Hank said, there was a machine that could do that now too.

JOHN'S LETTER STILL TUMBLED around her mind. Jenny looked at the doorknobs on the kitchen doors. The Tinkleys never used their doorknobs – almost all the doors in their house remained ajar or wide open. It was a parental habit – to keep an ear out for the troubles of toddlers – and they hadn't outgrown it. Having door-knobs didn't feel as liberating as John might think. Hank considered it safer to have internal doors that didn't lock. Jenny, on the other hand, longed to be able to lock a door sometimes. But the house was programmed not to allow anyone to lock major internal doors, except the bathroom doors.

Jenny went to her bedroom, tugged up the pillow from her bed and took the bottle of water from her bedside table and made for the bathroom. She closed the door and locked it with a jerky vehemence that was lost on the equable metal and reconstituted wood of the door. If this bathroom was your habitat, how would you use it? she asked herself. You could mouth words of assurance to the face in the mirror. There was a fluffy mat on the floor to remind you of the grass you remembered from your childhood. The bathtub was dry and would make a perfectly reasonable bunk; its cold, hard, rounded surface would ground her lightning bolts. She embraced the pillow in her arms and put her face to it. The pillow would represent a cloud. But clouds were deceptions, as anyone knew who had travelled in an airplane. You think they are soft, sometimes feathery, sometimes cotton-fluff, but they are in fact the thinnest of wet air, and they will not catch you if you fall.

CHAPTER 8

THAT EVENING, JESSE AND Luke were upstairs in their room. Jesse's headphones were accidentally pulled out of their socket when he made a wide backwards gesture with his torso as his avatar evaded the swing of a sword. He was in the throes of an epic fight on Battlesite.

'Fucking little girl – die!' one of his team-mates shouted into the room as the speakers blared sounds of gunfire and metal slinging.

'Nailed,' Jesse replied, and fired off several rounds of ammunition himself, unable to let go of the controls to plug the headphones back in.

'Cunt,' said his team-mate. 'Fucking pussy.'

'Those are pretty bad words,' Luke said from his bed. 'You shouldn't be around that stuff.'

'Shut up,' Jesse said in a glancing blow.

'Another bad word,' Luke said, looking back to his tablet.

Jesse plugged in the headphones and the room was silent again, apart from Jesse's grunting, and the shunting of his swivel chair.

The walls of their room were light blue, and each boy had their own wall to himself. Jesse had posters of skateboarders in mid-air, and some peeling T. rex decals. The posters above Luke's bed showed varieties of lichen and moss. There was a planet lampshade on the ceiling light, and curtains printed with rockets and asteroids on the small window between the beds.

Luke was scrolling through images on a tablet, trying to find out about nuclear power.

'Home, are you afraid of thorium?' He raised his face to the ceiling.

'I'm sorry, I don't know,' the house-voice said.

'Well, I don't think I am. Its radiation is stopped by just three feet of air.'

'Fuck!' Jesse shouted as he flapped his fingers furiously.

'I don't know how to respond to that,' the house-voice responded to Jesse.

'I mean, a thorium reactor can't really melt down.'

'I'm not sure I understand.'

'Home, you can go to sleep now,' Luke said.

'I can't sleep.'

'Why not?'

'There's not always an easy answer,' said the house-voice.

'Okay, shush now.'

'My lips are sealed.'

The glass wall panel dimmed its glow to black and Luke smiled.

Jesse shouted at him. 'Will you shut her up? She's making me screw up!'

'She's off! Why do you always get so mad on that game?' Luke said, walking out of the room.

THERE WAS SOME OUTRAGE in the Bentonville community because there were tentative plans to build a thorium nuclear power plant nearby. Jesse said that the Tinkleys could finally achieve their aspirations to be like *The Simpsons*. Jenny wondered if her frizzy hair was anything like Marge Simpson's. At least it wasn't blue, but if her brown curls continued going grey then she might have to resort to a blue rinse of some sort. Then Hank could go bald, and they could really become some Bentonville version of the yellow family. Except of course that Bart's smart little sister was a girl, and Luke was a boy. But otherwise, Jenny could kind of see Jesse's point. Not that it was an aspiration exactly, but still.

When Jenny had written to John about the proposed plant, his response was to ask if she was ready to take on 'the man'. And he joked, 'I thought you were already living in a nice nuclear family?' and then he apologised for being so crass. 'You must be concerned,' he wrote. 'Of course you're concerned. It's nuclear radiation.'

Jenny had replied saying that yes, her family really was nuclear. 'In fact, you could take an X-ray and look at all the houses on our street, and you'd see all the moms running around their own houses, all doing the same things in their little atomic units,' she wrote. 'The positively charged Mrs Proton saying, "Brush your teeth, do your homework, don't talk to your brother like that. Be good, work hard".' And then, she continued, 'Don't get me started on the massive hulking neutrons. They just take up space. And then all you have left are the crazy little electron charges whizzing around causing reactions . . . You see what I mean?'

She didn't want to sound resentful, she wanted to keep John on her side. 'What is radiation anyway?' she wrote. 'All I know is that mothers are damned by a nuclear force, a gravity of responsibility, which means that everything sticks to you, everything ends with you.'

FROM THE OPEN DOOR of her bedroom, Jenny could hear that Luke was playing 'house clock' at the top of the stairs. It was a game the kids had invented where they get the house to talk to the clock. First you had to get the house's attention. But you had to keep the house talking until the clock struck, and the cuckoo came out and cuckoo'd.

'Home, where did you go to school?'

'I was home-schooled in a galaxy far, far away.'

'You didn't go to school?'

'I'm an automatic auto-didact.'

'Have you seen a cuckoo?' Luke asked loudly and with a broad smile.

'Not yet,' said the house.

Just then, a little wooden window opened above the face of the clock, revealing a little bird that started dipping forwards and backwards.

'Hook-hooooo!'

'Did you see that?' Luke asked, and pointed at the clock.

'I have not.'

'You don't see anything,' Luke said, shaking his head.

'Indeed?' said the house.

A FEW MINUTES LATER, Jenny heard angry shouts from Jesse and Luke's room.

'Mom, he is saying the worst words!' Luke shouted, red-faced as she entered the room. 'He's been swearing constantly!'

'Shut up, you dummy,' Jesse said.

Jenny made wide eyes at Jesse. 'Jesse, that is unacceptable.'

'But, Mom, he's interrupting me, I hate it.' He clenched his teeth. 'He made me get killed. Don't you understand? It's the furthest I've ever made it.' And he kicked at a Jenga box that was on the floor. 'You don't get it.' Jesse pushed past her out of the room.

Jenny wasn't sure what to do with Jesse's rage. That game made him furious. And for a moment, it made her furious too. How could a game undo all the good she had sown in him? She looked at Luke, and he half smiled matter-of-factly at her.

'Teenagers, right?' he said to her, and her eyes softened at him.

'I guess so,' she said.

'Those are the kinds of words that will make you end up in jail,' he said.

Jenny wasn't sure if she had overdone the warnings to her children about the consequences of rude behaviour. There were a million things being thrown at her kids every day – rude outbursts they heard in the supermarket, bratty tantrums they watched on their TV shows – and she just couldn't buffer it all. 'Absorb, absorb,' she said to herself, as she turned to find Jesse and talk him down.

CHAPTER 9

H ANK COULDN'T BELIEVE HOW naive people could be sometimes. And that applied to the government too. And the security
services.

First off, who was in charge when the president was sleeping?
Presidents usually went to sleep at about midnight Eastern Time
(though Hank had read that Bush went to bed at 10.45 p.m.). So
that meant that all over the world, enemy forces knew that a lot of
important Washington people would take at least an hour to scramble
to their posts in case of an event. There should be a night shift, a
night president and a night CIA chief.

And someone should consider the water systems. Even Hank
could poison a water system if he wanted to – he went for jogs around
the reservoir just outside Bentonville, and, for a start, who's to say
he didn't piss in it at 6 a.m.? That wasn't the point. The point was
that you could add anthrax to the water. Or a radioactive substance.
And Hank knew that they couldn't be testing the water every minute

for every kind of contaminant. They'd probably detect it – but not until a lot of people had been fatally poisoned.

Was he the only one thinking about this stuff? He had heard that they were putting up a bomb-proof wall around the Eiffel Tower in France and he felt that was smart. But what took them so long? There had been portable explosives for decades and they were only now protecting their most recognisable national symbol. Seemed naive. Hadn't anyone read the Trojan Horse story? You let silent enemies into your country all the time and then you're surprised when they open fire? Not to mention the dangers within: they had only just reported on the news that Hillary Clinton had sent over a hundred emails containing sensitive government intelligence through her personal home server. What was wrong with the woman?

Hank wasn't paranoid, he was realistic. Apart from stockpiling water, peanut butter and batteries, he was trying to figure out how to react to a nuclear event. When they announced the plans for the nuclear plants, he bought a Geiger counter on eBay. He was also now assessing which hazmat suits were the most comprehensive. You could buy potassium iodide, but that only protected the thyroid from radiation. It was hard to find out about all this stuff, so Hank had downloaded an onion router to get access to the dark net. It was kind of illegal but, on the other hand, it was the only place where people were honest about what was really going on. He figured it would be useful if there was ever another 9/11 event. Plus it had all the information on how people were hacking smart homes – and this was information he needed to know. If you weren't careful, people could have you under surveillance in your own home.

Hank had his own section of the basement for his survival apparatus. On Friday morning, when the children were at school, he pulled the light string at the basement entrance and descended the plywood steps. His job at FINDASERVE gave him Fridays 'on the road' to sell to businesses in the area, which gave him a little latitude.

To get to his doomsday hoard, he had to pass through Luke's basement playroom. The shelves were deep with carefully arranged rows of objects. Hank knew that Luke was like most kids – wanting to know where things come from. But other kids looked at books about it. He'd never heard of a kid with his own private museum of obsession. He blamed Jenny. She was always encouraging them to be curious. And telling them they were good at things. Life's not like that. She was doing them a disservice by pumping them up, only to face the pricks of the big wide world. She didn't understand what it was like to be male.

The underground space had a pacifying effect on Hank – there was privacy here. He stood still. He looked around. This was a glimpse into the mind of the son he wanted to understand. Jars of powder, chunks of rock and shards of metal. What could he read in the arrangement of these articles? Hank thought. Was this so different from the baseball-card collection he'd had as a kid? He put his hands in his pockets. Hank had to admit: if you took care to see how ordered the objects were, it showed a serious work ethic. The boy had been as methodical as a beetle. Hank approached the row describing the origins of chewing gum. He knew Luke was phobic about chewing gum – the boy had explained that he didn't like to chew latex. He said you could just put the flavouring in your mouth, if that was all you wanted anyway. But he'd researched the stuff anyway. The gum was cinnamon, and Hank was tempted to unwrap it and pop it in his mouth, but he didn't want to screw up his son's work. Luke's mind was strange but it was smart. Hank had never been smart, so he felt an awe in the presence of his child's logic.

Something caught Hank's eye: lipstick. He plucked it from its place next to a jar labelled *Carnauba* and opened it: it was not only real, but it was used lipstick. What? Where had the boy got this? Was he using it for some weird activity, or . . . had Luke actually tried it on? He wouldn't put it past him. You never knew with Luke.

Hank put the lipstick in his pocket. His gaze sharpened. There were nylon stockings on the shelf above. He pulled them down, stuffed them into a wad and into his back pocket. What else? What *was* all this? Now he was nudging items aside and knocking things over. Bottles leaked, and a marble rolled onto the concrete floor. Something sizzled. Then Hank found an unused, unwrapped tampon. Shit.

The basement was cool and silent. Hank felt he had literally unearthed something significant. The survival store would have to wait. Something totally weird was going on with his younger son. It was probably from something the boy had heard in the playground. Maybe he was curious about girls' stuff. But a tampon? Oh God – was Luke, like, preparing to turn 'trans' or something? Or could some pervert have got to him? Wait – had Jenny given him these things?

Hank's mind was switching rapidly, trying to put it all together. He had to think clearly. Lipstick, tights and a tampon. It was obvious he needed to spend some more time with his sons. Jenny would have to move aside. This wasn't a game of 'playing house' anymore.

what's the number for the school

why? what's up? she replied. She couldn't answer the phone because she was at the plastic-surgery clinic on Fridays.

never mind

what's up?

nothing, he tapped. She was hysterical at the slightest hint of trouble.

He flipped up the lid of the trash can and chucked the tampon, lipstick and tights into it. Then he returned to the basement. He didn't want to overreact like Jenny did. Be logical. Okay, the girls' stuff was a problem. But what else was going on down there? This was a map to his son's mind, and he was never allowed access to that boy's thinking. Luke gravitated to his mother, and she pulled him to her too. Hank was so often left in the cold.

As he sat on the section of tree trunk that Luke used as a chair, Hank could see that the boy had principles. A particular and peculiar view of ordinary things. But being peculiar was only likely to get you grief, and Hank shook his head for his strange son.

He picked up the specimen jars from the gum process one by one: tree resin, frankincense, aromatic twigs, spruce gum, beeswax, pine rosin. There were other words he didn't recognise: chicle, jelutong, gutta-percha. It gave him an idea: he'd take the boys camping, without Jenny. Maybe he could teach them what they would need to know. His father had taken him camping once, and it had been a rite of passage.

It was no wonder that Luke was a little confused. The problem was that Jenny was always more impressed when Hank did stuff like make pasta or go to classical music concerts. He tried to tell her about the time he lifted twice his bodyweight, but she seemed to look right through him and turn her attention to her Instagram feed. He thought she would be interested in the story of how he settled a rowdy dispute in a parking lot with a total asshole in a Ford Bronco. But Jenny said to him, 'When you're calm, you're in control.' She said she was sure he could hold his ground in any good fight, but she was also sure that he wouldn't even have to – and she smiled at him, touched his bicep.

But Hank knew – he instinctively felt it – that sometimes 'being in control' was a matter of physique. He was getting sick of having to back down and be civilised. Jenny didn't even let the boys have toy guns. All she did was talk about chivalry and knighthood – and the 'nobility' of it – but Hank knew that the boys just wanted to roughhouse sometimes. It was in their chromosomes. Males were built for violence. Boys like toy guns, and he didn't want to have to explain it all the time.

Hank had never really been in a fight. Judo at high school didn't count. There was one time at school that he had pushed a guy who had cut in front of him in the lunch line. He hadn't really been mad, but he couldn't just stand there. A teacher saw it and Hank got in trouble – but in actual fact, he didn't really want to fight the guy so it was no bad thing that Hank was led away and made to sit out his lunch hour in the hall.

As he sat in the hall for that half an hour, fourteen-year-old Hank had fantasised about the punches and the kicks he would have imposed on the guy. He went through the fight over and over in his head. But the truth was: he wasn't really angry enough to go through with it. All he knew was that if he had to, he would give it his all. He had read *The Art of War* at about that age, and he reminded himself to give it to Jesse now that he was a teenager. Every guy needed to read that book. It told you how to manage opposition without losing ground. It prepared you for feats of the future. It told you how to conquer new territories.

The thing was, he was just so sick of having to behave all the time. Why did he have to feel so guilty for being a white male? Sure, he could see that there was a kind of patriarchy going on, but he wasn't really sure if he was actually a part of that patriarchy. He wasn't a CEO. He wasn't in control of any industry. He didn't suppress people. He was semi-successful at best. Anyway, if he was part of the patriarchy, then it was a double-edged sword. You have to protect. You have to provide. You have to be tough. You have to face the bullets when they come. But then you also should be ashamed of those impulses. It's toxic masculinity, they tell you. But whose poison is it? First, you're told to be strong and tough all your goddamn life, then you're told to lock it in – and you get patted on the head for all your good behaviour. Where was the dignity in that?

He only needed to look at his gnarly knuckles to know they were good for a fight. You learn that when you're the red-faced raging boy with the broken bike, furious because you can't cry, and you know that vengeance is your only option. That hadn't changed. His boys would still have to suppress their tears. He knew the awesome spectre of Superman that would hover above them their whole lives. And he understood that, like him, they would always be on the verge of failing to be that hero. Damned if you do, damned if you don't.

He had asked Jenny what the headline of her magazine meant by 'reconstructed men'. He'd heard it so often in Woody Allen movies but hadn't ever really understood the term. Not really. She had laughed at him, said something like, 'It's erasing your memory card and trying to start all over again.'

'I'm not a fucking device!' he said. 'The protocols are real.'

'Oh, come on, Hank, haven't you ever heard that gender is a social construct?' she said. 'It's imaginary.'

'I'm not made of goddamn Lego bricks,' he shouted at her.

CHAPTER 10

LUKE KNEW WHERE TO sit in the therapy room. He was fiddling with the ink bottles lined up at the low table. Mrs Paxton had her back to him and was jotting quick notes in his folder.

'So!' She turned around with a bright smile. 'Nice to see you, Luke.'

She was kind, and he liked her, but her games were pretty boring. He was still trying to figure out why she was so interested in him. What was he supposed to do? What was she waiting for him to do? He answered her questions with the words he could find.

'We're going to have some fun with ink today – what do you think?' She sat down opposite him, with her knees spread around the edges of the small table. She was tall, and the table was low. He didn't need such a low table, he wasn't a toddler. He had noticed lots of toys for little kids in the room – and he was suspicious that she thought he was younger than he was. Eight-year-olds don't play with buses and dolls. But anyway, there was no other table in the room, so they pretty much had to sit there.

She asked him which colour he wanted, and he chose the turquoise.

'Now, take this long, pretty paintbrush and dip it in the ink and put some ink onto this piece of paper.' She slid a sheet of thick paper onto the table.

This could be a little bit fun.

'Do you want me to draw something real?' He paused.

'No – no, you don't have to, you can do whatever you want. Anyway, we're going to make something special out of it.' She smiled and nodded at the paper.

He dipped the brush in the ink pot and lifted it out. A drop fell on the page. 'Oh no,' he said, tipping his head. He'd dripped ink. And ink stains.

'No! That's great!' she said. 'Keep doing that, that's exactly what you need to do – lots and lots of drips.'

He looked at her, and she nodded at him again: 'Go ahead, honey, just drip the ink.'

So he dripped and dripped the ink, until she indicated that he'd done enough. Had he passed the test? Was there something about the way he dripped the ink that told her something about him? She pinched the top and bottom edges of the paper, and proceeded to fold the inky paper in half carefully, trying not to spill the ink.

'It's kind of like something called a Rorschach – and we are going to use our imaginations and look into it.' The sides of the folded paper stuck to each other and she peeled them back, yawning, on the patch of table before Luke.

Luke rotated it ninety degrees and looked into it.

'That's interesting. Why did you turn it? Is there something there that you can see?' she asked.

He turned it again. 'So –' he checked with her – 'you want me to look at this and tell you something?'

She nodded. He sniffed the paper.

'Paper mills smell like giant farts because they use sulphur to soften the pulp.'

This was his first fact for her. She waited. He needed to tell her something interesting.

'Green ink is made of chlorophyll.' He sat back and looked at her.

She leaned forward and pointed to the ink splotches. 'Look at these interesting shapes – I bet you could find some pictures in there. Can you see anything?'

He leaned over the paper again. He wished he knew what she wanted him to say.

'Saturation?' He looked up.

'Oh right, yes, saturation. But you know, some people think these look like butterflies. Do you?'

He hadn't got the answer right; she was being nice about it.

'Butterflies. Because of the colour. Because of the shape?' he offered.

She stayed silent, looking down at the inked paper.

He was tensing; he thought he must be getting it all wrong.

'I don't like ink,' he said to her, and pushed the paper towards her. And before she could answer he added, 'And I don't want to play with your dolls either, sorry.'

Mrs Paxton straightened up. She was very sympathetic.

'That's okay, Luke, we don't have to do anything you don't want to do.' She reached for his shoulder. 'Why don't you tell me anything interesting that you would like to tell me. Doesn't matter what it's about. Like, what happened this week?'

'Oh, that's easy. Yes, I can tell you. We had a burglary,' he said, checking her reaction.

'A burglary? . . . At your home?' Now she was interested.

'Well, yes. And no one knows about it, only me.' He folded his hands in his lap. 'Unfortunately,' he added, lifting his thumbs from their clutch.

'Really? What did they take?' she asked.

'They came into the basement and scuffled around looking for something, and I'm still trying to figure out what's missing – I think my cotton sample, my nylon sample, some coloured whale blubber. Which is basically lipstick. But they knocked things over and they put things in the wrong place. And they spilled the hydrogen peroxide too, which could have been dangerous. We could have all died.'

Mrs Paxton seemed confused, so he continued. 'I didn't tell my parents because I didn't want to scare them. Not until I figure out what happened . . . There was an intruder, but I still don't know what they wanted. It was probably a girl. Because, you know, whale blubber is made of lipstick.'

He thought he'd explained it pretty well but Mrs Paxton was still confused.

'Are you sure, honey? Are you sure it wasn't your pet that knocked things over, or some mice in the basement? Maybe your brother moved your things?'

'No, no, it happened when we were both at school. And my mom never goes down there. And my dad was at work . . . and we don't even have gerbils anymore since they died!' he explained. 'I know what happened. I just don't know *why* it happened,' he said.

Mrs Paxton moved carefully to her desk and made some notes in his folder again. She distracted him with another question. 'So, that sounds alarming – were you scared by this burglary?'

'I'm not scared . . . I'm not scared,' he repeated. 'But, it was a strange event.' He looked up at her again. He was doing something right. Maybe he should tell her more scary things, and she would have something to write down in the folder of notes.

'Another thing I saw. My neighbour smokes cigarettes. So he is going to die,' he said.

The door cracked open and they both looked over. Jenny poked her head through and smiled. 'Everything okay?' she asked, opening the door and moving into the room with her bag.

Mrs Paxton brightened. 'Yes, everything's great. We did some ink painting and Luke told me some interesting things.' Luke shot her a look of warning, which she caught.

When Luke had his coat on and they were leaving the room, Jenny and Mrs Paxton were exchanging short phrases, spoken quietly, about 'being in touch'. As Jenny and Luke were heading into the reception, Luke held his mother to stop her, and dashed back towards the therapy room. 'I forgot something!' He pushed open

Mrs Paxton's door, bent over a little and whispered loudly to her: 'Don't tell her about the burglary!'

She nodded a loud whisper back. 'Okay! I won't!'

Jenny was waiting in the reception area, where one little girl was lying on the floor face-down and another child was trying to rock his chair, with little effect. Luke returned and presented himself to Jenny.

'Got everything?' Jenny asked as she took his hand.

'Sure,' he replied, showing her a rock from his pocket.

In the car, he told her that he had done a 'roar-sack' with Mrs Paxton, and it dawned on him that there was something quite particular he was supposed to have seen in the ink splotch: a lion roaring in a sack. He wished he'd been smart enough to see that at the time.

CHAPTER 11

JOHN'S LETTERS WERE COMING weekly these days, and Jenny started to see a pattern. They came in on a Monday morning, and she replied on a Tuesday. The next Monday, there was another.

Dear Jenny,

Thank you for the God-phone number, I wasn't expecting that.

My cell has a desk and that's where I sit to write to you, and it's uncomfortable cos the furniture here is fixed down and metal. You want to pull up a chair somewhere but you can't do that. They're cemented to the floor. You want to catch a spider high up on the wall, so you can put it in a jar and get some damn sleep, but there's nothing to climb on. Nothing bends either. Two flat beds with green sheets and one hard pillow each. There's a metal toilet and a small sink and no window but that's obvious.

So, there is something I didn't tell you and I'm sorry about this. I have a wife. I don't know why I didn't tell you, I guess

I got all caught up in my own stories here. I also wanted to protect her, to keep her secret and away from this hell-hole existence. But actually I didn't protect her. She's in jail too, Penn State Penitentiary. She's the one who was an 'accessory' to my crime. She's the one that I need to tell that I am sorry and I know I should probably think up a better word than 'sorry' but it's all I can think of. I know she doesn't hold it against me or maybe she does now. I can't get in touch with her because prisoners can't write to other prisoners. Shona's a good person, she is a medical professional. Maybe you can tell me a nice way of saying it? Something that wives like to hear husbands say. You know I'm no good with words. I would really appreciate that. I'm getting urgent about it, it's keeping me up nights, because she gets out in a few weeks and I don't know where she's going when she's out.

    Peace out,

    John

PS. She likes fancy ground coffee.

A tiny envelope tumbled from the bigger envelope with a name on it: Shona Brendon. Jenny sat back in her chair and held the letter in a hand on her knee. So, he has a wife. She is called Shona. A real wife. Jenny tugged at her collar; her earlobes burned and her throat pinched.

Shona. Jenny tried to take a deep breath but it huffed in and puffed out; she held the envelope up and fanned herself with it briefly. The name sounded African American to her, but she quickly chided herself mentally for making assumptions. It might be Irish, she supposed. You had to do that – you absolutely had to check that you weren't lapsing into subliminal racism. White people were still prone to that, she knew it. Only assholes were overtly racist but she knew there were wrong undercurrents in most people's minds.

Bentonville didn't have that many African Americans in it. There were second-generation Indians, and several families of Chinese Americans, but not many black people. She remembered taking seven-year-old Jesse downtown for a musical and that there were so many African Americans that Jesse had become distracted, and dragged on her arm, absorbed in the city's people. He said to her, 'There are a lot of brown people here,' and she had reacted quickly, perhaps a little too quickly: 'You know, Jesse, if we went to Africa, the children there would look at us and think we'd been bleached. They'd think that we'd had all the colour drained out of us. Maybe even that we were albinos . . . So it goes both ways, you see.' He looked at her as though he'd been reprimanded, but he was angry because he didn't understand why he had been scolded. She let it stand though – because who knows what messages their mostly white community was sending to him? There was room for correction, she was sure. 'We call brown people "black", by the way,' she said. 'They call themselves black too, just so you know.' She felt like maybe explaining that white people weren't actually white either – and the significance of the damnable black-and-white dichotomy – but that might confuse him. He just needed to know that he should tread carefully when it came to skin colour.

AS JENNY FOLDED JOHN'S letter, and pushed it back into its envelope, she wondered just what difference it was making that they didn't know each other's race. It was something she'd requested at the beginning – that they didn't exchange photos of themselves. So they had the delicious freedom of the mind's eye. He had agreed, though only with the response 'Okay, fine by me'.

In the morning sunlight of her kitchen, Jenny was still. A stripe of sun fell across her face and chest and the warmth of it felt like a gift: to be warmed by the sun that came and touched her through her own window. Shona's envelope was sitting on the table and Jenny picked it up. It was so light. What can he have said in the card? She held it up to the sunlight. A prayer card. According to the sunlight, he hadn't written anything on it. Jenny wondered if some couples have private romantic signs; maybe for John and Shona, the prayer had some story to it – that he was sending her a prayer to remind her of invisible love. But he was Buddhist. It was a little weird. Well, it was none of her business. No, it was not. That's right.

She took the sharpish end of the J of her key ring, and slid it along the adhesive strip of the card, breaking the seal cleanly and gently, bit by bit. It came apart easily for her, and she prised open the envelope slowly. Yes, there was a card, she had been right. It was a prayer for the lonely. And written in light pencil: *I can't live without* you. *I won't live without you. You are my freedom. Wait for me, we'll start again*. And, at the bottom, written so lightly you might miss it, were the words: *Taste me*.

Jenny recoiled. That was a little gross. And rude! She looked into the corners of the envelope for anything else. She sniffed the card – it smelled of linoleum floors, and, strangely, Fruit Loops. She placed the card on the countertop, and took a sip of water from a glass that had been sitting by the sink all morning. After swallowing, she felt a surge of guilt and tried to reseal the envelope with some spittle on a finger. It wasn't working. The orange glue on the seal of the envelope wouldn't come alive again. And her finger had turned orange. An orange finger. That was odd.

Her phone was buzzing; several messages were coming through, so she picked it up, started to flick at them with her thumb, and without thinking, she put the orange finger into her mouth. It tasted sweet. She looked up from her text messages and frowned at the orange finger. And she put it back in her mouth. *Taste me*, he'd said to his wife. *You are my freedom*. Except it was Jenny who was tasting now. She kept the finger in her mouth. She hadn't known he had a wife. She held her finger in her mouth for as long as it took for the taste to abate – it was a good taste, it was clean and she felt her chest relax. The taste of freedom, she thought. But it was lovelier than that. It felt as if kind sun had finally come round to her and it was warming her roots.

CHAPTER 12

MARCH HAD BEEN SO changeable that year that the shoots of unborn flowers kept pushing up into the sunshine, only to be paralysed by night-frost. And so, by late April, the flowers were in disarray and the lawn was patchy as Hank packed up the car with camping equipment and set off with Jesse and Luke to the Endless Mountains. Easter was late this year, so they had a good opportunity to go camping during the kids' vacation week. They drove up through the state, the highway to the mountains was neat, cutting into rock, shooting cars between newly hewn cliff faces. The trees at the edges of the highway were still wiry, their leaves not yet unspooled, and they pushed up their branches like cracks into a white sky.

The boys were silent in the car. They each had their windows and Hank had the windscreen – views that offered them horizons for their thoughts. Hank wondered if they were heading for rain – not that it mattered, because the whole point was that they were going to face the elements, whichever they were. He checked the boys in his rear-view mirror, as if to check that they were prepared for what lay ahead. He was glad he remembered to warn Jenny that there is no cellphone signal in the Endless, so there were no expectations to manage there. The drive was several hours, and Hank had promised they would stop for pretzels in Cresco. He remembered them to be pretty good pretzels; he'd been camping up in the Endless about fifteen years ago with a bunch of friends, and they had stopped there. Hank thought that if they decided to go camping every year, the three of them, it could be a ritual, the pretzel-stop ritual.

'You boys falling asleep back there?' Hank looked again in his rear-view mirror.

'Nah,' one chimed, and the other repeated it.

'You think we're ready to face the bears?' He chuckled. And the boys said nothing.

After a while, Luke asked, 'Are there really bears? . . . I mean, do they come to the campsites?'

Hank chuckled again, and rubbed his chin with one hand.

'Well, yes, there are. That's why you tie your food up in a bear bag, hang it from a tree,' he said, checking Luke's face in the mirror.

'But I thought bears could climb trees – isn't that what they're good at?'

Hank was turning off at an exit, indicating, and looking into his wing mirrors. He didn't answer immediately. 'Well, yes, but the point is that you hang it from a branch that would be too thin for the bear to consider climbing, and too high for him to reach . . .'

There was silence as this fact was absorbed by the back seat.

Hank continued. 'But these days they have bear-proof lockers in the main campgrounds, I believe . . .' He was following signs onto a different highway. 'But we're not going to one of those, are we? This is a *real* wild camping trip – right, boys? We're going to be like Neanderthals. Grrrr!'

The boys didn't answer, their eyes again trained through the windows.

Hank gave up. They would soon get it. This would be a trip to remember. He might finally be able to teach them something useful.

IT DIDN'T REALLY MATTER, but the ground was damp – the park ranger had told them that a sudden April snow had fallen and melted a few days back. The boys were red-faced and sullen when they finally heaved their backpacks off their backs and sat on a stone outcropping. Hank had decided that this little clearing in the woods was the perfect size, and there was a trickling stream a few paces away – good for washing dirty plates, or sweaty feet.

'First thing to do is get the tent up – come on, boys,' Hank said, emptying the spokes and fabric from the tent bag. The boys slid from the rock, came over and picked up spokes.

'You boys're not exactly springing to action . . .' said Hank as he pushed a spoke up through the spine of the tent's fabric. 'Tents these days are so quick to put up – you should have seen how complicated they used to be when I was young,' he said. The tent leapt up into its correct geometries.

'Now. A fire. We need to go get some kindling and wood. Follow me.'

The three of them scattered into the nearby woods and picked up broken pieces of fallen branches. Hank thought that if he could get them to think of it as a competition, they would be quick and successful at this. 'Boys – whoever gets the most sticks, wins,' he said.

'Wins what?' Jesse said, bored.

'Yeah,' Luke joined. 'Wins what?'

'Wins the challenge. You guys, don't you get it?' Hank was pulling up a big branch from under a bush. The boys continued picking up sticks and carrying them back to the campsite. They seemed to think the pile was big enough, and sat there again, on the rock, waiting for more instructions. Hank was scrabbling around in his backpack. He couldn't find matches. Did he forget the matches? Of all things.

'You guys, I'm going to the camp store to get matches before they shut.'

'You forgot the matches?' Jesse grimaced.

'I don't know where they are and we'll need plenty, so you guys prepare firewood like I told you, and I'll come back and see whether you got it right.' He zipped up his jacket and set off through the woods. The camp store was an hour's hike away so he'd be gone for two hours. It was only three o'clock though, so the boys would be fine.

'You want us to come with you?' Luke asked.

'No, kiddo, you keep the camp safe.'

He probably should have made the boys come with him. He was

in two minds about it – to toughen them up with the physical exercise of it, or to leave them to their own devices and let them fend for themselves for a short while. He had to figure out how to get them on track. They couldn't go through life so pathetic. No matter how much their mother watched *Oprah*, or read those parenting books, the real world – city people, poor people – still followed a man's code. Eat or be eaten, and that was the bottom line, he thought as he trudged downhill. He was working up a sweat and it felt good. He felt strong when it was just him against the natural world. The crack of pine needles underfoot; the bracken parted by his stride.

The man at the camp store didn't look up when Hank walked in. Hank didn't need anything else much besides matches, he was pretty sure. He picked up some marshmallows.

'You . . . probably want a lighter,' the man said as Hank stood at the cash register with a large box of matches in his hand. 'If that's all you have, I mean.'

'Oh, right, sure. One lighter then.' Of course. If the matches got wet, they would need another source of fire.

'Colour?' the man asked. Hank paused, not quite understanding, so the man took the cardboard tray of lighters down from the shelf and placed them in front of Hank. 'Which one d'you want?'

Hank picked out the yellow one, gave it a thumb-strike and paid for everything with five bucks.

He checked his cellphone one last time and there were no messages. He thought perhaps to send Jenny a text message but she knew where they were, and there wasn't anything more to say since they had pretty much said it all. It had been a grand fight, one of those that clears the air completely but so much so that light shines starkly on the remains of life afterwards. She had been swearing at him under her breath for a day or so, to keep the kids from hearing but also to make sure he knew he had crossed one of her lines. Her many putrid lines. 'Boundaries.' But so what if he hadn't picked up the phone? So what if he came home late? He was just working things out with a potential client. Well, it turns out that she wasn't just mad about all that, but also, according to her, and to Luke's shrink, he had 'burgled' Luke's playroom. It was just too much. He had burgled his own son's playroom.

When he had told Jenny about the female stuff he found there, she just exploded. Told him just how stupid a man he was.

'You're so . . . you're so . . . small-minded!'

'Thanks a lot for your understanding.'

'No, you're just a Neanderthal,' she shouted.

'Well, that's not necessarily an insult,' Hank had said.

He was a Viking though, and he almost reminded her of that. In fact, the more he read the issue of *National Geographic* about Vikings, the more he understood them. Some of them were traders and farmers. They had an amazing ability to shrug off their losses in battle. Hank could be like that sometimes. So he had brought the magazine with him to show the boys. It turns out that Vikings were big on hygiene and were well-groomed too – another strong piece of DNA. They were strong, fearless, just, honourable. This was why they needed to go camping. To honour their heritage.

When Hank approached their campsite, he decided to slow up and quieten down. And he needed a slash. And to give his sweaty nuts some air. As he pissed against a birch tree, splotching the white peelings with his dark yellow urine, he decided he wanted to see what his boys were getting up to while he was gone. Just wanted to spy on them for a minute. This would tell him something. Anyway, it had taken him far less than two hours to get to the campground and back – with the boys, and carrying their packs, they had been slower to get here.

The walk had done Hank some good – he was feeling it now. And, moreover, he was glad he had left the boys to fend for themselves. They could feel proud that they had faced the wilderness alone for a while. Maybe Jesse would face his fear of insects. Maybe Luke would stop his counting when he saw that nature has too many things to count. They would be fine. Bears didn't come out until evening anyway, so there wasn't really a concern there. And other hikers were few and far between – what were the chances? All the same, he was glad Jenny wasn't there; she would be fussing about it and protecting them. She wouldn't let them have the freedom that was necessary to make boys into men.

But, as he approached the campsite, he could neither see nor hear anything. He stopped to hear a little better. Not a sound. He worried for a second – would they be so stupid as to follow him, and get lost? Yes, they could be that stupid. Then he smiled; maybe they were hiding from him. Yes, that would be about right. So Hank circled the campsite, quietly treading through the woods like a Native

American hunter: placing his feet down toe-to-heel, toe-to-heel. He stopped behind a big tree and looked around either side of it. And he looked up, in case they'd climbed a tree. He rested there for a couple of minutes. Sometimes you just had to be quiet to stir up your prey. They would crack up soon.

Hank looked around the tree at the clearing where their tent and kit lay. He could only see one backpack: his own. The other two were gone. Maybe they *had* actually followed him down? Hank tried to figure out which direction they would have taken. There was a lake in the valley; the stream led to it. They probably went swimming. Yes. That might be something they would do. Still, they could be skipping stones, or trying to fish, or something. He went into the clearing and picked up his backpack, which was leaning against a tree. A glance over to where the tent lay confirmed it: their backpacks were really gone. *Shit*. Slinging his binoculars over his shoulder, he headed down to the lake. He wasn't going to panic. These woods were not dangerous, and they weren't Little Red Riding Hoods!

When he got to a ledge from which the lake could be seen, he pulled out his binoculars. There were two small figures wading at the edge of the lake some distance away. He started focusing the lenses to get a clearer picture of what they were doing. *Damn* – those boys do not follow instructions. They should have stayed put. *Damn*. He was relieved, if a little pissed off. First things first, he was going to tell them, you set up your camp. Then you can go and play in the lake and all that stuff.

As the figures came into focus, frilly bikini bottoms and twisted ponytails came to the fore. Those were two girls catching minnows, not his boys. And their parents were sitting up on the grass watching them. *Shit*. Hank scanned the lake. There were big branches floating and rotating with leaves clustering at their joints. Waterbirds popped up here and there. Fish leapt and flopped, reaching for bugs, pushing wave-circles out over the water. What was he looking for in the water? He had to get down there.

'Say . . .' Hank gave a broad smile as he walked up to the girls' parents. They had seen him scrambling down the hill and trotting towards them. He wanted to appear relaxed about this though. 'You haven't seen a couple of boys around here, have you?' he asked, slowing down, removing his cap.

The mother, her arms resting on her raised knees, bangles falling and catching on each other at her wrists, was beginning to stand up. The dad was already coming to meet him.

'It's just that they went off to play, and I thought they were heading here, and I can't find them. I'm sure they'll come back to the tent – you know boys.' Hank laughed. 'They'll be hungry at some point! . . . But, uh, you haven't seen 'em around here?'

The parents looked concerned. The husband spoke first. 'I'm sorry, we haven't seen anyone. It's so quiet around here. Um . . .' He looked around the lake. 'How old are they?'

'Oh, they're eight and thirteen, called Luke and Jesse . . . Well, if you see them, I'm up there.' Hank pointed up the hill. 'Send them along, if you don't mind.'

'How long have they been gone?' the mother asked, pushing a forelock of curly hair out of her eyes.

'Oh, about an hour, I'd say . . . Not long.' Hank was already backing away, still trying to be friendly. 'I'm not too worried, my boys are pretty intrepid. Just, uh, keep an eye out, I'd appreciate it.' He waved a hand and turned to walk off.

'Good luck finding them. I hope they're okay,' the dad said. 'We have a first-aid kit if you need it.'

'We'll take care of them if we find them!' offered the mom.

HANK WALKED AS FAST as he could without seeming to rush. The boys must have followed him down to the main campsite. Maybe they wanted something from the store and they went after him. Dammit! He wished he had cellphone reception so he could call the store to find out if they were there. He cut across the hill to join the trail that led to the main campsite.

Hank clambered over rocks and fallen trees, stumbling, bruising his shins. When he got far enough from the parents with the girls, he started to call out for them. He whistled with two fingers in his mouth. He decided to cut back up to the tent. He could circle for hours, and his only hope was to go back to base. He approached, hoping they had returned. But as he tramped into the clearing, there was still no sign of them.

'Luu-uke! Je-ss-seee!' he sent a call around the clearing. When his voice subsided, he heard the tinkling of electronic sounds.

Luke's head popped out of the tent, and Hank jumped. 'Shit, you scared me.'

'Hi, Dad,' said Luke.

Hank bent down towards Luke and swiped the tent door aside. Inside, Jesse was propped up on a backpack playing a game on a hand console.

'Get out of there.' Hank spat the words at Jesse.

Jesse scrambled out of the tent, still holding the hand console that was beeping at him for further action.

Hank grabbed it and jabbed at it to switch it off as Jesse and Luke stood, stock-still.

'This —' Hank splayed his hands, jerking them in various directions at the trees, the sky — 'is *not for that*.' He pointed at the device. He was shouting now: 'Didn't you hear me calling for you? . . . Didn't you hear me even come get my binoculars out of my pack?'

'I thought it . . . was a bear,' Luke murmured.

'And what the heck is this?' He pushed his boot at the pile of sticks the boys had laid for a fire, and it collapsed.

THE BOYS SHIFTED FITFULLY in the tent while they slept, and Hank couldn't sleep for his back. Jesse was still dressed, because he wouldn't get changed. Hank had urged him out of the tent to get changed outside while he and Luke were inside, but Jesse said that was even worse — the woods made him feel watched. So he was going to wear the same clothes for a few days, and Hank said that was okay by him.

He could hear the boys breathe, and little sounds emerged in their breaths. In his half-sleep state, it seemed to Hank that Jesse had tiny screeching tyres in his exhales. Luke had the breathing of a cathedral, echoing and cavernous. God, he loved his boys. But as soon as that love surged in him, it was always superseded by an urge to drive them. The boys needed to be disciplined about their ambitions. They needed to be impervious. Hank was learning about all this too late in the game; he should have owned himself earlier.

After the console fiasco, Hank had rebuilt the fire pile, showing his sons how wood needed oxygen to burn. 'Don't suffocate it,' he chided, stern but now calm. 'You have to give it air so it can rage.' Before lighting it, he took the boys up to a ridge of rock overlooking the steep valley of the Susquehanna. They sat down, in a row. Hank was going to initiate a few minutes of silence, a sort of meditation session, but as he looked over at the boys, he saw they were still locked in the silence that began after Hank confiscated the console.

CHAPTER 13

A T FIRST, JENNY WAS relieved to have the place to herself.
Scouring the house for camping equipment, and trying to pack
their backpacks for every possible weather, had exhausted her. She
had tucked energy bars down the sides of the boys' backpacks in
case they were desperate. Hank tended to feed the boys only when
he himself was hungry; he didn't seem to understand the correlation
between the children's moods and their appetites.

She had spoken to Jesse upstairs before they all left. Alone in
Jesse's room, she sat down on the bed and said, 'I have two things
to tell you, and you have to listen – I'm counting on you, Jess.' First,
she told him about the energy bars, and told him to keep them in
reserve. Second, she showed him a small brown package. 'In here,
there are three flares. You must only use them in a real emergency.
Listen, they are very dangerous. They shoot fire, so hold them
away from faces. Point them at the sky.' She held them up high to
demonstrate, and then showed him the instructions. They were to

use them if they were too injured to get back to the main campsite. Or if a bear attacked. Or if they were totally lost towards dusk. 'I'm giving these to you so you can have some big-boy responsibility,' she said. 'Because I trust you.'

'Mom,' he answered, taking the package, 'you don't have to call me a big boy anymore. I am already a big boy.'

'Okay, fine, but there are bad guys out there, just remember,' she said. Bad guys who make bad choices, she thought. Jesse rolled his eyes.

The detritus of the packing storm littered the stairs, but her back ached so it could wait. She flicked on the coffee maker. She should have asked the house to make coffee, but she liked to override it as often as she could. But coffee made her prickly – maybe she shouldn't. Jenny was jagged with the thorns of disaffection and they sharpened with caffeine. She should drink tea, she knew that. Tea was an ancient cure. But there was this mood that coffee could sometimes deliver – an ecstasy of sorts. When the hit was right, she could fix everything, their lives seemed not only doable but conquerable. 'Coping admirably' was the phrase. It only lasted for about two hours, but the tasks accomplished in those two hours could sometimes facilitate events for a whole week. In those two hours she could tackle the tasks that she avoided the rest of the time, like hanging pictures on the wall, like replacing the doorknobs on the basement door, like hand-washing their delicates.

But this wasn't going to happen – she was beat. Lately, she had felt that she was on edge, that she was manic with the blizzard of details that she needed to keep in mind, so the coffee would make her frazzled, like she had acute ADHD – or OCD – or PTSD.

A lazy fly bounced and soared across the room – not lazy, probably, but barely alive. Hatched too soon from a cluster of eggs tucked in a windowsill somewhere. It looked like it was having trouble waking up. She hoped it wouldn't lay any eggs of its own, because she loathed those sticky fly strips they were sometimes forced to hang in the kitchen during the summer months. Fly graveyards that looked like Fruit Roll-Up – it was confusing to her that they looked both tasty and disgusting. She'd better kill the fly; it seemed logical, a mercy killing. John had told her he wouldn't kill a fly if one buzzed into his cell because he was a Buddhist. But she was technically a Christian, and so she could kill a fly without wondering if it was her grandmother reincarnated.

'Home, get rid of that fly,' Jenny said to the ceiling.

'I'm sorry I'm not sure I understand you.'

'Fine, I'll do it.'

She lunged at it with a rolled-up magazine but, moronic as the fly was, it still managed to outsmart her. She couldn't remember what she'd been told about the eyes of flies. Could she hover her magazine above it without it seeing, and then smack it down hard, killing it – or did flies have, like, 360-degree vision? Her only chance was to corner it, so she drove it towards a window with a flapping dishcloth.

The fly fussed and panicked at the sash of the window. Even though she hadn't started her offensive on it there, it knew she was after it. Well, of course it did. Jenny smiled lightly as she realised that we always think insects are blind to us, that they can't see us, that only the fly-swatter mattered. But this fly was probably watching every movement of her hulking presence and knew she was its predator. It was just so damn tired that it couldn't think clearly, and couldn't maintain any real flight pattern. Kept passing out, then rousing itself with sheer fear. Needed something sweet. Needed a sip of water. My kingdom for another nap.

She flattened it with her palm, on the window. The fly left a smear of clear juice, flecked with bits of wing. Gravity peeled its corpse off the glass surface and dropped it to the ledge. Jenny got a paper towel and removed it all, washed her hands. That was not as satisfying as she had thought it would be.

She got a sticky fly strip out of the kitchen drawer, and its sweet smell reminded her of something. The orange glue of John's envelope. What had she done with that letter? It was weird that prison glue smelled like Fruit Loops. She left the fly strip on the kitchen counter, unopened, and fished John's note to Shona from her purse. She'd better mail it. But since the envelope wouldn't stick anymore, she got a new one, a large one, and copied down Shona's name onto it, with the address of her correctional facility that John had mentioned in another letter. It was in Pennsylvania, across the state, but actually only a few hours' drive from Bentonville. Jenny put her post office box address on the back of the envelope as John had told her. And after stuffing the prayer card into the new envelope, she added a short note from her kitchen pad saying: *Hi Shona, this is for you. I'm a pen-pal and my name is Jenny.* She added her cellphone number at the bottom of the note just in case. She pushed a small packet of ground coffee from her kitchen cabinet into the envelope too – John had said that Shona liked coffee. She could still smell John's original envelope, even though it was now back inside her bag – what a delicious smell. Kind of like the Flintstones vitamins she used to take when she was little. She wondered if that was what had attracted the dozy fly.

Leaning on the countertop, she typed the words 'orange glue envelope' with two thumbs into the search engine on her smartphone and the results listed stationery retailers selling orange envelopes. 'Orange seal envelope' gave her the same results, pretty much: a string of images of orange paper for correspondence. She had never seen orange glue before, but then again, it reminded her of kindergarten. Maybe they didn't let prisoners use regular glue in case they sniffed it.

John's last letter was still bothering her – annoying her, in fact. Did she know what his incarcerated wife wanted to hear from him?

Dear John,

What do wives want to hear? I hate the word 'wife'. But I might as well have it branded on my forehead. Please don't ask me what a wife thinks because I have no clue. Husband is a pretty ugly word too. Are you maybe asking about love?

I heard a story once about a husband who saved his wife's life. They were in the woods, and I guess they were walking upwind, and they encountered a mother bear who attacked them. She had cubs. The husband gave the wife a flare and pushed her up a tree. He himself didn't make it, the bear mauled him and killed him before help came. Maybe that was an act of true love. Or maybe it was just an accident.

I would probably try to push my husband up a tree if a bear attacked, but he is a lot bigger than me, so maybe he would push me up the tree instead. I would certainly push my kids up the tree and face the bear. I would even kill the bear if my kids were in danger. Mother love is a different kind of love. I would murder anyone, even a person, if I needed to defend my kids.

My children broke my heart when they were born, and my husband knows it too. I can't explain it, but it felt like heartbreak, or maybe heart-burst? Or maybe they just are my heart, now outside of my body, walking around in the world, with my blood in their veins, exposed to storms and sunlight. Love and death. Love and birth. It's weird because giving birth really is a deadly thing, you really feel like you might die. What I mean is that becoming a mother does not feel nice – it feels sacred and shocking. It still does.

I'm not sure why I'm telling you this. Why I'm telling you that I now feel capable of murder – which I never felt before. It's just that this love for children is frightening. It blasts a massive hole into the neat framework of life you have built – and you can see into distances of greater love, greater cruelty. What I mean is, I am not afraid of criminals, nor of the things you have done.

Your mother probably felt the same way about you as I do about my children. If you're lucky, your wife feels this about you too.

Jenny

Her cellphone pinged with a message. It was Terri.

Hey girl, want to get coffee?

Terri knew she was alone for a few days. Jenny decided the housework could wait. She picked up her coat, hanging on the back of a kitchen chair, and went straight for the door. She picked up the letters – she could mail them on her way there.

Yes, you wanna meet now at Dazzles?

Looks like she'd be having coffee after all.

Jenny got there first. Her coffee was made by a barista in training, and Jenny was fixated; it was an education she had never witnessed: the barista trainer was goading his trainee. 'Flower! Flower!' The trainee's hand was wobbling as she tried to follow his instructions. 'Push the milk in, push it in, push it in.' And she tried, plopping three dollops of foamed milk into the top of the coffee. 'And line . . . line . . . do the line,' he said. The trainee pulled her small jug from the back to the front of the cup, forming a line through the circles she made. They delivered the coffee into Jenny's hands with a smile. Jenny looked into her cup. It wasn't a flower. It looked like a giant penis blooming from a pair of pendulous testicles.

Moments later, Terri arrived.

'So.' Terri clutched her coffee with both hands, her silver thumb rings like bolts at the articulation points of her gripping fingers. She raised her eyebrows at Jenny. She clamped her lips closed to stop a smile that anyway billowed from her eyes.

'Ye-es?' asked Jenny.

Terri and Jenny had met at the school where their children were pupils. Terri had girls though, so Jenny didn't feel she entirely faced the same family issues. Still, Terri was fun, and didn't take herself too seriously, and Jenny found this refreshing. Terri was younger, and a rebel – probably still smoked pot sometimes. She definitely let her children eat ice cream for breakfast. That kind of thing.

'Okay. Well . . .' She began her delivery. 'You know how at the church they do confession by text message, right?'

'Right,' Jenny repeated with a long nod. She had forgotten that Terri had been making occasional efforts to go to church with her children – a raggle-taggle group, filling up the back row noisily.

'Well, it seems that there are some pretty major sins happening in Bentonville,' Terri said, and leaned in. She whispered: 'One of the acolyte's mothers – Mrs Trevear, I think . . . you know, the one with the fifties hairstyle? She was helping in the back room after the service, and she saw the phone – you know, the "God" phone.' Her fingers provided quotation marks. 'And, well, let's just say she saw some freaky things coming through on it.' A pause. 'Well, okay, so there was kinky sex, which Mrs Trevear thought was heinous . . . but there was something even worse! Some kind of cardinal sin.' Terri sipped her coffee. Jenny waited. 'She won't tell anyone though. Which is *so* annoying,' concluded Terri, sitting back.

Oh my God, Jenny mouthed. 'That is wild,' she said. Jenny looked around the coffee place as if to check for Bentonville's sinners. Some people had their noses in their phones, thumb-typing rapid-fire into their screens. Laptops were placed on tables, some open, some half open, like a bed of confused clams. The looped coffee-shop soundtrack was interrupted by whirlpool-flushing sounds of the espresso machine.

'Apparently, Mrs Trevear spoke to Father Brian and he told her it was not a sin to have seen the messages but that she was to be silent in the matter of other people's transgressions. Those were the words he used. And she used. Can you believe it?'

Terri had silver-glitter nail polish, perhaps something she had put on with her daughters, but quite likely a nail polish she had chosen herself. Jenny was still trying to read the tattoo on the lower edge of her forearm – but it didn't seem to be in English. She had felt it was too invasive, even a year into their friendship, to ask about something that was written on Terri's body. Terri was beautiful, she had lovely eyes, and her skin had a kind of permanently tanned look from many summers by the beach. She had a tiny hole where a nose-ring used to be and Jenny thought that this absence was her one concession to Bentonville.

'B-ville,' Terri said, 'is like, all happy on the surface, but I never trust that.' She stirred the remains of her coffee with a small wooden stirrer-stick. 'I think it's better when people show all their shit on the outside, you know – show who they are up front.'

'This isn't the place for that,' Jenny conceded.

They both looked out the window onto the parking lot, carved with concrete edges containing small and hardy bushes. It dawned on Jenny that it could be John sending those sin texts to the Godphone. Maybe she should tell the priest. Then again, who knows what things happened beyond the trimmed lawns and singing doorbells of B-ville's homes.

There had been a handful of scandals in Bentonville over the last couple of years – namely, a family called the Evanses who had made a big show of collecting money for a cancer charity – with fundraisers of baked goods and bouncy castles – and then were found to have pocketed it all for themselves. They couldn't return the money to all the donors because by the time the scam was discovered, they had spent it all on an expensive vacation to Disney World and a kitchen renovation. The townspeople were in an uproar, but upon realising there was no recourse, they took to helping themselves to things on the Evanses' property. Their mailbox disappeared, their swing was removed from their maple tree, their bench was removed, and once someone walked off with their lawnmower, which had been left idling on their lawn while Mr Evans went inside for something.

'The Evanses don't go to church anymore so it couldn't have been them,' said Jenny. The coffee had made her nervous after all, and she needed to go home, to do something active to work off the jitters.

The truth was that Bentonville had just as many good people as bad. There was the time, for instance, when James Sturton, a firefighter, was killed in a blaze at a warehouse on the edge of town.

One of their neighbours set up a crowd funder campaign and the town raised $113,000 for his widow and their two children. Jenny tugged at her T-shirt to smooth it out: that was the kind of thing that also happened here.

CHAPTER 14

THE SECOND DAY OF the camping trip, they spent their time getting to know the surrounding woods and Hank took the boys down to the lake. When they got to the edge of the water, Hank waved at the couple whom he'd approached the day before. They were cleaning up the ashes around their fire pit, the toddler picking grasses nearby. 'Here they are,' he shouted over at them, 'safe and sound!' And the couple smiled at him and waved.

In the evening, Hank had tossed them each a couple of red peppers. Man food, he told them, so they roasted them over the fire on sticks along with their hot dogs. Only Hank hadn't mentioned that some of the peppers were chilli peppers, and both Jesse and Luke had taken entire mouthfuls before they realised.

Both boys staggered to their feet and spat out the chewed pepper onto the ground. They looked at each other, panicked, rushed to find water and then glugged the little water there was left in their water bottles. 'More water!' they shouted at Hank. But Hank sat back against his backpack and chuckled, continuing to eat his hot dog. He wasn't going to help them. Before he knew it, they had rushed to the stream and pushed their faces into it.

'What are you doing?!' Hank shouted at them, sitting up. 'That water isn't purified!'

They didn't seem to care. They were sticking their tongues into the streaming water, red-faced and coughing.

Hank strode over and lifted them onto their feet, one by one. 'For crying out loud, is it that bad?' he said. He led them back to the campfire.

The boys were red-eyed and teary. Hank went to his backpack and got his water bottle for them. 'Take this,' he said. The boys looked up at him, their forelocks dripping with water. 'People in India eat hot food all the time, it's *not* going to kill you,' he said.

'You choked me!' shouted Jesse, his hand around his throat, his face contorted with outrage.

'It was supposed to be funny,' He said, and went over to the half-eaten peppers that the boys had thrown down in their panic.

'Look, I'll eat these and you can see how it's done.' And with that Hank blew the dirt off the two discarded peppers, popped them into his mouth and started chewing. The boys watched intently, wiping their eyes and sucking air across their tongues.

Hank's face turned red. His mouth rounded with chewing, and he forced a swallow.

'Shit,' he said. 'Gimme that water.' Hank had started sweating profusely, and was sitting on a boulder, panting and coughing. He tried spitting but he didn't seem to have much spit left. His eyes, though, were streaming.

Jesse looked at Luke and smiled.

'That was just fine,' Hank managed to say, standing up and walking towards the stream. He took a glug of his water and knelt down, pushing his face into the stream. When he emerged, he let out a '*Whooo!*' sound and swore again.

'You boys weren't wrong,' he said without turning around, still on his hands and knees at the edge of the stream.

Jesse nodded to Luke to follow him into the tent. 'Let's go,' he said.

Once inside the tent, Hank could hear Jesse assuring Luke, 'Tomorrow morning we are going to figure out the way back to the main campsite where there is normal food and bathrooms. Let's do that before Dad wakes up, okay? We'll just escape.'

They were putting their pyjamas on. Hank could hear their efforts to remove shirts and socks inside the small space of the warm tent, and then Jesse's hushed voice: 'Dad is not going to like those pee-jays – with those fairies on them.'

After the boys had fallen asleep, he had sat tending the fire by himself for another hour or so, listening to the forest. Jenny said she felt watched in their 'smart home', but the house had nothing on the open forest. Hank didn't even want to look around at the shadows of the trees, and the sinister grey between their trunks – because he just didn't want to see anything. The stirrings of the woods were enough. He was wary of bears, he told himself, and that was just smart thinking, because there were bears in these mountains, and they were hungry in springtime. Plus there were bear-mothers with cubs and everybody knew how vicious they could be. As he sat there on a folded tarp, poking a stick at the coals and cinders in the fire pit, he thought about how Jenny had probably never given Jesse and Luke anything they didn't like, and so, effectively, she had limited their tastes. 'I know the fabric of their little tongues, I know when it's time to stretch them,' she had said, and Hank thought that was just about the stupidest parenting he had ever heard. Hank himself was still spitting and hucking anything he could from his mouth and throat, occasionally sucking air in and out of his puckered lips. Water wasn't that helpful for hot stuff, he knew that. But he took a few more gulps and spat some more. He was trying to be quiet. He didn't want the boys to hear him. Shit. Those peppers were as hot as freaking fire. He wondered if anyone ever went into anaphylactic shock from hot peppers. His head felt like it was swelling, his lips were burning, his eyes were watering and he was soaked in sweat. Shit. He took off his shirt and looked through their food bag for something to stop the effect. Packets of sugar. He tore off the top strips and poured sachet after sachet of sugar into his mouth, swilling it around and hoping that it would work. It didn't really. Twenty minutes later he was lying on the ground, cooling down, and starting to shiver in his sweat-wet clothes. The boys were quiet, probably already asleep.

AS A GESTURE OF apology for the red-pepper incident, Hank decided to surprise the boys with breakfast the next morning. He also hoped that a good feeding would escort the remaining chilli pepper seeds from his gut. A camp breakfast, which meant that they had to drink weak coffee out of metal mugs and eat dirty-looking scrambled eggs with bacon. He had rolls too. The boys would be hungry.

'The eggs look dirty because they are scrambled with the bacon grease,' said Hank, handing a plate of food to Jesse.

'Did you bring ketchup?' Jesse said, a flattened question.

'Well, yes, I did.' Hank lifted a mini ketchup bottle to Jesse.

They ate. Jesse and Luke ate everything on their camping plates.

'I want more,' said Luke, showing his plate to Hank.

Hank tossed a roll into the tin plate. Neither boy had tried the coffee. One after the other, they poured it away into the grass when Hank wasn't looking.

Jesse took his plate to the stream. He rinsed it gingerly, pushing the grease off the plate and swishing the plate through the water. The water wasn't purified.

'Where are the paper towels?' he said to Hank.

Hank had a mouth full of bread roll and gestured around him, pointing at the grass, the leaves.

'Gross.' Jesse went back to the small boulder to sit down. His trousers were already dirty and he told Hank that he couldn't get all of the slivers of brown matter from under his fingernails. And that his stomach hurt. He wasn't going to the bathroom in the woods, he said sullenly. He would hold it until they got home, he said, and Hank said, 'Fine, up to you.'

CHAPTER 15

JENNY TURNED ON THE TV in the bedroom in the morning as she got dressed. She could smell the coffee in the kitchen that the house was programmed to make every morning at seven o'clock. The boys had been gone one night. She turned on the TV, and it greeted her: 'Good morning, Mrs Tinkley.'

'Oh, get a life,' Jenny replied, pulling a T-shirt over her head, sliding her arms through the sleeves. The house didn't reply.

'Why are you so damn subservient?' Jenny whispered viciously at the walls.

Hank thought it was a neat feature, but Jenny found it creepy that the house knew her name. Mrs Tinkley. She remembered when they were first married and Hank told her he thought it was cute, hearing Jenny spell her new last name. He told her, however, that it was better if you kept the first four letters together – *Tink* – with no break. But Jenny always started with a simple *Tin*.

Jenny hadn't been entirely convinced that she was really a Tinkley, but the taking of his name had seemed like some sort of historical exercise at the time. She was curious to find out how it would feel. Likewise, when they were married, she had let her father walk her down the aisle. At first she had told her brothers that she wouldn't – but they convinced her. Dad had waited to do this since she was born, they said, and he would feel seriously rejected if she didn't let him do his one important part. She thought she could accept that – she could pretend just once that her father was giving her away to her husband as a sort of transfer of possession. It wouldn't matter, would it? But, secretly, it had mattered, and though she bride-smiled throughout her wedding, she felt humiliated. And estranged from herself. It was a performance, she came to understand, and she had played her part; she was a thing, and she was given away. She would have made it different – she would have stepped out of her role – but the cogs of the wedding-day machine are well-oiled and there just wasn't a good moment wherein she might have any agency. And so she was married. And her own house identified her as Mrs Somebody Else.

'My name is Jenny,' she said to the ceiling.

She switched to the news and turned up the volume. The newscast showed a gawky teenager, wearing black; neighbours described him as a quiet boy, a shy boy. There had been another school shooting, somewhere in Rhode Island. Parents were rushing to the school, grasping at their children if they could find them, mothers giving sound-bite interviews to news journalists, in tears, calling upon God, unable to stop and say more as they ran to their cars. Later some fathers would be interviewed, and their voices wavered with emotion, then steadied with pronouncement: 'There's something wrong in a community where this could happen.' And: 'This can never be allowed to happen again.'

She remembered Obama's words at a previous school shooting: 'I react not as a president but as anyone else would, as a parent . . . I know there's not a parent in America that doesn't feel the way I do.' He was breathing in sips, catching his breath to hold back the tears. He pressed at a tear by his eye with a long elegant forefinger. Then his voice turned matter-of-fact. She could see that it was the only way he could get through this speech. To make it sound, for a sentence or two, like a scolding. 'We have been through this too many times . . .' he said.

She loved Obama for his tears.

The plastic surgery opened at eleven. Jenny liked her Fridays at work. But the morning was so uncluttered she really didn't know how to use the extra time. Usually she groaned at the lack of time for her own personal grooming. The boys would cast requests at her from every side ('Where are my socks?' 'Can I take this jar to school?' 'No, I mean my other socks!'). And Hank would start putting things away – to be helpful – things that she had placed just so, in order to grab them when she needed them.

She still had half an hour to waste before work on doing something semi-useful. Like Hank joking that he was 'semi-successful', Jenny was often 'semi-useful' – in that most of the things she did for people were something that the person could have done by themselves. She just made it easier for them. But it wasn't essential help. She was the oil that made the cogs run more smoothly – a woman pushed and smeared along the paths of action.

But there was no one at home so she picked up her car keys and headed out. She loved driving, loved the swinging motion of pulling out of a driveway – that certain swerve, the long pull at the wheel, and the release as it slipped back to straight inside her tunnel of fingers. Jenny rolled down Maple Drive, trying to see how far she could get before she had to use either the brakes or the gas pedal.

She wondered about the mothers of those school shooters as she drove to the post office. What did those wretched mothers understand of what happened to their sons? The shame – you would never be able to wade through that every day. Jenny felt a hard hollowness inside her even considering it. But that wasn't all – the sheer agony because you could still love him, your monster son, even though he was a murderer. Somewhere in your mother-heart you would rescue his image, your poor child who turned bad. The guilt. Was it something you did or didn't do? Or was it your husband's fault? Shit. It made parenting feel like a dangerous act. Jenny turned the car radio to Smooth FM.

SHE RECOGNISED JOHN'S HANDWRITING among the colourful tatter of advertising that was shoved in her post office box. When she got back into her car, she opened the envelope.

Dear Jenny,

I appreciate you writing to me, I do appreciate that. But there are certain things that I don't appreciate. Like what you're assuming about me because I'm here. First of all, you don't know me, excuse my French, and you should respect that. What I don't like is that you don't even know the main fact about my being here. No offence, but your life has no similarity to mine. You can keep your murder ideas to yourself from now on. I mean that. Stop it. I don't know why you would want to murder anyone anyway and you have no idea what you're talking about. You should just be nice and normal like you are, and not going into stuff you don't understand.

And also, if you think it's so bad being a wife then you should have some sympathy for the people we call 'wives' here in prison. It's one of the worst existences you can imagine. But I guess there's some protection in it. Maybe you don't have it all that bad?

John

PS. If there's one thing I know, it is this: crime defines. If someone tells a lie, they're a liar. If someone takes something, they're a thief. If someone kills, they're a killer. That's what happens. Thinking about shooting is basically playing video games. Not the same thing.

JENNY FLUSHED WITH ANGER, sitting in her car in the parking lot of the post office. The letter had fallen from her hands, spilling into the passenger-side footwell. She stared at the entrance to the post office, people walking in, coming out, passing the door to each other with their fingertips. What was he so angry about? She didn't accuse him of murder. She was just telling her own truth. People like to pick on mothers because they create a gravitational force: everything sticks to you, everything ends with you. What would he know? He wouldn't even kill a fly in his cell.

She picked his letter up from the footwell and threw it onto the passenger seat. Crime defines? Jerk. She gripped the steering wheel. If that was true, then could he please tell her exactly what crime she had committed that made her nothing more than 'mother' and 'wife'?

She had to go to work. There wasn't time to waste on John and his jailbird wife. This letter-writing was getting annoying. She wasn't sure she wanted to write to John anymore. Who did he think he was? And, moreover, who did he think she was? She flipped down the sunscreen flap and looked into the mirror there, wondering what she could possibly do to her appearance. She pinned back some loose hairs with a barrette. She didn't know how to apply anything other than mascara and lipstick anymore. She unzipped her purse to get the make-up and the smell hit her again, the fruity, sweet smell of John's first envelope. She thought she'd thrown it away.

Damn it. She swiped at angry tears that sprang at the edges of her eyes. Jenny picked it out, took a long smell of it. Fucking criminal. She could betray him too. She licked at the bottom corner of the envelope seal. The orange taste spread across her tongue and she closed her eyes. This time she recognised the warmth it gave, and, as she opened her eyes, she felt a tingling rise up the sides of her neck. 'It isn't really glue, is it, John?' she said aloud.

THE OFFICE WAS STUFFY when she arrived. April was relatively warm so far and the heating had been blazing all night long. She jammed the doorstop under the door and left it open to let in some fresh air. The magazines were looking a little tired, so she replaced them with a new batch that had come in the mail. But she was feeling a little dizzy so she sat down in one of the waiting-room chairs and flipped through a magazine. All those beauty magazines and men's magazines with their promises. Oh the promises! (Did she say that out loud?) Lord knows, people who came into that surgery had enough problems as it was – did they even need these magazines? She dumped them in the visitors' trash can.

After a while, Jenny settled down at the desk. Boy, it was nice to be at work, she thought. And boy, was her chair nice and comfy. The first patient was a lady who came in about her feet. The woman wanted perfect feet and had had seven surgeries already to adjust the shape of her foot, her instep. Her toenails were re-formed and lasered. She had an ankle mole removed. And she now used high-potency lactic acid on her heels. Today she was there about her pinkie toenail, which apparently was so small that she couldn't paint it with nail polish nicely. She liked the new shades of polish, the beiges, the purples.

'Do you think,' she asked Jenny that morning, 'that baby-blue nail polish looks a little . . . um, medical?'

'Medical?' Jenny was trying to work out what she meant by that.

'I mean, a little like Pepto-Bismol for toes? Something about the pastels I don't like anymore.'

Jenny smiled at her, 'But it's not medical, is it?' She hadn't painted her toenails in years.

THE PATIENTS AT THE clinic were mostly men these days, and Dr Simmons was considering paired waiting rooms, so that all the patients didn't inspect each other too much. Some of them had had terrible plastic surgery work – by other doctors – and he didn't think it was good advertising. Plus Bentonville wasn't all that big a town and people didn't like to see people they knew in the waiting room. The worst, recently, was a series of men who had been injected with too much filler by a doctor in the next county. They had cheekbones from a horror flick, and bee-stung lips. Unfortunately you can't remove filler, he told them. But you can push your face into a basin of ice-cold water every morning, and use ice-packs to keep them to a minimum. The fillers would wear off in a few months. He recommended that they avoid fillers altogether. But everyone could benefit from some Botox, he would tell them.

There was a small mirror on her desk, used mostly to reassure patients before they left, and Jenny had been staring at her face for most of the morning. Botox, she thought. Why not? She had wrinkles like everyone else. Day in, day out, she assured patients that it didn't hurt, you could barely feel it. But then, she really didn't know if that was true, and she hated needles.

'Jenny,' Dr Simmons said from the doorway of his clinical rooms. The waiting room was now empty.

'Okay.' She stood up. 'Here I come.'

When she sat in his chair – which was essentially the same as a dentist's chair – she couldn't help but ask, 'Is this going to hurt? I mean, I know they always ask that – but does it actually hurt?'

'Jenny, I can't believe you're asking me this – have you ever heard screams coming from these rooms? Of course it doesn't hurt.' He turned and prepared the needles behind her head.

'I know, I know . . . it's just . . . well, you know, I've never had it myself.'

'You can close your eyes if you want,' he added, and she did.

He warned her that he was about to start. She was surprised that the needles didn't bother her at all. 'Just a little Botox,' she had said to no one in particular, as she leaned back. She hadn't quite thought it through; getting Botox for her frown-lines was something she'd only casually mentioned at lunchtime and Dr Simmons had said he'd do it for free after the last patient left.

'Honey, you're late to the party,' said Amy, the clinic assistant.

The needle had to pierce the skin each time it landed on her forehead. She thought she could even hear the piercing sound. It did not seem as tiny a needle as he had described. And it did hurt, but she didn't really mind. He dabbed each needle-prick site with a tissue – there was blood, which she hadn't expected.

With each dip of the needle, she could feel a bit of cold liquid spreading into her forehead. She knew, because she was always informing patients of the fact, that she might have headaches for a few days afterwards.

'What surprises me . . .' Dr Simmons was speaking from beneath his mask, syringe in hand. 'What surprises me is that I am getting so many more requests from men for gynaecomastia. Used to be that you'd hardly ever see it, but these days it's one in five appointments.'

Jenny should have known what the word meant but she didn't. Sounded like something that women should be having. He did occasionally have women coming in to alter the appearance of their vaginas. She had to file the anatomical photos so she saw things.

'Huh. Why do you think that is?' She hoped for a clue.

'Well –' and he turned to the table behind her to pick up a new cotton pad – 'I'm wondering if there's something in the water – it's hormone related. Men aren't supposed to have breasts.'

'They're embarrassed,' said Jenny.

'Well, they say that their breasts hurt, and that seems a fair enough reason to me.'

He was finished now, just dabbing any dots of blood that had re-emerged on her forehead.

'Moo-oobs,' said Jenny, imitating a cow. 'That's what they call them.'

Dr Simmons turned from her, replaced his equipment on the papered tray and started pulling off his rubber gloves. He didn't react to the word but asked her how she felt. 'You're a worry-free woman now,' he said, and flipped open the trash can with a foot.

IN THE CAR ON the way home, the radio continued its reporting of the Rhode Island school shooting. There had been many guns in the house of the boy who did it. Jenny was relieved that at least she had banned toy guns in her household. Even if that seemed so trivial compared to the Rhode Island boy's circumstances.

She'd held a real gun once. As a young woman, in her twenties, she had visited a shooting range. It was a date, and the young corporate fellow who took her thought it would be a cool surprise. His name was Dave and he was dressed in a striped shirt and chinos, which seemed oddly formal for a Saturday morning. They drove in his SUV to an industrial building on the outskirts of Pittsburgh and she saw herself as though in a true-crime show on cable TV. The windows of the black SUV were blacked out, that was the first thing. And the building that they seemed to be approaching looked abandoned. Some windows were broken and there was no sign above the front entrance. You really shouldn't go on dates with men you meet in bars, she thought. Where did he say he worked? Deloitte and Touche or something like that.

'You know,' she piped up, a bit too cheerfully, 'when I first read the name Deloitte and Touche, I thought it said "Toilette and Douche" . . .'

'What?' He was distracted, trying to decide where to park.

Several other serious cars were parked beside the building.

'Don't you work for Deloitte and Touche?'

'Bear Stearns,' he said, cranking his head around to reverse into a space between other SUVs. But he swung in too acutely and the car rolled up against the kerb. He swerved out of the space and moved on towards a longer space he could enter without reversing. Jenny was really good at parking – it was one of her skills and she wished she could have parked the car herself. It was a nice and inane thing to be good at.

'So, here we are,' he said, looking over at her, pulling the key out of the ignition. He could see that she was neither impressed nor upbeat. 'Don't worry.' He touched her knee lightly. 'It'll be fun, I promise.' He gave a nice smile. He didn't seem dangerous.

When Dave opened the entrance door, she could hear loud noises coming from the building.

'It's legit,' he said. 'Come on in.'

'What is this place?' she said as she stepped inside.

'It's a shooting range.' He smiled. 'I come here every weekend to blast some rounds and unwind . . . You'll see, it's really fun.'

And it was kind of fun. Upstairs, there was an enormous and long room. Where they entered, there was a row of shooting booths, separated by rough wooden panels. At the equipment table, her date picked her some earphones and ammunition. On a small ledge, in each booth, lay a pistol.

Dave wanted to show her how to do it so she stood behind him with her earphones on. He cocked the pistol and planted his feet apart.

He looked like someone from *Magnum, P.I.* or *Miami Vice*, with his arms outstretched. He aimed and fired. Guns were louder than she had imagined. He fired a round, six shots, and pulled in what Jenny assumed was a re-purposed laundry rope, the paper target flittering towards them. He had sprinkled the edge of the target with his shots, but he seemed proud. He showed it to her. They weren't removing their earphones so he indicated to her that she should aim for the centre of the target, a target that was contained within the vague silhouette of a man.

So this was the romantic part, she thought, as he stood behind her, helped her load the gun from underneath, and steadied her outstretched arms with his own arms, coming around her from either side. He was standing close to her – she could feel his chest, his belt buckle at her back. He pushed one finger at her index-finger knuckle, telling her to pull the trigger, and the gun went off, shunting her shoulders backwards into him. He steadied her and they looked at the target – the bullet hadn't touched it. Dave crooked his neck around to see her face and mouthed *Are you okay?* at her. She nodded. *Cool*, he nodded.

He stood behind her for all six rounds, by which time she was hoping he'd lay off and let her try it for herself. Only one of their shots had skimmed the edge of the target paper. He started to help her reload but she took the ammunition magazine and shoved it into the gun herself. He took a step off and made a gesture of *Be my guest*. Jenny raised the pistol and fired.

It probably wasn't such a smart thing to do, Jenny thought

afterwards, as they tried to eat fajitas neatly at Mexico Ranch; it wasn't smart to excel at anything sports-related on a date with a guy. She had hit the target with every shot, many into the dark, middle circle. Her hand was incredibly steady. He was impressed at the time, but overall it had annoyed him and he went off to his own shooting booth and did some of his own shooting. She didn't check to see which target was his – so she didn't know whether he had been any better than her, but she suspected not. Her shooting was good, so good that some of the other guys congratulated her, joking that she must be an FBI trainee in disguise. Meanwhile, their fajita lunch was only lurching along with little forays, seeking common ground.

'So, Bullseye Jenny.' He leered a little. 'That's what I'm going to call you from now on . . .'

She was just taking a bite of her fajita, a sliver of onion fell from her lower lip and she tried to react smilingly.

'Where did you get your steady arm, and your eagle eye, eh?'

HER HEAD DIDN'T ACHE yet. When was that supposed to kick in? She found it hard to drive though. It was weird. She was gliding, like she was in charge of a hovercraft and not a car. By the time she got home from the clinic, she slightly regretted getting Botox. Botulism injected into her face. That was as crazy as the women who used to drink arsenic to make their skin pale in the nineteenth century. Wait until we find out that it makes you get dementia, she thought, or become incontinent. She needed to pee so badly that she rushed into the house, forgetting to disarm the alarm. As she sat there in the downstairs bathroom, her underwear at her ankles, finally relieved, the alarm started howling. Shit, shit, shit. She half pulled up her trousers, and ran to the alarm panel. *It's connected to Hank's phone and when he's away it switches to manual.* She typed in the code and nothing happened. She tried again – ERROR, the screen told her. And it was so loud, and drew so much attention to her. She pulled up her trousers properly and buttoned them; her knickers were wet but it was too late to do anything about that. Through the kitchen window, she could see Mrs Salton open her front door. The other neighbours would start to come out now too.

She tried the alarm panel again with the code 4–6–7–6–7–6–2–7–8, which Hank had chosen because it spelled 'I-M – S-O – S-M-A-R-T' on the keypad. ERROR, it replied, and then KEYPAD DISABLED.

Jenny went outside with her cellphone. She pointed back at the house: 'It's malfunctioning!' she shouted out to Mrs Salton, hoping everyone else would hear too and she wouldn't have to explain any more than that. She fumbled for the number in her phone – the alarm was really loud. She still felt a little dizzy, and possibly nauseous.

She would have to walk away from the house in order to speak to the alarm company – which seemed sort of illogical, badly planned on their part. She wondered if she should explain to Mrs Salton why she was walking away from her screaming house and talking on her cellphone. Mrs Salton was standing at her door, surveying the cul-de-sac, possibly pretending to let some fresh air into her house, as though she had been cooking onions or something.

Jenny walked down the Maple Drive and sat down at the edge of a particularly wide patch of grass where two houses seemed to have been designated a wider space between them. The grass seemed more neutral and less owned than the rest of the lawn area on the Drive. International waters, she thought. The alarm company had said that they couldn't get to her until about 9 p.m., which was a few hours away. Hank was out of range so she couldn't call him. Had he changed the password? Her fingerprint didn't work – only Hank's did.

After busying herself for a few minutes with her cellphone as she sat in the no-man's-land of Maple Drive, she walked home, taking care to purse her lips and look dejected for the many neighbours who would be twitching at their curtains by now. When she got in, she wondered if her hearing was getting damaged by the shrilling, wondered if she might go deaf early as a result of this damnable alarm. She didn't think it needed to be quite so loud to be effective. The longer she stood in the sound, the more clearly she thought she could hear the house-being howling.

'But you haven't been violated,' Jenny shouted. 'It's only me!'

She couldn't even hear her own voice.

She saw John's envelope at the opening of her handbag, and picked it up, holding it to her tongue to get another taste of the orange sweetness. Just a little lick, she said to herself. She then put her fingers in her ears to brave the crossing of the house, up the stairs, to her bedside table where the ear-protectors were. Gosh, they were good, she thought as she placed them over her ears. The alarm was reduced to a gentle drone somewhere beyond. A perfectly suburban hum.

She closed her front door, pulled the curtains closed all over the house, hoping that it might dampen the sound. In fact, she wasn't even sure where the sound came from – it had never occurred to her. And it was so loud that you couldn't discern its source. There might be a box on the outside of the house, but if it was the one she thought it might be, it was too high to reach and she wasn't sure what she could wrap around it to silence it. She wondered if bubble wrap might work. It was weird wearing earphones – her life seemed suspended in some kind of liquid, the edges of things smoothed in the fog of inaudibility. The sound of her breathing showed her she was calm. She decided to have a shower to think about what to do.

But could you take a shower with ear defenders on? She put on two shower caps, overlapping, each covering one of the ear-pieces. She wasn't sure that would work so she decided to lie down in the bath and think about it for a time. The cool tub was a nice antidote to the heat of the alarm-shrill.

SHE AWOKE TO SEE a man standing in the doorway of her bathroom. Jenny did not know this man and her heart leapt. He was wearing a black woolly hat with thick ear flaps. She thought it could be the alarm mechanic, but he wasn't wearing any kind of uniform. Was it a burglar? Was she being burgled? She was still lying there, motionless, eyes open, earphones on, wondering if she should close her eyes again. It occurred to her that it could be John, escaped from prison. She sat up in the bathtub and snatched up her robe.

The man jumped in surprise as she rose – and she frightened him so much that he stumbled backwards. Jenny looked at him again and realised it was Mr Salton, the pharmacist, her neighbour, who now was waving his arms and looking away. He was embarrassed. Jenny was swift to get up, push into his field of vision, mouthing *I'm so sorry* into his face. He waved that comment away, and pointed to a pad of paper in his hand: *I can disconnect your alarm – would that be okay?* She nodded enthusiastically and thanked him with her hand on her chest. He also nodded and went out. As she followed him down the stairs and through the kitchen door, Jenny saw that he had already leaned a ladder against the side of her house. He motioned at her to hold the ladder still as he climbed it to the top, braced himself against the edges of the ladder with his legs and pulled at the box that contained the alarm bell. It wasn't removable, evidently, and he then pulled garden secateurs from his back pocket and cut the wires leading to the alarm.

Silence. A giant exhale. Jenny hesitated to remove her headphones. With the sound gone, even under ear defenders, all colours seem to grow blunt and take on edgings of fine white. She had got used to the camouflage of sound, to the aggressive pushing away that it had somehow achieved for her. There was a peace in that alarm, like being underwater, and now she was thrust into the lemon-bright and tinkling world and she was compelled to say something. 'Oh wow.' She took off her ear defenders to be polite.

'Well, that should do it for now – and they can replace the wire when they come, shouldn't be all that much trouble,' he said as he was climbing back down the ladder.

'Well, thanks, thanks so much,' she said. 'And sorry for the disturbance . . . I'm not sure how it happened.'

'Oh, that's no problem. Just that Jill gave me the idea of helping you out, and I can see that Hank and the boys are away.'

'Yeah, they're in the mountains.'

'You must have been pretty tired to fall asleep in the tub, and with all that noise.'

He was struggling to recover from the scene in the bathroom. His grey hair was spiked up on the sides of his head where he had been sweating and his glasses had pushed up sprigs of hair. She saw boyishness there – with his ears sticking out. It lent his orderliness an endearing ruffled-up look.

'You know, I wouldn't have come in . . .' He paused, looking for the right way to put it. 'But I couldn't knock or ring the doorbell. I didn't mean to startle you – in your own bathroom. I'd been calling your name . . .'

Jenny appreciated his efforts to normalise the encounter.

'I was wearing headphones.' She smiled and closed her eyes briefly. 'I fell asleep.'

They both looked up Maple Drive at a car that was lazily turning into a driveway.

'Shame about the news today,' he offered.

'Yes, oh . . . yes, it is. So unbelievable. Those poor kids.'

'Never happened when I was young,' he said. 'That sort of thing.' He shrugged. 'It just didn't happen as much. Like a lot of things.'

She waited for him to explain what other things he meant.

'Like all the abuse you hear about. The violence. We didn't have that growing up,' he said quietly, slightly shaking his head.

'Well, it's something to do with video games probably,' she said. 'My kids play video games sometimes. Which I should probably stop.'

She could see he was fidgeting, replacing the catch on his secateurs, pulling at his shirt cuffs, trying to find a way out. 'Anyway, thanks again.' She cast a look over to his house. Mrs Salton's face was visible between the curtains of the small window of their front door.

'That's some rash you got there,' he said, with a low wave, indicating her forearm.

'Oh, that,' she said, covering it with a hand. 'It's nothing.' She had been getting rashes recently but they usually disappeared as quick as they came.

'Okay then,' he said. 'You know where to come if you need any emollient or whatnot.' He turned down her driveway and walked over to his own house. Mrs Salton opened the door for him just before he could open it himself.

She had stood there with her hand over the rash, watching Mr Salton walk away. He had no real body evident within his loose-fitting clothes, and he walked like a set of hinges and planks. There was a meekness in it, in the flatness of his behind, in the regular mechanics of his gait, and Jenny thought how nice it was that older men seemed slightly drooped, like all that bulging had subsided. It looked more comfortable somehow to be an older man than a young one.

She had once asked Hank, 'Is there anything hard about being a man?' She knew it was an odd question so she explained herself.

'I mean, I can tell you what's hard about being a woman ... there are body issues, age issues, the periods, childbirth, the problem of being taken seriously, glass ceilings – you know that sort of thing. But, I'm just thinking, what about for men?'

She really wanted to know. Was it hard to have to be brave and strong – what if you didn't want to? Was it hard to feel like you had to be successful, the 'breadwinner'? Was it hard to have to worry about the size of your muscles, your penis? It looked stressful to be a man, it looked like there were all kinds of rules you had to uphold.

Hank answered, 'Seriously?'

'Seriously.'

'Well, seriously, then no. Not really. Being a guy is actually pretty great.'

Jenny wasn't going to judge him for this. She was fascinated. Maybe he hadn't understood her question exactly?

'I mean, you know, sports, promotions, the kind of car you want to drive ... baldness?' She was wondering what would trigger a little understanding from him. She wasn't going to mention penis size because although his wasn't small, it wasn't enormous either, and the territory felt as treacherous as the does-my-butt-look-fat-in-this question.

'Well, I'll tell you honestly, it's still no.' He adjusted himself in the leather armchair. 'I mean, the good thing is that when you want that stuff, to be big and manly, you can do it. But when you don't want it, you don't have to be that. It's not all that hard,' he explained.

Jenny was blown away.

'Huh, interesting,' she said casually. She didn't want to get his back up. She would be very careful here, not to press too hard. Otherwise, he'd clam up and get defensive. 'So, what I mean is, I'm not wondering what it's like to be a particular person – not what it feels like to be Hank, or Bill or Jerry. It's not a personality question I'm asking. Just like, what is it like to be a man? You know, the gender. There must be good and bad things – right?'

Hank was smiling a little, he was actually very relaxed. These questions did not seem to be irritating him at all, Jenny realised.

'Yeah, I see what you're asking. But I don't have a problem with being male per se. It's like asking an orange if they have a problem being orange. They just are orange.'

'But are you a colour or a fruit?' she answered, now turning away from the conversation.

'You sound just like Luke,' Hank said.

CHAPTER 16

Not only had Hank stopped for Lotto tickets at the gas station on the way there, but he had also brought some old pans from the garage and instructions on panning for gold. There was no native gold in the streams of the Susquehanna River but there was glacial gold – Hank had researched it online. This was bits of gold that had been pushed around for a few ice ages and mixed into glacial sands and gravels. Rivers and streams concentrate this gold in their bottom layers. Some people had found gold nuggets the size of Cheerios in the Susquehanna River there. That's about all he knew about the gold in the Endless Mountains, which would hopefully suffice. And the Lotto would have to wait; they wouldn't get the results until they got back to an area with data reception. Probably not until they hiked out of there in two days' time.

The day was bright, just the kind of day that would make a good memory. They walked upstream along the sandy banks of the Susquehanna to look for a smaller stream to follow. The smaller streams, particularly those with bends and boulders, would be a likelier spot for gold-panning. Hank told the boys they could lead the way; he remembered liking to be the leader when he was a boy. In fact, he still liked to walk ahead of other people on any grouping. Usually he forced himself to keep in step with anyone he was with – although both he and Jenny apparently enjoyed striding ahead of the other and they often walked that way, for example on the way to a restaurant from the car. It didn't happen all that much anymore that they went on date nights.

Hank could see the gold of his wedding ring glinting as his arm did its part in his stride. He hadn't realised that there were so many grades of gold. Jenny had wanted a rose gold; she liked that it was gentler in colour. But the jeweller had explained that rose gold was rare – and not because it was in any way finer, but quite the opposite, rose gold is a cheaper gold and he would have to find some old piece of jewellery to meltdown in order to create such rings.

'Surely, sir, you want the best-quality rings,' the man said. 'As an expression of your respect.'

The jeweller was an immigrant, still carrying an accent, so he must have been first-generation something, possibly Armenian, Hank thought, since the man reminded him of Charles Aznavour. 'Respect' was a good word, and Hank couldn't fault it. But he hadn't thought of it in those terms. Rings were more like a promise, he thought, a promise, probably, to stay faithful. He remembered the phrase 'in sickness and in health', and that seemed fair. And then came 'for richer, for poorer'. The jeweller seemed to see that Hank was thinking about marriage, and he stood patiently, watching, somehow without intruding or interrupting his customer's pause. For richer, for poorer.

'Yes, of course, the yellow gold,' Hank replied.

'Very good,' said the man. 'And you have one more consideration.' The jeweller was being so gentle in guiding him to do the right thing. 'The carats.'

'The carrots?' Hank realised immediately his error. 'Oh, yes, the carats. Twenty-four carats.' It rolled off his tongue and he hoped he had got it right.

The jeweller made this final note on his jeweller's pad.

'Curved, three-millimetre thick, yellow and twenty-four carats.' It almost sounded like he said 'callats', which was as wrong as 'carrots' but it sounded elegant to Hank. He stood a little straighter; he didn't want the jeweller to think that he'd never bought any decent jewellery before.

'WHAT KIND OF GOLD do you think we might find?' Hank raised his voice so the boys, who were some five paces ahead, could hear him.

'Um, isn't gold an element?' Jesse cast back at him.

'You know – how many carats . . . ?'

'Twenty-four-carat gold – rings, rings, rings!' Luke was mimicking something he must have heard on TV. There were lots of commercials everywhere for companies that bought gold. They would take anything gold-ish and melt it down – for cash. Gold was a safe haven in these volatile financial times, and Hank wished he had a bar or two of gold stashed away in the attic. Other people probably did, and they were smart. Hank decided he would buy some gold as soon as he had the money.

Hank had already told the two boys that gold cost $1,200 an ounce and explained that if they found a Cheerio-sized piece of gold, they'd have about $600 to spend. Not bad. He looked at their faces when he said that, wondering what that wealth meant to the boys: were they counting it in their own currencies – the latest in cellphones for Jesse, and some weird materials that Luke might want for his archive?

THE STREAM THEY CHOSE was wide and low, and the trees grew sparsely from its edges, gradually forming into forest. It was a sunny length of stream, and Hank and the boys took off their shoes, rolled up their trousers and waded in. Hank had watched a video online and tried to re-enact the motions of gold-panning. Dip the pan in the sand, take up a little water with it, and swill gently. The point was to swill it around until the gold dust gathered at the edges of the sand in the pan.

'Just watch me,' he said, but Jesse wasn't paying attention.

'Jesse!' Hank shouted. 'Get here and watch how this is done, or you won't ever know anything.'

Hank was here to impart knowledge and Jesse wasn't taking it seriously. He was thirteen – only just a teenager and already acting like a pro. The boys now stood behind Hank, watching him lift and swill. He tried to make it look easy, like he'd done it before – after all, he'd told them he had.

'I can do that.' Luke took a pan and got started a few yards away.

Jesse picked one up too, and walked upstream silently. Hank carried on swilling the sand in his pan. The glinting sunlight on the water in the pan, which sparked inside the water and ricocheted around the metal of the pan itself, would make it hard to see any gold.

And so the three panned for gold. They had to wade into the little sandy pools and then crouch to perform the panning – and it was tiring work. The crouching above the burbling waters especially. After a time, Luke seemed to be digging in the sand with his pan, and that did seem logical to Hank, since a nugget was a nugget and you wouldn't have to pan through sand so carefully to find a nugget. He considered correcting Luke's technique but didn't bother – Hank was now thinking of how he would plant the fool's gold he had brought. Originally, he had wanted to make it a treat for the boys; he had a plan to set them up with a pan of sand into which he had slipped one small rock of the pyrite so that they would find it. But he didn't think they deserved it – particularly now that Jesse was sitting at the stream's bank, throwing stones into the stream and not making any effort to pan for gold. Luke, too, was just digging now – so Hank thought he could teach them something about persistence, stamina and respect.

'Well, what do you know!' Hank stood up, looking at his pan. 'Jesse, Luke, come here and see this.' His hands made a gesture of sweeping them towards him. Luke was curious, Jesse was slower to react. And when they came up Hank wasn't sure of exactly how to pitch it – total amazement, or cool achievement.

'Whaaa-at?' Luke said gently, looking into the pan and up at his father.

'You see that?' Hank said, and as Luke went to touch it, Hank pulled the pan back. 'Wait,' he said. 'Jesse, get over here and look at this,' he called to his elder son. He had a point to prove before they headed back.

Hank wasn't sure that they had been adequately impressed. And he didn't want them to hold the pyrite in case either of them, especially Luke, figured out that it wasn't real. Hank told them it was too precious to play with, and anyway, he told them, when you find gold in a national park, it actually belongs to the government. It would be a crime to keep it, he said as they walked downstream towards their campsite, and they didn't want to be criminals, did they?

Luke was lagging behind as they made their way down the riverbanks. The river was busy at this time of the year. The melts had charged through it in March and passed into its many streams which watered the flatlands. But the melts continued and the river was prone to surges and movements. Rocks had been moved recently, prodded along by the flow, and new material gathered like horseshoes pointing downstream. There were branches and piles of mud shoved up against river boulders. There was no evidence of beavers or otters – were there ever any here? Hank wondered. He suddenly wished he knew more about nature, and scanned the landscape for elements he could name. Pine tree. Or was that a fir tree? He didn't know. He certainly couldn't name the bird he could hear chip-chipping in a nearby tree. He tried, at least, to locate it – like a survivalist would – but he couldn't see it among the bushy pine needles.

The deciduous trees were still mostly bare – the little beginnings of green had sprouted but the trees had not reached their full expression – and this made it harder to identify them. Leaf shape was the big clue. He would know a maple leaf of course, and probably an oak leaf. But were any of these maples or oaks? Okay, so he wasn't good on trees. They all looked pretty familiar.

He looked up at the sky and saw a bunch of clouds that chuffed along like steam engines. Cumulus clouds. Yes, they were puffy. He knew that much. He considered telling the boys about the cumulus clouds in front of them. But he didn't know the name of the wispy ones that followed behind them, and his children were likely to ask.

'Come on, boys.' Hank felt it was time again to teach them something. 'Now, what if . . .'

They looked at him, unwilling to enter the conspiratorial space he was suggesting. 'Come closer,' he said.

'What if we were US soldiers in the Vietnam War and we were trying to get back to our base camp without being detected by the Vietcong? The bad guys.' Hank was already hunching his shoulders and looking around.

'Here're your guns.' He collected long sticks from the ground, gave them one each and held one himself over his shoulder. 'Don't make any noise.' He bent down and set off.

Luke looked around tentatively and held his stick-rifle with both hands in front of him. Jesse followed quietly, not exactly playing along but still holding the stick he was given. Hank motioned them to move towards the edge of the forest. 'This way,' he whispered with force.

CHAPTER 17

JENNY HADN'T WANTED TO greet her in-laws alone. But Hank wasn't back yet with the kids and so she steeled herself. The house was clean. She had been to the supermarket. She had brushed her hair.

The neighbour's dog, the one also called Jenny, was sitting on her front lawn and she thought it was somehow a fitting omen, given her in-laws were coming. She remembered telling Hank's parents, that first weekend together, how she and Hank had met. She was hoping to make it a funny story – something cute, something from a rom-com, and she hoped they might like it. That they might like her.

'A dog?' Sally said.

'Well, yes,' said Jenny. 'It was the dog's fault for running into the street, of course.'

'What car did he have then?' Sally said after a moment. Jenny's story was already derailed.

'Uh, it was a blue car, I forget.'

'I guess it was pretty dented.'

'Well, yeah, it was . . . but well, we didn't talk all that much about the car at the time.'

'Whose dog was it?'

Jenny lied. 'Oh, I don't know, some neighbour.'

And that was the extent to which Sally was interested.

The truth was that Hank had run over her own dog. Her beloved boxer called Triumph that she had rescued the year before. When the doorbell rang and she opened her front door to see a handsome man carrying her bloodied dog in a blanket, she was confused. Where had the dog been? Did you see what happened? How did you know it was mine? All these questions she asked as he entered, and gently took the hot, limp animal from his arms into hers, carrying it to her sofa, speaking the questions pleadingly to the dog, into his silken ear, and not to the man. At first, she was grateful to the handsome man, assuming he had found Triumph, injured, somewhere in the neighbourhood. But she busied herself over the dog for a minute or so, cooing at him, lifting his muzzle, before realising that the dog was dead. Warm but dead. The dog had soiled the blanket, and the smell of dog shit was seeping from the folds of the orange blanket.

'Aw,' she moaned, peeling back part of the blanket. She could see the dog was broken in so many ways. Its spine had snapped. 'Poor guy,' she exhaled.

'I . . . My name is Henry. I'm sorry . . .' He offered her a hand-shake and she extricated her hand from among the dog and blanket to take it. What an oddly formal fellow.

'Your neighbour – the older lady – told me that he was yours,' Hank said.

'Oh. Right.'

'Do you want any help?'

'Uh, I don't really know.' Jenny looked up. 'I guess it's too late for the vet.'

Hank nodded, drawing up his bottom lip into a formation of regret. Jenny was cradling the dog and her eyes were welling up. Triumph's tongue was hanging from his mouth, falling between his side teeth, over his thin lip. She stroked his cheek, the top of his head.

'What do you do when they die?' Jenny asked him in a whisper. Her tenderness for the dog was souring into extreme repulsion at the dog's corpse. She thought she might be sick. 'Can you take him to the backyard?' She offered the dead dog to Hank. 'Just for a second . . . I . . . I know you probably have to go.'

As Hank took the dog, Jenny saw that her clothes were wet with Triumph's effluence. She pulled the shirt away from her body, fingers crooked and splayed, and stood up. The beige carpet was splotched with the same rust colours. The sofa was disgusting.

Hank left the dog in the backyard but he had to go. 'I'm on my way to the dentist, sorry,' he said, and told her he would come back later to help with the dog. If she wanted. Which she did. She sat on the steps to her backyard, looking at Triumph. 'What did you do?' she whispered at him.

She showered, threw her soiled clothes in the trash and sprinkled baking soda over the stains on the carpet and sofa. Made a cup of coffee. Who did this to her dog? She would probably have to have the carpets professionally cleaned. Her heart hadn't yet risen again to its place, and all she wanted to do was take him in her arms, but whenever she got close she was repulsed by the pool of blood and his sagging lifeless muzzle.

When the doorbell rang, she thought it would be that nice guy who had brought Triumph home – but it was her neighbour, Anna, the former schoolteacher with the elaborate front yard.

'I'm sorry about your dog,' she said immediately through the screen of the door.

'Oh, yeah – I'm still so shocked.' Jenny urged the woman to come in.

'I was only worried. I came because that jerk who hit the dog seemed to stay a while with you and . . .' Anna stood in Jenny's hallway looking at her.

'Who?'

'That man, the one who hit your dog. He almost left him there, poor thing . . . was ready to drive off, but then he saw me. I was dead-heading geraniums. Well, I saw him. And he knew it.'

Jenny frowned, looked outside.

'Hope he didn't bother you,' said Anna.

'No. No, he didn't. Thanks for coming though.' Jenny wasn't sure if the day could get any worse. 'I don't really know what to do with a dead dog,' she offered in a faint voice, and looked through to the kitchen. Was the woman going to need coffee too?

*

'YOU MIGHT HAVE MENTIONED that you killed my dog,' Jenny said as she pulled the door open for Hank a few hours later. But the guy was so friendly, and wanted to help. He looked so clean-shaven.

'Oh. I'm sorry.' He held his jaw. 'Novocaine.'

He tried again: 'I didn't know how to tell you.'

And: 'I didn't see it. I just heard the sound. I didn't see what it was until I got out of the car.'

He was moving into the hall as he spoke. Jenny was now picturing the crash scene in slow motion.

'You were probably on your phone or something,' she said, offering him half an accusation and half an excuse.

Hank dug a hole for Triumph in Jenny's back garden. It was a rented place but she didn't know of any other place to put the animal. She wasn't sure if there was anything administrative that you had to do if a dog died. Did the authorities need to know? So, Hank dug the hole, and they put the dog into the hole. Her landlord never visited so hopefully he wouldn't find out. As long as Miss Anna didn't tell him. And she would buy some fresh turf to cover the grave-site.

BILL AND SALLY TINKLEY pulled up in a brown and square Chevrolet. Jenny marvelled that such cars still existed – it was as though they were driving in from the past. She wiped her hands and walked out to greet them, still holding the tea towel in her hands. She looked down at the tea towel – ah, the performance of wifehood had begun and she hadn't even realised it. 'Helloo!' she called, waving, and she gave a wide, wide smile.

The senior Tinkleys did not like fancy coffee. Jenny made them some instant coffee and added a teaspoon of evaporated milk. She had stayed with them often enough to know that was how they drank coffee. And, accepting their cups, they seemed to think that some of their good habits had rubbed off on Jenny – she was even drinking a cup herself. Mr Tinkley – Bill – had not taken off his beige driving jacket. Sally Tinkley had removed her light green coat and hung it on the hook Jenny had made available for them by the front door.

'That's very nice,' said Sally, sipping her coffee. 'Strong,' she said after swallowing and clearing her throat, giving a little cough. Jenny watched this and thought her mother-in-law's wattle was wobblier than she remembered it. 'You know, I tend to dilute my coffee with decaf – you know, I make it "half-caff". I think that's what they call it,' said Sally, and she turned to Bill. 'Who needs all that jittery caffeine anyway – right, Bill?'

Bill nodded without looking at his wife and took another sip. 'So, where are those boys?'

'Oh, didn't I say?' Jenny started. 'They're coming. They've been camping.'

'Aw, that's nice. Real nice,' he replied. 'They go to the Poconos?'

Jenny was putting the evaporated milk into the fridge – she hoped that that was what you were supposed to do with it.

'Uh, no, not the Poconos. They went to the . . . oh, hold on.' She had forgotten.

She went to check her cellphone. Hank had messaged her this morning saying they would be back by four o'clock. He mentioned they were coming south.

'Somewhere up north,' she said. 'Anyway, they'll tell us everything when they get back – which should be any minute.' She turned to them both. 'Do you want to freshen up before they come crashing in?'

Her in-laws mumbled and protested, they were fine, they might like to go outside for a few minutes and get some air. 'See how your garden plants are getting along!' Sally said, and the pair walked out onto the lawn.

Jenny wasn't aware that they had any particular garden plants. The Maple Drive association was in charge of planting and most people's gardens were variations on the same theme. There was a bush of some kind by the driveway, which Jenny thought might flower at some point in the year. There were some coloured flowers planted in the island in the centre of their turn-about section of the cul-de-sac. She watched Bill and Sally from the kitchen window to see what they were looking for, and the couple seemed to be walking along the neat edge of the lawn, prodding it with an occasional shoe-tip. They were admiring the way the lawn was mown? Okay, well, never mind.

Jenny went to her phone and texted Hank: Your parents are here. When are you getting here?

CHAPTER 18

H ANK WASN'T IN MUCH of a rush to get home. He was going over his camping experience with the boys and hadn't finished talking yet.

'So when I gave you the hot peppers – some kids woulda been, like, "Whoa! That's cool!" and you guys were almost there, I swear. So now, next time you eat a chilli pepper you can be all cool about it and nobody needs to cry anymore, you know? It's just a chilli pepper. And actually, you might even get to like them.' Hank was driving along, tried to catch a glimpse of their turned faces in the back seat. He hummed something, a handful of half-notes, possibly from a song.

'And then, when we were playing war games, and you guys shook me off your trail . . .' Hank braced his arms and turned quickly to look at them directly. 'Are you guys even listening?' He was now glaring at them in the rear-view mirror. 'I just want to get it into your heads that you would have been fine, it was just foggy . . . you were *not actually lost*. Got it?'

The Vietnam War game had ended with Hank stalking the two boys. But Hank lost track of them at one point and the boys had been walking in circles, unable to read the compasses he had given them. They had given up after a time, and when it had started to drizzle, they took refuge in the entrance to an old gold mine. Several hours later, Jesse set off one of the flares which summoned a park ranger who, based on their descriptions, led them back to their campsite. The man took Hank aside and exchanged some serious words with him, ending with a warning: 'Those old mines are a serious danger and you're lucky anything more serious didn't occur. You were smart to have emergency flares – but those aren't for kids to handle.' The boys were out of earshot but they were watching, so Hank smiled and patted the ranger on the shoulder. The ranger shook his head.

The car was silent – the boys had some kind of silence pact. 'There is no point in saying anything because it just makes you talk more,' Jesse had said to him that morning at breakfast.

'We're almost home.' Hank checked his phone. 'Grandma and Grandpa are waiting for us.'

The boys looked at each other. Hank didn't mind that they were silent; silence was good for them.

The radio was reporting something about a school shooting. 'Aw, Jeez, not again,' Hank said to no one in particular, and he switched off the radio so the boys wouldn't hear.

*

HANK WAS DRIVING AT the speed limit, which seemed unnaturally slow but gave him time to unwind before getting home. He was really pissed off at Jenny for giving Jesse the flares. Undercutting him, yet again. He thought about how mad she would be when she found out about the boys going into a mine, and he remembered the Chilean miners again with their sunglasses and cookies.

'You guys brush your teeth today?'

'Yes, Dad,' they said.

'Once there were some miners trapped in a mine, and when they got out at last, the president of their country said they were born again.' Hank looked back at his sons. 'You hear that? Born again.'

Hank was still going pretty slowly and wasn't really concentrating on his driving much at all when he changed lane and happened to move in front of a red car that was accelerating. The blaring of the man's horn startled Hank and he adjusted the steering wheel quickly to centre himself in his lane, checking his mirrors, looking side to side. The man leaned on his horn again, right up close to Hank's back fender. Hank hadn't meant to cut him up. He'd been distracted. Enough already, he thought.

But now the man had driven up beside Hank and rolled down his window. Hank waved at him, in a gesture of apology, but when the man's car stayed level with theirs, Hank could see that the man was actually trying to say something to him. He looked over. A vast mouth was billowing at them, screaming, with its teeth gnashing and tongue rigid. Hank looked straight ahead again. Wild arms were flashing across Hank's peripheral vision. Both cars were now going

55 mph and other cars were passing them on both sides. Everyone was looking at them as they passed.

Hank tried to acknowledge the guy, and mouthed the words *Okay, okay*.

Jesse and Luke in the back seat were riveted. 'I don't think that is a good guy, Dad,' said Luke.

'Epic,' said Jesse. 'You should race him, Dad.' It was the first volley of enthusiasm Hank had heard from Jesse the whole trip.

The man was still going off. Hank could now see that he was mouthing *Pull over now, you asshole*. He wanted to take it outside. He was slightly swerving towards them, back and forth. Hank fixed his face forward. He needed to do something. He wanted to fight the guy, he really did. He didn't want to look like a coward in front of his sons. But, even from the side, he could see the guy was big. Hank wasn't all that sure he could beat him. He might get knocked out, and where would that leave them? Fear was crawling up his neck and he was itching to react. Jenny would not approve of any of this.

The guy was bellowing curses at Hank. But couldn't he see that there were kids in the car? Hank shook his head and changed lanes from the middle to the slowest lane. He wasn't pulling over but he wanted to get out of the middle of the highway; figured he could veer off if need be. For a moment, he wondered if the guy actually thought Hank was pulling over. The man continued his fevered pursuit. Once Hank had settled into the slow lane, the man pulled in front of him and slowed down. Hank had no choice but to change lanes. The red car pulled in front of him again. There was an exit coming up and Hank needed to get off this freeway.

The kids were scared and silent by this point and Hank felt emboldened by them. He needed to protect them. Was it flight? Fight? Or just, like, protect your offspring? The thought darted across his mind: what would a Viking do?

Hank slowed down and when they approached the exit, he made as if to drive past but swerved and pressed the brakes and took the exit instead, leaving the red car to continue along the highway.

He drove straight to the International House of Pancakes that he saw as they turned off the exit-ramp. He parked in the back, by the dumpsters. They were just on the outskirts of Bentonville now. The kids were looking at him for guidance.

'We did it,' Hank told them, and smiled. 'Some people are deranged.'

A pause, and then he laughed. 'Never trust people in red cars!'

He looked at the little faces in his rear-view mirror.

'You gotta know when to fight and when to get the hell outta Dodge.' He took hold of his door-release handle.

'C'mon, guys, let's get pancakes before we get home,' he said to them, and they scrambled out of their seat belts and out into the parking lot. Hank hoped they were still young enough to get excited about the chocolate pancakes on the weekend menu that were decorated with whipped cream and candied cherries, all made up to look like a face.

CHAPTER 19

'THE CHURCH SERVICE WAS nice,' Grandma Sally said.

'Wasn't it?' Jenny said. Silence. 'I made cookies,' she said, rising.

'Did you?' Grandma said.

Grandma followed Jenny into the kitchen and stood by as Jenny unwrapped the cling film from around a plate. The cookies were not pretty but they were home-made. Grandma put her hands out to help carry them.

'We could put them on a nicer plate, maybe,' she suggested.

'Of course.' Jenny pulled the platter they had given her out of the cupboard. She was barely keeping up with the tests presented to her. But her face was serene, and she had noted with satisfaction that while her mother-in-law was ageing, she herself was looking a little younger since last week.

They hadn't all fitted into one car to go to church, so the boys travelled in the SUV and the women went in the Honda. Since the senior Tinkleys did not eat raw fish, they decided that Hank and his dad would stop and pick up some food from one of the restaurants in Bentonville. 'That's nice,' Grandma said. 'That you get a little break from cooking on a Sunday, that's nice . . . for you.'

When the male Tinkleys processed into the house with aluminium boxes of food, Grandma cooed over them, but, to Jenny, upon opening them, she said, 'Baked ziti? Well, even you could have made that.'

Jenny had cooked her lentil casserole the night before, and they had reminded her that she had cooked this the last time they visited. As far as Jenny remembered, she had never claimed to be a great cook.

Hank and Jenny were on edge. Everyone was a little tense. Going to church had been complicated. Grandma had whispered forcefully throughout the service.

'Why is everyone looking at their phones?'

Luke whispered back the word 'peace', followed by a 'shush'.

Later, at no one in particular: 'God's phone? This is wacky.'

And at confession, a little louder: 'I'm not sure about this at all.'

And then: 'Oh my Lord God, what the bejesus?!'

The teenagers in front of the Tinkleys were sniggering and pretending to cough. Hank was separated from his parents by Luke and Jesse so couldn't control his mother. When the pastor had made a special announcement about the unusual sins that had come through on the God-phone, Grandma groaned. He was concluding his sermon with a plea for the sinners of the congregation with particularly heavy burdens to come to him, to confess in person. 'I am deeply concerned for your spiritual welfare.' He wiped the sweat from the edge of his eyebrow. 'I am worried on account of your eternal life.' He paused again – clearly this was the improvised part of his sermon. 'It's my job, right?' He tried a chuckle. 'But seriously, we confess to be cleansed.' And he launched into a sung prayer to which the congregation sang a wavering '*Amen*'.

Now they were back at home, and while Hank and his father settled in front of the TV, their wives were putting out the food. They sat at a reasonable distance, never side by side. They needed to pick a channel and Bill was annoyed that Hank was holding the remote control. 'Put it on ABC, Hank,' Bill said. Hank ignored him and started to flip channels. 'ABC, Hank,' Bill said again. Hank stopped at a football game. 'Who's that?' Bill asked. 'Beamers,' Hank answered. And they watched that until Sally called them over to the table.

Jenny was out on the front lawn talking on her cellphone, and Hank rapped on the kitchen window, gesturing to her to come inside. She glanced back and nodded.

'I don't know who it is . . .' Sally said to Hank. 'She walked right out that door as soon as she answered it.'

There were sins in the air and everyone knew it.

Grandpa started a tirade about sins and neighbours. 'You want to know what I think that priest was talking about?' No one answered but they were waiting to be told. 'Well, I'm going to say that there are a helluva lot of perverts around these days. Don't know where they came in from – foreign parts – but things are happening now that never existed back when I was young. Never existed!'

He leaned in to Luke who was always good at listening to his pronouncements. 'You know, Luke, I don't mean to be racist or nothing, but different people are different, if you know what I mean.' He sat back in his chair. 'And I'm not saying all other nationalities are bad, you know.' He chuckled. 'We got a real melting pot here. And me and your grandma know people from all kinds of places – good people. But what I'm saying is when the bad element gets in, well, let's just say it can take hold. Say, Hank,' Grandpa boomed. 'Maybe you should consider moving, you know? Down to somewhere nice and friendly like Florida.'

WHEN SHE FIRST MET his parents, Jenny did her best to appear like a nice choice of girlfriend. There was a performance to the event and Jenny felt for the first time as though she were entering a ritual. First of all, she was amazed at how interested in her body they were. They didn't exactly show it, but they were very aware of her bodily – his mother, for example, tried to give her some girly clothes, not having daughters herself, she said, as she held them up against Jenny's torso, measuring this new girlfriend from the front, the side, the back. 'Turn around,' Sally Tinkley told her. 'Hmm, not quite right,' she said. Hank's dad was overly polite to her, helping her with her bags, taking the collar of her coat to help her remove it, helping her to sit in her chair. 'Are you comfortable?' he asked her. 'Do you need the bathroom?' She smiled to herself, reminded of indigenous tribes whose habit it was to inspect the teeth of their future daughter-in-law. Did the Tinkleys think to themselves then that she had child-bearing hips? She didn't know, but she knew there was fierce and furtive assessment in progress. She wasn't at all sure if she had passed or failed, but Hank soon enlightened her.

'My mom thinks you don't like them,' he said on the drive home.

'Did she say that?' Jenny was horrified.

'No, but I could tell.'

CHAPTER 20

'I'M SORRY, I HAVE guests, I wasn't expecting your call – but hi, hello, thanks for calling . . .' Jenny had left the house while the others unpacked the food, and she was walking a little ways down Maple Drive. She smoothed down her hair, buttoned her jacket; she had forgotten that she had slipped her phone number into the envelope she sent to Shona.

'Look, I only have five minutes' allowance – this is my one call for the week,' Shona said. 'You sent me something that was a little terrible.'

'Right, yes, yes, I did,' Jenny said. 'Did I?' She had stepped somewhere in between them. Jenny was embarrassed now that she had Shona on the phone. Who was she to be meddling in their lives? And how would she explain why she was writing to this woman's husband?

'I, um, am taking part in a programme to write letters to prisoners.' Jenny tried to sound courteous, there was nothing else for it.

'Uh, oka-ay.' Shona's voice contained menace. 'But . . . I don't understand who you are. Like, who are you exactly?'

Jenny hadn't foreseen this. She had been asked to pass on a message and she had done that – but yes, it did look very weird that she had a private dialogue with this woman's husband.

'Oh, right. Uh . . .' She faltered. 'I'll send you the letters if you want. It's just, you know, letter-writing to inmates.' But that sounded pretty bad too – like a pity parade, like Jenny was some kind of charity worker, counselling people that had erred. Bad choices!

'Okay, it feels a little weird, okay?'

Jenny was silent and so was Shona. She was going to apologise but she was not sure what for. She had to walk a little further along Maple Drive because Mrs Salton had come outside wearing gardening gloves, holding garden shears.

'I sent you some coffee,' Jenny said quietly. 'I'm just a regular person . . . a wife. A mother.'

'You what? I can't hear you,' Shona's voice sounded far away – she had apparently tipped her head away from the receiver.

'Okay, okay, I just wanted to get that prayer card to you . . . and so I did. Before you get out. So you didn't disappear.' Jenny looked back at the house; she knew that the family was sitting down for lunch and this phone call would be hard to explain.

'Aw, shoot.' Shona sounded less annoyed now, a little plaintive. 'Okay, look, I'm running out of time. But I can tell you one thing – you *have* to not contact me.' And then, after another pause, Jenny heard a quiet 'shoot'.

Jenny waited.

'I don't know if you're trying to help or what is going on, but you know, I'm getting released. I can go see him myself soon.' Shona shouted something at someone nearby but Jenny couldn't hear what she said. There was a hellish echo coming from Shona's end of the line.

Shona got back to her. 'Look, just keep me out of this.' And a pause, and then, quiet but tough: 'No more prayers. Please.'

'Okay, right, no prayers,' Jenny said. She had to remember these words because they might mean something more if she thought about it later. Was 'prayers' some kind of drug-slang maybe?

'Okay, bye.'

'Okay, right, sure . . .'

Jenny looked down at her phone, the call had ended after four minutes and fifty-four seconds. So that was Shona. She'd seen the pencilled words on the prayer card Jenny sent, but there had been nothing to taste. Maybe she was mad that Jenny hadn't sent the correct envelope with the orange glue stuff. But, God, Jenny was relieved she hadn't sent the envelope. That would have been actually breaking the law. Who were these people anyway? Jenny looked at the house: what was she going to tell the family when she went back inside?

'WHERE YA BEEN, SUNSHINE?' Hank asked her as she walked into the dining room. They had started eating without her – in all of four minutes and fifty-four seconds.

'Why do you always call Mom "sunshine" when Grandma and Grandpa are here?' asked Luke.

But the tableful of Tinkleys were all looking at Jenny for an answer to Hank's question. Where had she been? 'I've been out there,' she gestured. And they all looked at her, waiting for more. She turned and got herself a plate, busied herself with the various shapes of pasta they had brought.

'Well, that's nice. It's a nice day,' Grandma said. She was eating the baked ziti, and spoke with some food still in her mouth. She seemed to have a very mobile tongue, licking at the insides of her mouth to clear out the little pieces of pasta lodged there. This would annoy Hank, Jenny thought, and might be enough to distract him from interrogating her. Jenny saw Hank was frowning in his mother's direction.

Hank never insisted on mindful breathing at mealtimes when his parents were visiting. They wouldn't understand, he told the boys, they're old-fashioned, they just breathe, you know, the regular way. Nonetheless, Jenny and the children could hear Hank's rhythmic inhales between each mouthful. Church always made people hungry, for some reason, and their moods would all ease when they got some food into their stomachs. They passed around the pre-cut garlic bread, and then the paper napkins because the garlic bread had been so greasy on their fingers. Jenny was a little disappointed to waste such nice paper napkins on a family lunch, but Sally had put them out and it was too late to fuss about it. They were ornamental; they matched the nice tablecloth in wine-red and black. Paper towels would have been fine. She breathed it out, and the boys looked at her, assuming she was doing *pranayama*. Let it go, Jenny thought. And that stupid Disney song fired up in her head, so she rolled her eyes, disguised under a quick half-blink.

Bill asked the boys about the camping trip. 'So, you meet any bears up there?'

Jesse laughed; he was so much more boyish with his grandparents than with his parents. 'No bears,' he said. 'But we did have some scrapes with danger – right, Dad?'

Hank glared at Jesse. Luke looked from Jesse to his dad and back again.

'We found gold,' Luke said.

'Go-old?' said Grandpa. He turned to Hank.

'Aw, no, well, we went panning for gold is what we did . . . right, boys?' Hank seemed pleased the subject had shifted.

'Yeah, and Dad found gold,' Luke said.

'Show them the gold, Dad,' added Jesse. He sat taller in his seat. 'Basically, we were swirling sand around with water in some frying pans and looking for little flakes of gold. But we didn't find anything, just some black silt. And then Dad found two huge chunks . . . worth a *lot* of money,' Jesse explained.

Hank's parents had stopped eating, their forks placed carefully down on their napkins. Sally looked a little amazed and a little annoyed: 'Why haven't you told us this yet? You've been back since yesterday.' She looked at Hank, and over at the boys too.

It was the first Jenny had heard of it, and she was glad to hear that they'd had some fun together. She had been dreading the details of their trip – they'd said so little so far, and that wasn't a good sign. And she hadn't had any time alone with either of her children to ask them privately if they had enjoyed themselves or not. Panning for gold sounded like fun. That was something.

Hank wasn't getting up, he was the only one still eating. He shoved a big forkful of ziti into his mouth and looked up at them, around the table, as he chewed, grinning. He would make them wait while he chewed, and they did.

Luke turned to Grandpa and asked him, 'Grandpa, gold happens in veins inside the earth. Do you think that the gold is the blood of the rocks?'

Grandpa wasn't listening though; he glanced down at Luke and cast a short 'Sure' at him. And then: 'You found nuggets in that river there? The Susquehanna, was it?'

Hank nodded, and continued to chew. He would have to say something now; his mouth was emptying. 'I put it in the safe,' he told them, and consumed another mouthful.

'Well, that is lucky,' said Grandpa. He knew a thing of two about gold-panning since one of Grandma's uncles (she had seven uncles) had been a gold prospector. The method, he told them, was to take up some pay-dirt and some water, and shift it to the left and to the right so that the heavier matter – the gold – would settle to the bottom. Slowly and gradually, you needed to sweep off the top layer of dirt and gravel.

'At the bottom of your pan, you're gonna find some black sand,' he said.

'We found black sand!' Luke chirped.

'Yes, but did you find garnets?' Grandpa asked. 'Garnets are a real sign that there's gold there.'

Grandpa was getting going now, and once he was onto a story, he laughed and teased his way through it. 'You know, the only thing I ever found was a couple of old bullets – down there, on the Sallany river. But, Grandma will tell you, I am not what you call lucky when it comes to the lottery or buried treasure.'

Hank was listening to all this, and was happy to let his father direct the conversation.

'So,' said Grandpa, 'did your dad actually get his hands dirty to find that gold? If I know Hank, I'd say he would not exactly want to get his hands into that black silt . . .'

Hank kept on eating and Grandpa ran out of steam. No one really answered his taunting. He turned to the boys and continued. 'So, Uncle Ted – now he was a real frontiersman. Do you know that one time he found a piece of gold that was so beautiful that he couldn't bring himself to sell it? I remember, it was in the shape of a beetle and even had a natural loop to it – you know, like a beetle's antlers? Well, he put it on a gold chain and gave it to Aunt Trish. You remember that necklace, Sal?'

'Oh yes, yes, I do. It was a big piece of gold.'

'Why don't you give your gold to Mom?' Luke said.

'Sure,' Hank said. 'Sure I will.'

'But, Mom –' Luke turned to Jenny – 'you know you will have to give it back to the government in the end, right?'

Jenny might have raised her eyebrows, if the muscles in her face weren't now variously unavailable.

'Yes, honey,' she said, and walked some plates to the kitchen. Standing at her counter, she could hear the Tinkleys discussing gold. She counted the flies on the fly strip: seven. She then reached into her purse and slipped John's envelope from it. Those rushes of love that she got from licking the envelope – these were meant for Shona. But Shona didn't want them. *Don't send anything*, she said. *No more prayers.*

She took up her smartphone and her thumbs brushed and tapped at the screen, she googled 'orange prayers' and it came up with prayers for orange trees, and Islamic websites for a mosque in Orange County. Then she googled 'orange drugs' and the list was long. There was something called 'orange crush', a term for cough medicines that contained dextromethorphan and were often delivered in an orange-flavoured syrup. Dextromethorphan – it relaxed you, eased your breathing, soothed your cough. She'd heard of people abusing cough medicine, but the image in her mind was of lame junkies chugging bottles of the stuff when their usual drugs weren't available. That's probably something people do in prison, she thought.

Jenny took the envelope up to her nose and nuzzled the envelope. The smell spoke to her; it said: *All things bright and beautiful.*

CHAPTER 21

MOST OF JESSE'S HOMEWORK was online. But today they had to handwrite their work – it was something to do with Easter. Or resurrection? At least, that's what he thought the teacher said. Anyway, the homework was to write a letter to your older self: you, at twenty-one years old. Eight years into the future.

He had seen the movie *Back to the Future*, and he had thought a lot about time travel. Especially time travel into the past. For example, what if his dad hadn't killed his mom's dog all those years ago? Jesse just wouldn't exist. He would never have even been born. Sorry, dog, he said to himself, but your murder was my lucky break. Maybe he was the dog, just reincarnated. Or, he thought, maybe I would have been born but just to different parents. But that sort of wasn't possible when you considered DNA.

He was sitting at the desk in his room. He was trying to spin the pen in his hand over the top of his thumb knuckle; he had seen Mr Dillon, the math teacher, do it. It was harder than it looked. And when he started trying to write something, he realised that it had been a while since he'd written with a pen – and he couldn't really control the tip. His handwriting looked like a first-grader's. That was bad. He googled 'good handwriting' and watched a video on the formation of letters on fast forward. He tried to slant his writing and to join up his letters, but that was almost worse – the lines between the letters made them look like they were all lined up in a game of tug of war. Anyway, joined-up writing was kind of girly so he started again with plain, upright letters.

Dear Jesse, aged 21,

You don't know me. But you used to. I'm you, eight years ago. How are you? I'm hoping you did something good with your life. Did you? You are pretty old now, and definitely an adult. Did you at least graduate from high school? If not, then you better do that – try again. (Only losers don't graduate from high school, so don't be that.) But I'm guessing you pretty much aced school. And that you're in college now and you're free, and you can do whatever you want. Do you keep candy in your room there? Do you go out when it's night-time? I bet you do.

The only things I want to tell you is this. First, never do drugs. Drugs will make you stupid. And also, try to get as much money as you can so you can retire early. Then you can really do whatever you want. That's what our Dad says. And try to be normal and NOT a loser.

One of the main things I want to know is if you have got your expert driving licence. And what kind of car do you have? Is it a Porsche? I hope it's a Porsche.

Also, I hope you have not forgotten how to skateboard because it is a life skill. Remember that.

Over and out and see you on the other side,

Jesse

Now that he was done with his homework, he could go out skateboarding. Grandma and Grandpa were out at the drugstore so it wasn't like he was being rude. Downstairs, his mother was sitting watching TV and didn't really notice when he walked past. He told her was going out to skateboard and she replied with a simple 'Okay'. It was weird that she didn't check what time he would be back, and that she didn't insist that he wore his elbow and knee pads. She used to always make him wear them. But lately she was not so careful. Maybe she thought he had finally grown up and didn't need all that parenting anymore.

Skateboarding was as close to religion as Jesse got. He believed in God and all that, but there was something about skateboarding that was more wonderful than he could explain. Even the sound of the board hitting the street, the *clack-clack-clack* as he rolled over the cracks in the sidewalk – it made him happy. It was like hearing the music that they play at the beginning of movies – when you just know you're about to have a good time.

He set off, and pushed himself fast with his back foot, then ollie'd down from the sidewalk and veered around the street. There were almost no cars on Maple Drive so you could make whatever shape you wanted with your skateboard. That was the thing: everyone skateboards differently. You don't know that until you're into skateboarding. Everyone just has their own style – kind of like walking. And that's why it felt so free, because, in a way, you're just doing it for yourself.

As Jesse careered down the street, he realised that skateboarding was a little like time travel. Like time wasn't happening anymore. There are no limits, no scores, and no time-outs in skateboarding. There is no pressure. You coast. You leap. There's no team you have to impress.

The only thing you had to remember was that in skateboarding the small obstacles were the worst. Big things like stairs and banisters, or kerbs, or railings – these were challenges, and they were good. But pebbles, and cracks in the sidewalk, were the biggest dangers of skating. The point is that you can dodge big things but the small things can make you fly off your board and land on your face.

The nicest thing about skateboarding was that you just didn't have to think about anything else. The skateboarding kind of consumed you, it took all your body and your concentration. You were really living, in 3D, and there was no extra thinking that would bother you.

He had a lot of extra thinking going on these days. He kept thinking about the images he had seen online. The cartoon vaginas, all blue and smooth, and the big, elastic tits that seemed to swing around. He was more surprised by the huge purple cartoon penises he had seen. They were usually dripping and writhing, and he just thought it looked like something from the *Hulk* cartoon, but much, much worse. Everywhere he went, he lapsed into these cartoon sex scenes. He'd see a girl and then wonder about her smooth, blue vagina, that spewed rainbows and candy. Of course he knew that real vaginas didn't look exactly like that – he'd seen real ones on the internet too – but the cartoons blasted their way into his world. It was like *Roger Rabbit* – but much, much worse.

He had it with guns too – and even on his skateboard he sometimes wanted to be holding an Uzi and skating around spraying gunfire in great arcs. He could kill everyone he passed if he wanted to. He could blast stop signs from their posts. He could shoot the pine cones off trees. Blast the tyres off trucks. Mow down a line of pedestrians – not that there were any pedestrians in Bentonville. In fact, he never really saw anyone at all when he was skateboarding, except people in cars. None of his friends were out – they were all inside on their consoles, hanging out together online.

He lifted the tip of his skateboard, and flicked up the back wheels. Someone was shooting at him now, and he was dodging bullets, high and low, and leaping over landmines, veering away from grenades.

CHAPTER 22

S HE HAD BEEN AVOIDING her in-laws all morning. They were sitting around, observing family life and formulating their judgements. Luke was in his basement, dressed in overalls, busy with his archive. Jesse was in his room, on some device or other, his whole little soul wicking into his phone.

Jenny left to run some errands – groceries, the drugstore, the dry-cleaning, and then to the post office, where she found another letter from John. She lowered her window, tore the envelope and unfolded the paper, promising herself she'd throw the letter out of the window if it was more of the same abuse.

Dear Jenny,
Now I need to say sorry to you. I'm apologising for my last letter I know you didn't mean what you said how I took it. This is a hard place, and your letters are so fresh and so innocent. I shouldn't have broken that. You love your kids and that's

174

beautiful. Nobody needs to get on that. What I guess I need to tell you is that I have a soul on my conscience so I don't like to talk about taking away a life. But I guess you knew that from my profile. That I am down for manslaughter. I should tell you how it happened then you'll understand a little more. It was a terrible accident.

I was living in an apartment complex in Philly with Shona and we were working jobs. We had a nice place with two bedrooms and good living room with some nice furniture. One night, I hear a noise in the hallway and I go out but there's no one there, so I check down the hall. It was a weird noise, like a kid or a woman, or maybe a cat, you know like a high howl. But there's no one there. Except my neighbour comes out and he's always been a little crazy, shouting and dressing up in weird costumes. He says I'm watching him. Asks me who I am and what I'm doing there because he doesn't recognise me. He's really worked up and he is screaming and he's a big guy and I don't expect it but he grabs my neck and gets me in a headlock and I'm telling him to calm down. Shona comes out and tries to push him off me, and the guy is starting to pound at my head saying that I was following him and what was I watching him for and Shona shoves him and I'm holding onto his arms trying to release my neck, and I get out of the headlock and push him off me and he falls over. Well you see then he cracks his head on the concrete floor and he's unconscious and he's bleeding. And we tried to help him.

We called the ambulance. Shona tried to risusitate him. The ambulance came. There were no witnesses, no one saw it or heard it so when he died a few days later in the hospital, the police came back and then we got convicted of manslaughter. You can look up the details of the case. There were reports of it in the newspaper.

I'm giving you a wooden spoon that I made. It's maple wood. It's for all that you are. And to say sorry.

Peace,

John

The spoon was smooth. She held it carefully – it was an object straight from prison, and without sniffing it she could smell prison coming from it. A metallic and oily smell. A male smell. The spoon had a flat diagonal head, the kind that is suited to mixing; you could get into the corners of a pan with this spoon, she thought. The wood was yellowish and lined with maple fibres. The lines followed the length of the spoon and spread slightly at the spoon end into the shapes of pods and almonds. She wanted to wash it. She didn't really want to feed her family with any prison matter, any atoms that came from the inside of a jail. Could eating a little bit of jail put the essence of jail inside you? She didn't want to risk it with so many males in her house.

The day was rainy and cool, and she really didn't want to rush home. It was the last day of her in-laws' visit and she was hoping to just get back in time for their departure. Jenny had told them all that she was so sorry but she had a long-held appointment at the jeweller's to get her engagement ring fixed. The stone was loose and she didn't want to risk losing it. She didn't wait to hear Sally talk about how expensive the stone had been, and how, in her day, people didn't go around wearing diamonds all day, that they just wore them on special occasions. It was a less showy time, she would say.

So Jenny played with the car radio and went through her handbag, removing all the cough-drop wrappers and stray coins, and shaking the crumbs out onto the parking lot tarmac.

'WELL, THAT IS VERY kind of you,' Sally was saying. She was rubbing the head of the wooden spoon with her thumb. 'And what kind of wood is that?'

'Maple,' Jenny replied quietly. 'It's maple, I believe.' It was so much easier to converse with her parents-in-law with a forehead full of Botox, not to mention a lick of the orange stuff.

'Oh?' Sally dipped her chin in acknowledgement. 'Is that something they make around here? They have maple farms?'

'Yes. Sure. Yes, I think they do,' Jenny answered, and started opening her kitchen drawers and shifting things around. The boys were still upstairs and Hank was in the bathroom, while the senior Tinkleys stood in the kitchen in their light travelling jackets, with their packed bags. Jenny was offering last-minute helpfulness: did they want a drink before setting off? Did they need some mints for the car journey? Did they know their route? She had a map somewhere . . .

But no, they were fine. The Tinkleys were very organised people. Jenny looked at her father-in-law and wondered if his hair had some kind of old-fashioned hair oil in it or if it was simply greasy. It was slicked into place, with comb tracks from roots to tips. And had his ears always been that large?

Sally was still looking at the spoon. 'You know, Jenny,' she said, pointing the spoon over to Jenny's stove-top where a collection of wooden spoons stood in a tall jar, 'I think you should have this spoon. It really is a nice spoon. And your spoons look a little cracked up.' She smiled at Jenny. 'They're so well-worn, I mean.' And she offered the spoon back to Jenny. 'You need it. Not us.'

'Oh? Oh, okay,' said Jenny.

'It's just that you have a whole family to feed here. We're only two people. We don't eat much.' Sally said this with such sympathy. 'Isn't that right, Bill?'

Jenny would have to ignore it because there was no reply she could think of that didn't involve spitting. So she walked across the kitchen and pushed it in among her other wooden spoons. For a split second, she considered pulling out her oldest, crappiest spoon and shoving it at her mother-in-law. *There you go, you old hag.* But she just walked back and started to fuss around with a dishcloth, rinsing a fork that had been left in the sink, and mustering whatever remained of her small talk.

Hank came into the kitchen, talking. 'So, you all set?' He went for his mother's small bag but she pulled it to herself. Bill had already packed the car with their suitcases.

'Why don't you come visit this summer?' Sally said. 'It would really be nice. The kids could swim.'

'Sure, okay, Mom,' Hank answered. 'We'll see what we can do.'

Bill was standing in the doorway looking at Hank. There was something passing between them but Jenny couldn't catch on to it. Bill directed a stern glare at Hank, and Hank was avoiding it and trying to get them out the door.

'You ready?' Hank said, with his palm at his mother's back. Sally moved towards Bill and they filed out towards the driveway.

Jenny was slow to follow. Let them get settled in the car. Let them smooth down their jackets and set their jaws. Let Bill turn on the engine. They weren't people who liked to hug anyway.

CHAPTER 23

HANK HAD SET LIMITS on how much time Luke could spend in his basement room. He wasn't allowed to 'stew down there anymore'.

Meanwhile, Luke had been interested in the bricks that formed the walls of the basement. Was there really just dirt behind them? He knew he was underground – but dearly wished he had X-ray vision to see through to the dirt and its contents. There would be rocks. There would be roots. There might even be archaeological findings. There had been Indians around here. Native Americans. He didn't know what kind. There would be arrowheads at the very least. The earth held secrets.

So, a few weeks back, he had removed a brick by scraping away at the mortar. And another. He removed seven bricks before he could see that behind the bricks were concrete breeze blocks. He tapped at them a little with his mallet and chisel. He scraped the mortar with a plain spoon from the kitchen drawer. The bricks and blocks weren't all that hard to break either. Only you had to do it in little pieces at a time. Bricks break in slices; they offer themselves as sculpture. Concrete falls apart into clusters, it gives itself granularly. Luke made two piles. The brick shards and the concrete lumps. He would have to hide this rubble when he was called upstairs. He hid the hole in the wall with his enormous poster showing *The Process of Smelting*. The hole was only about two-foot wide, and only about six inches deep. He had yet to get to the soil.

'Luu-uke, honey!' his mother called from upstairs. She had told him they were having a meeting with Mrs Paxton. Jenny had said that it would be just to check in, that lots of kids had therapists and it was helpful in this 'confusing world'. Luke wondered again if he was saying the right things to Mrs Paxton. Maybe this time he would get some clues about what she actually wanted to know.

Hank and Jenny were waiting in the kitchen. When Luke emerged, slightly dusted with mortar, from his basement playroom, Hank looked at Jenny. He seemed to be proving himself right about something.

'I wasn't stewing,' said Luke to him.

Jenny moved forward and swept at Luke's clothing to clear the dust from him.

'You must be very busy down there,' she said quietly.

'Go change your clothes,' Hank said.

But Jenny countered, 'He's fine. He's fine as he is.' And to Luke: 'I'll just get a cloth to get some of this dust off and we can go. You're not hungry, are you?' She had already given Hank a cheese sandwich.

'A cookie?' Luke answered. Jenny got the cookie and the cloth, and she brushed her son as they walked out together to the SUV. Luke hated the SUV. He had told them before what he thought: it smelled of the bottom of suitcases. The part that gets dragged through airports.

Mrs Paxton was smiling as usual and invited Luke into the therapy room. The Tinkley parents would wait in the reception area for half an hour.

'Show me the ink test again – I know the answer now,' Luke told Mrs Paxton.

'Oh, don't worry, honey, we're not doing anything like that today. Your parents are here. We're going to have a little time together and then show them the games we play. And then I'm going to talk to them while you play in the room next door.'

'Please can we not play with the dolls.'

'Of course, honey. What would you like to play with?'

Luke looked around the room: paints, baby dolls, knights, soldiers, puzzles, crayons, toy food, board games.

'Can I ask you some questions?' he asked.

'Yes. You can. Of course you can.' She seemed happy.

'What was happening on the earth in year zero?'

'Hmm, interesting question. Year zero? Well, let's see. Year zero . . .'

Luke thought that surely she must know.

'Well, you know,' she went on. 'Year zero is the year when, I think, Jesus is supposed to have died. That's how we count the years.'

'Jesus?'

'Right. Well, anyway, it's just how people in the olden days decided to count the years. But we can imagine what it was like then. What do you think it was like?'

'Well, I guess it was dusty and hot. And they had shekels.'

'Yes, well, maybe in parts of the world it was hot. But it was probably not so different from today – the nature parts of the world, I mean. Not the cities. Cities in those days were small, and had houses made of clay mostly.'

She seemed unsure to Luke about the clay houses. 'Do you actually know, or are you just guessing?' he asked.

'Well, the problem is that we don't have videos and movies about that time. We have to imagine it because the only thing we have is a few books.'

'You mean scrolls.'

'Right, well, yes, I suppose I do. They didn't really have books in the same way as we do now. That came later. But I think they had monks who wrote books. Or maybe that was later.'

'Okay, so you don't really know – that's okay. I just want to find someone who can tell me.'

They sat in silence for a moment.

'I guess someone must know. We can always google it. I tell you what, I'll google it and tell you about it the next time we meet.'

'Sure.'

She clapped her hands on her knees and started again: 'So. Why. Don't. We . . . Why don't we play something?' She looked around the room.

'I can help you organise your room if you want,' Luke offered.

And so he organised Mrs Paxton's room – which had looked quite ordered as it was, but Luke had some better ideas. The baby dolls, which she had of every colour of skin: Luke felt they should be arranged in order of shade, from dark to light. But then he paused and turned to her. 'The first people were probably darker-skinned – I think humans started in Africa, and they might have had brown skin. Which they needed because the sun there is very bright. The ink in their skin protects them like suntan cream.'

Mrs Paxton watched and listened. 'What is it, Luke, about the beginnings of things? You really like beginnings, don't you?'

He felt, for the first time, that she understood something. He didn't actually like beginnings, but he liked to know where the beginnings were located.

'I just want to know, how did a thing get to where it is now. You know? Like, it's more obvious when you're panning for gold. The gold is there. An element. Lying in the soil layers. The river washes over it. And it's been there for thousands of years. Maybe millions. Maybe dinosaurs walked over it.'

'Panning for gold? That sounds interesting!' Mrs Paxton said, eyes bright.

'Yes, I have done that. I did that in the Endless Mountains.'

'You did? When was that?'

'Oh, you know, a week ago, maybe two. I went with my brother. And my dad.'

'Do you want to set up the figurines in a camping trip?' She had walked over to the shoebox that held the little people. And without him answering, she placed it on the table and picked up some male figurines, placing them on the table, on their feet, arranging their hands by their side.

Luke rearranged them. He put them in a row. Two boys, and a man beside them. Luke looked into the box and picked up a lady figurine and put it on the table. 'I don't need no Crafts,' the male figurine said gruffly, 'I am the Arts – okay?!' Luke placed the man figurine back into the box. 'But we like Crafts – don't we, boys?' squeaked the lady figurine to the two boy figurines.

'Okay,' Mrs Paxton said, rising. 'You do the people, and I'll see if I can find some trees and a tent in my drawers – okay?' She was listening though, and watching him as she went to her drawers.

'Okay, and we need a cave too.'

'A cave?'

'Yeah, a cave where they have to hide, and then they turn blind,' he said.

Luke started tapping the feet of the figurines against the table. He wanted them to walk in a line, holding each other at the shoulder. But they kept falling into each other, letting go.

'Did you know that Vikings abandoned their children if they were weak? They left them in the wilderness or threw them into the sea,' he told Mrs Paxton.

WHEN MRS PAXTON INVITED the Tinkleys to sit on the tiny chairs by the small table, Hank didn't know who was supposed to speak first. 'So, how does this work then?'

Luke was in the reception, looking at magazines.

'Well, thank you for coming. I wanted to share some impressions I have of Luke,' she began.

Hank would be relieved to know just what the point of this therapy was. 'You play with him?' he said.

'Yes, that's right, we use play to access what's going on inside the child. Among other things,' she added, bringing Luke's file to her lap.

'Luke is an intelligent child.' She looked to each of them.

Hank was immune to flattery.

'Has he told you about his hoarding problem?' Hank pressed her.

She looked surprised. The play therapy was a pretty weak method, as far as he could see. Jenny shot him a look that told him to back off. It wasn't quite the frown she would usually pull, but there was warning signalled somewhere in her face. He was a reasonable man – he would let the woman speak and see what she had to offer. He hated Mrs Paxton's orange nail polish; it was a bad sign.

'Luke has an urge to be in control. He seems to have a hard time relaxing. This is, of course, an artificial environment, but we can observe his approach with the games we play. He wants to keep a certain order. Is that something you notice at home?' She was possibly trying now to blame them for his issues. Was Luke like that at home? Shit, she had no idea.

'Luke is very interested in tracing the history of things,' Jenny said. 'He, um, feels sorry for inanimate objects.'

Again, Mrs Paxton was clueless.

'I wonder –' Hank's voice was loud – 'do you think he displays the signs of autism? I mean, we know it's a spectrum.'

Mrs Paxton put down her notes and took off her glasses. She squared on Hank: 'I do not think Luke is autistic, no. Not at all. In fact, he may be almost opposite to that. He is a highly empathetic boy, and, in my opinion, spends an awful lot of time trying to read adult cues. He tends to overthink, I would say.'

'What about OCD then?'

'Have you observed some obsessive behaviours?'

Hank harrumphed. She really was an idiot.

'Yes . . .' Jenny was almost whispering. 'Yes.' She cleared her throat. 'He is compulsive about ordering things. His playroom . . . is rows and rows of ordered items.'

'Oh, I think that's a nice way to put it! The room is evidence of a seriously problematic mental state. Look, Mrs, uh . . .'

'Paxton.'

'Mrs Paxton. I am telling you that there is something not right about him. He is a hoarder. He speaks in tongues. He only wears cotton. He talks about plastic like it's his own grandmother, for Chrissake. You must have noticed something – something we can call it, help him.'

Mrs Paxton heaved a breath. 'Well, it's early days. I think we need more time to see how these behaviours will pan out. He exhibits traits of being obsessive compulsive, yes. And he has unusual interests. He is an unusual kid.'

'You mean, not normal.' She needed help getting to the point.

'Ah, that's not a word I tend to use. But, certainly, he is a special kid.' She was sounding particularly reasonable now. 'He told me that he is part Viking, and that seems to mean an awful lot to him. Would you have a clearer sense of why that is?' She was directing her attack at Hank. She was turning the tables. He hadn't done anything wrong. He hated her orange fingernails.

'Hank is a Viking,' Jenny said to the therapist. Her face was still, calm and knowing.

Hank looked at her, and then at the therapist, and back at Jenny. 'What?' he said. 'What the hell is this?'

'I'm just saying that the Viking thing, it comes from you.'

'Yeah, okay, but what was that?' He waved back and forth between them.

'You root for a football team called the Vikings?' the therapist asked.

'What? No,' Hank said with disapproval.

'I'm sorry, I don't understand. You say you're a Viking, but Vikings don't exist,' the therapist said.

Hank did not need to be humiliated like this. The therapist looked at him and did not see a Viking in front of her.

'It's in my DNA,' he said, crestfallen and angry. 'I have Scandinavian roots. That's all.'

ON THE WAY BACK home, Jenny told Hank and Luke she needed something from the drugstore, and she pulled into the parking lot of Mr Salton's pharmacy.

'Why don't you just drive through?' Hank asked.

'I need to browse for a second – I really won't be long,' she said, getting out of the car. 'Just wait a minute, okay?'

Jenny entered the pharmacy and immediately turned down into the aisles of the store, heading for the coughs-and-colds section. There was a long row of cough suppressants, but she didn't need to browse, she just needed to pick out a few of the orange-flavoured ones. Desprex, Demisol and Soothinx – these looked good. She checked the ingredients to make sure they all contained that dextrometh-a-something. And before going up to pay, she made sure that Mr Salton was busy at the drive-thru window. She paid a sensible-looking young woman, saying that her husband had a cough and he'd asked for the orange one. 'And I don't want to drive back here three times if I didn't get the right one – he's pretty fussy,' Jenny said to her. 'Here's hoping!' she chirped, holding the paper bag of cough syrups and hoofing it out the door.

CHAPTER 24

H ANK'S DESK WAS NEAT. There was very little on it. A framed picture of the family on vacation in Florida. A hole from which two charging cords emerged. A coaster for his coffee mug. Hank wasn't entirely sure what he was supposed to be doing that morning. He checked his email. There were some sales situations that needed resolving but they weren't easy fixes. He scanned the incoming mail – 131 emails – he was looking for easy fixes to start off his day. A few slam-dunks before he had to make some complex plays.

An email landed from his boss: *Hank, have you got those reports yet?*

His sales reports for the month were due.

Yes. I'll get them to you asap, he replied. He stood up. It occurred to him that he better go out for some meetings. There were people to meet and sales to make.

Hank felt better in the car. First, he'd stop to get a Huge-o Coffacino at the drive-thru Dazzlebucks.

The drive-thru attendant was chatting to her colleague as Hank waited at the microphone. You were supposed to speak into a panel that looked like the chocolate sprinkles on the froth of a cappuccino. He could hear her words: 'I was like, no way! Mn-mm! That is *not* happening . . . Welcome to Dazzlebucks, can I take your order?'

These drive-thrus weren't all that much more advanced than when Hank was a kid in the seventies. The disembodied voice that blared at you. You shouted back, your head craned out of your car window. Had they heard you? You started to repeat your order and they interrupted you: 'Can I take your order? Hello? Your order, sir?' All of this, jumbled about with the negotiations inside the car about what each passenger wanted. But Hank was alone and deciding whether to have a Danish pastry.

'Hell-o-ow?' the voice sang. She had a nice voice, actually.

He had worked for the company for a couple of years, since leaving the medical supplies company. It was a start-up – though people didn't call them that anymore. It was a web company: *FIN-DASERVE: A Web Portal for Providing Services*. But that never explained it.

Hank was working on a new pitch: 'Any service you want. Anything. Find it here, and request it. Wife forget the ironing? We'll pick up and deliver it done. Drain need fixing? The plumber is on his way. Need a massage after a long day's work? She'll be there in a jiffy.'

It was long but it was catchy. He probably should have been in advertising. Making up slogans came pretty easily to him.

He opened the paper as he sat in the parking lot, splinters of frosted sugar falling from his Danish onto the words as he read. There was an initiative in Pittsburgh to provide women-only subway cars. This was to deal with the apparent rise in reports of covert molestation on the T. Hank looked up, lifted his paper and swept a cluster of icing slivers out of his window. It wasn't such a bad idea actually.

The girl who gave him his coffee and Danish hadn't been quite as cute as her voice. He never liked nose piercings – couldn't help wondering how the inner part of the ring wouldn't get tangled up in nose gunk – it sort of grossed him out. But her skin was clear and she had a lot of make-up on. Neat eyebrows. He liked that. Jenny liked the natural look, and although he had told her in the early days of their marriage that he liked that about her, that she looked beautiful without all that stuff, he sometimes wished she would smooth out her complexion, put on some mascara or whatever. Make-up sort of shows respect, he thought. Respect for everyone else. Self-respect.

Hank checked his smartphone. Eleven new emails. He'd get to them at some point. But he hadn't checked Facebook in a while, and he figured he'd better find out what was going on. He had to be connected – he was a sales associate.

But he hadn't checked Facebook in so long that he was a little bewildered by his feed. All these people on family vacations with their kids. All these people who were enjoying glasses of white wine before a semi-beautiful sunset. All these satisfied people. With so much to celebrate.

'Got something to celebrate? We'll serve the champagne.' Yet another good tagline.

Shit, Hank thought, he should really post something about the camping trip. There must be at least one happy photo where the boys are smiling and somebody at least appears to be having fun.

First, he needed to check his privacy settings. He looked over his shoulder. It was hot in the car. The coffee was getting to him. He tossed the phone onto the passenger seat and turned on the ignition. His gestures were calm and soothingly mundane as he pulled out of the parking lot and proceeded along the street. He took the exit for the highway. Highways were smooth and wide; a place to relax.

He drove for a while down the slow lane of the highway. After some time, Hank realised he was near to the church. He would have to make some sales calls at some point to prove that he'd been productive. He could do that. He needed to call the alarm company anyway to repair the severed wire that the old man across the street had cut without Hank's permission. But, he wondered, maybe he could make a sales call here after all?

The vicarage was a pleasant white house just off Route 43, and Hank could see Father Brian's Honda parked outside.

'Hello, Hank.' Father Brian was portly and slightly red-faced. He was wearing his dog-collar in a light blue priest's shirt, and he wiped the side of his forehead with one hand while offering Hank the other.

'Thank you, Father. I wonder if you could spare a few minutes,' Hank said, stepping inside.

The priest's house was shady and neat. There was a sour and dusty smell in the hall that gave way to a living room that smelled faintly of furniture polish. Father Brian gestured at the sofa while heading to the front window curtains to open them.

'I'm afraid I don't use this room all that much,' said the priest.

The two men settled. Hank sat on the wide sofa, and Father Brian sat in an armchair to the side. Cool light from the window gave an edge to the furniture and brought to light the minute dust particles in the air that they would now both be breathing as they prepared to speak.

'How can I help?' said Father Brian, hands loosely clasped in his lap, thumbs touching.

Hank wished he had a folder or something. He opened the leather cover of his phone and laid it on the coffee table.

'It was me,' he said, aiming his words into his lap.

'It was you,' Father Brian repeated, and paused. 'What was you?'

Hank looked up at Father Brian.

'The text messages . . . The sins.'

A light surprise spread through Father Brian's expression, followed by a swift pallor.

'I see,' he said nervously. 'I'm glad you came.' Father Brian set himself more rigidly, more upright now that he understood. The noises of the two men's movements seemed unusually loud. A juddering: one shifted in his chair. A light puff: the other sat back against a cushion. Some shuffling: both of them adjusted their foot positions.

Hank expected the priest to laugh, but he hadn't. 'Just kidding, Father,' Hank said. 'I'm not your big sinner.' Hank placed a hand on his chest and grinned.

The priest looked confused.

Hank dropped the grin, cleared his throat, set his feet closer to the phone on the table and began. 'I'm just, um, wondering. You know I'm a sales associate at a web company, right? Well, it's a really terrific site that offers services, and it just occurred to me. It occurred to me that you offer a very valuable service here, Father. It may just be that it's the most valuable service of all. I mean to say that you offer support to the living and the dying – and I think, I think you would really benefit from being available online – you know, to people who don't know it, they just don't realise it, but they need help. They might be looking for a psychiatrist – but then they see your service. I don't know what you'd call it, but maybe a "soul-saving service"? And they might just think, yes, yes, that is exactly what I need. Do you see what I mean, Father?'

Father Brian had been nodding and raising his eyebrows throughout Hank's pitch. He didn't speak straight away and Hank waited for his reaction.

'Hank, that is a really smart idea – just up my street really.' Brian smiled. 'But doesn't your site require that money changes hands? I mean, my service, it isn't a paid service,' he continued. 'And, as such, I couldn't pay the commission that you likely take.'

'Yeah, Father, of course,' he began. 'I'm just thinking outside the box here, stirring it up, and wondering whether you need the synergy that we can provide. Internet outreach. In any sort of way.'

Father Brian may have been preparing a reply. Hank flushed and sent his gaze through the window, then said: 'You know, Father – well, you probably don't know, but I read a book called *The Answer Is Now*. You heard of it?' The men were looking at each other again.

'Yes . . . well, no, but I'm familiar with the type of book you mean.'

'Well, you see, it says that if you can imagine yourself as rich, then you will probably become rich. It's about the universe and believing. The power of powerful thinking.'

Father Brian listened. Hank swiped at his short hair.

'And, well, I guess it's like prayer, Father, you know? The universe is like, God, right?' He looked at the priest, who was moving his head, almost nodding, a wide nod with minor reservations. Hank went on. 'And, well, I was doing this visualisation thing they recommend where you put yourself on a cloud and surround yourself with what you want. So I had all this gold around me, and I could really see it, I really could.' Another pause. 'It sounds stupid now I'm saying it.'

'Not at all,' the priest said softly.

Hank gathered himself again. He was sweating; the priest's house was strangely warm now.

'Well, I just wondered if that was a sin,' he said. 'You know, greed or something.'

Hank had fixed his gaze on a point on the floor. There was a squashed raisin or a piece of old gum stuck to the rug about two feet from his own feet, and Hank thought that it was probably stuck to the fibres of the carpet, that it resisted any vacuuming. You could scrape it with a knife, or use some harsh soap to dislodge it, but whoever cleaned the priest's house had not thought of that, apparently.

'Sometimes I just want to be free,' he said quietly.

The priest leaned in, and his face opened into curious concern. 'Free?'

'Do you ever think about how hard it is to be a man these days?' Hank asked Brian.

'A man?' he responded. 'Well, now, what do you mean?

'Well, like . . .' Hank was struggling. 'What was Jesus like?'

'Jesus? Well, he was a man of compassion. Forgiveness. Healing. Love. Nurturing.'

Hank shifted in his seat again. 'Exactly. And then you look at him, crucified, and you think, why did you let them do that to you?'

Father Brian didn't seem to understand and Hank realised that male priests had different rules to live by, and that maybe the guy just wouldn't get it.

CHAPTER 25

THE DISTURBING TEXT MESSAGES had been coming into the God-phone at a rate of one a day for two weeks now. At first, he thought they were a prank. But they were so vehement. Someone in his parish was not okay. But he would look out at the congregation during various prayers and scan their faces. They all looked so healthy. They looked so, well, professional. He knew it was a man writing to him, because the message-sender referred to his 'wife'. (There was one lesbian couple in his parish, but Brian was well-acquainted with them since they'd struggled when they first started attending the church. Brian was impressed on the whole with his hetero-congregation for making them feel welcome. But he somewhat suspected that his parishioners' readiness to talk to the lesbians was judgement-tinged curiosity – at coffee mornings, he heard questions like 'So, who is the real mom of your daughter?' and cringed. Still, he had welcomed them into his parish and that was a start.)

The message sender wrote with increasing vehemence, as if Brian should know what he meant. The first one came in on a Tuesday:

I confess to my sins. I confess to many bad choices.

This wasn't alarming, Brian received many vague texts on the God-phone during the confessional. I have sinned, people would write. I have broken two commandments, wrote others. He suspected certain adolescents of sending texts like I have a sinfully big penis and I fantasise about you, Father Brian, you are so hot.

But when this same phone number sent text after text, Brian realised there was someone in particular, slotted in among his chaste and goodish parishioners, someone who was fallen, someone who was imploring for his help.

Is this really God?

GET ME OUT OF THIS PLACE.

I CAN'T HEAR YOU.

I don't eat meat. No more lives.

My wife should take none of this karma.

AM I NOT GOOD ENOUGH FOR YOU TO ANSWER?

WHERE ARE YOU GOD?

Protect Jenny's way, don't involve the donkey.

This punishment isn't really enough for me.

GET ME OUT OF THIS PLACE.

Don't get me wrong, it's good that I'm here.

How am I supposed to make up for the life I disappeared?

I DIDN'T DO IT ON PURPOSE. It was his flipped up world that I walked into.

AM I NOT GOOD ENOUGH FOR YOU?

Lord, I am trying but maybe you aren't. Why aren't you helping me?

Can you hear me? Can you hear me?

What did I do?

BRIAN HAD BEEN HOPING all along that this member of his flock would come to him in person. But when this last message arrived, he realised he would have to write back. This person needed help coming forward. The message landed as he was having his dinner. He usually ate at about six o'clock, and he cooked for himself. That night, he was having a pork chop with onions, some reconstituted mashed potato and a big sour pickle. He would also make himself eat a carrot that he had peeled and cut into sticks. He didn't watch TV while he ate – he found it gave him indigestion – but he did listen to a podcast of other people's sermons and gathered ideas for the forthcoming week. The sermon he was listening to when the text message came through was about 'actor–observer bias'.

'We see someone else do something bad and we say that's who they are. They are what they do. But when we do bad things, we blame the situation, or say it was because we'd just spilled coffee on our new jeans,' said the sermon-giver. 'We're biased. We give ourselves every excuse, and yet condemn other people as bad people when they make a bad choice.'

Ping. The text message lit up the screen of the God-phone, which was charging on the kitchen counter. **Lord, I am trying but maybe you aren't. Why aren't you helping me?** And then another: **Can you hear me?**

Brian placed his knife and fork facing downwards on the lip of his plate. He wiped his mouth with his brown cloth napkin as he rose to get the phone. The sermon was still rising and falling in the background when he read the message. He put the God-phone by his plate and sat down to eat again. He chewed and he thought. He chewed with his mouth closed, eyes directed at the seam where the wall met the ceiling, knife and fork aloft in his hands. *My God, my God, why hast thou forsaken me? Why art thou so far from helping me, and from the words of my roaring?* That was what the message was saying – just with different words. A cry of dereliction. And what was God's answer in scripture? He chewed the unrelenting pork and tried to remember. Psalm 22, yes, but did God ever reply in words to Jesus on the cross?

Brian never normally did this. He never answered the messages on the God-phone. It was supposed to be a direct line to God. But he took up the phone and typed. This was getting to be too much. Maybe something from Corinthians would help bring the man forward: **If I could speak all the languages of earth and of angels, but didn't love others, I would only be a noisy gong or a clanging cymbal.**

The phone made the whooshing sound of flight as the message sent, and Brian felt that at least he had sent the true words of God, instead of improvising. It seemed fitting that the scriptural words he had typed flew so vigorously, away into the ether.

He wasn't expecting it so soon, but within seconds a message came back: Are you God?

Oh dear. This was not what he meant to do. He set the phone down and went back to his meal. He thought the person would know from his urgings at church that he read these messages and that he wanted them to come and see him. Maybe the guy was hallucinating.

He texted something he remembered from the seminary: My son, peace be unto thy soul; thine adversity and thine afflictions shall be but a small moment; And then, if thou endure it well, God shall exalt thee on high; thou shalt triumph over all thy foes ... Know thou, my son, that all these things shall give thee experience, and shall be for thy good.

Wait, is this an app or something?

Again, Father Brian was stumped. He wanted the guy to come and see him; that way, he could help him. But the guy was clearly tripping, so Brian tried to figure out what was the best way to make this happen.

He wrote: Go to your priest and let him help you.

Which one? The baptist or the methodist?

Okay, this guy is hallucinating, thought Brian. He better be clear. Maybe the guy would read the messages when he came off whatever he was on, and then he'd know what to do.

Father Brian.

Who is that? I'm sorry God, you should know I can't do that. Why don't you know that?

And that was it. No more messages came from the phone that day.

Brian didn't know what to reply. He didn't want to masquerade as God anymore before this suffering man. In fact, when he was allocated the episcopal parish of Saint Peter's in Bentonville, he expected he would mostly be dealing with marital problems. He knew there would be plenty of that, and he felt competent in that area. He would tell whichever partner was the dominant to respect the other. He would tell them to follow each other, in parallel. He would tell them that marriage is not easy.

But mental illness was always challenging. He never knew how things would go. And he never knew if they were being themselves or whether it was the illness or the drugs talking. This was the problem. Whose voice was it?

Like this guy who couldn't, for some reason, visit him. Like it was an impossibility. But hadn't the guy been to church? Or maybe he was a lapsed churchgoer. Brian's brain was hurting from trying to figure out what was going on. He would have to bring it up with his superior, Father Adam. Someone in his parish was in crisis, had a wife, had a donkey called Jenny and was possibly hallucinating. He just couldn't, for the life of him, think who it could be. But he had to solve it, because the man was a real danger to the community. And yet he wasn't allowed to tell anyone – that was the oath he had taken.

First he googled the phone number that was sending the messages. It was a pre-paid number. No dice. Then he wrote a list of all the men in his parish. He crossed out those he knew it couldn't be.

*

FATHER ADAM HADN'T BEEN convinced by Father Brian's digital ministry. 'Sometimes,' he said, 'simplicity is best.' But Father Brian had argued that he saw his parishioners looking at their phones such a lot during his services, it seemed like a case of 'If you can't beat 'em, join 'em'. Plus he needed to get the youth engaged, and he knew their lives were semi-digital. He didn't understand it, but he knew they were a generation who had a second consciousness, one that was outside of their physical and mental selves. Phones and computers are human addenda, he told Father Adam. They are an extension to our very selves now, he said.

So when Brian turned up for his monthly meeting with Father Adam – the meeting in which the more experienced priest guided the less experienced priest in matters of pastoral care – Brian knew that he would have to explain the God-phone incident. Worst of all, he would have to explain how he had masqueraded as God, sort of accidentally.

But Father Adam was not disapproving; he was fascinated.

'You answered with scripture?'

'Yes. Well, I didn't want to intrude on his confession. I wanted to prompt him to come and see me, without asking directly in a text message . . .' Brian was faltering. 'I didn't know what to say, so I drew on God's words.' He was in confession himself now.

'This God-phone is interesting.' Adam was starting a soliloquy now. 'It reminds me of a medieval fellow called John Dee.' He paused. And then: '*Sigillum Dei*!' he exclaimed, in the jubilant way people who know Latin tend to deposit wisdom. He lowered his tone again: 'He used a sort of medieval computer to align with God's vision.

It was a kind of disc with symbols inscribed onto it.' He looked up and made a circle with his fingers. 'And upon it –' he removed his glasses at this point – 'was a crystal ball.'

'A crystal ball?' repeated Father Brian.

'A crystal ball,' the elder said, with perhaps excess gravity.

But Brian could explain. 'The drugs, the man – I wasn't sure who I was talking to.'

And then: 'I did invite him to come and see me. But, you see, he replied that he couldn't. He just couldn't come.'

After a moment: 'I'm not sure how to reach him.'

Father Adam had been listening, hands loosely clasped in a semi-praying position. He inhaled with emphasis. 'You don't know who this fellow is.'

'Right.'

'On Sunday, look each of them in the eye at Communion. Make them face you and acknowledge you when administering the body of Christ.'

'I've done that. I have. I can't find him,' Brian said.

'Perhaps he is not attending? You might think about who hasn't been to church recently.'

Father Brian was embarrassed because fundamentally he really didn't know half of his parishioners. He just knew that many were familiar-looking, and he knew those that came to the coffee hour. He also knew those that had had marriage problems. But a drug addict or disturbed psyche? Surely he would know a disturbed psyche when he saw one?

'Perhaps this person has already been to confession,' Father Adam started up again. 'That is to say, it has sometimes happened to me that someone comes in with a test-confession. They use it to lead up to a bigger one. It's a testing of the waters. They're looking to see what kind of reaction you give them.'

Brian hadn't considered that. As he drove home, he shuffled through several recent in-person confessions in his mind. It wasn't all that common to have in-person confessions in the Episcopalian Church – this was the function of prayer and Brian's God-phone innovation. But sometimes people did come, and most often those that came were fantasists confessing to disturbing thoughts, or sometimes confessing to acts that they didn't actually do. He had become good at teasing out the truth of these bogus sins, often encouraging the confessee to draw a line between what happened and what was imagined: crimes, burglaries, betrayals. It was as though, by confessing to them, a person could experience a frisson of guilt, a little thrill – but these were exercises of the imagination, not sins. Brian often dealt with confessions that weren't actual, real sins.

There was the married guy who had fallen in love with his next-door neighbour. He watched her make toast in the mornings. He watched her wash her windows. His own wife was a 'career woman', he said. Instead of confessing, the man was cataloguing the ways in which he loved the neighbour. (Brian had to stop him after a time.)

And there was the woman who had a secret penchant for eating food from trash cans. She said eating was the most intimate act there is. The consumption of a living or post-living thing. She said it made her feel connected to other people. (He suggested she limit herself to the body and blood of the transubstantiated Christ. Communion; it was Communion. He'd never heard it so weirdly explained before though.)

There was the pizza delivery guy who arrived at one doorstep and was greeted by a lady customer who was naked. He bolted and, in his embarrassment, he dropped the pizza onto the front step. Later, the lady complained to the pizza place about the deranged pizza she found in the box. (Father Brian told him next time to ring the bell and leave the pizza on the doorstep.)

Brian's mind returned to Hank. The man had been sweating profusely during his visit. He was nervous and a little jumpy. The joke about being 'your big sinner' was simply odd. The weird sales pitch about soul-saving services? And then the anguish of wanting to be free? How hard it is to be a man? He'd lost his kids while camping – but the boys had been found eventually. Hank spilled the story, said he was in a rush, checked the time, said he had to go, said he was thinking of becoming vegetarian. The man practically ran out. Hank. Maybe it was Hank. The name Jenny was mentioned, and so was the word 'wife'. But How am I supposed to make up for the life I disappeared? – what on earth was that about? Oh Lord, maybe it was Hank, and Brian had completely fluffed it as the poor man came to give his test-confession. Darn it. He bounced the heel of his hand against the steering wheel.

He arrived home and told himself he'd have to leave the matter aside for the rest of the day. He had to mull it over, and he had a sermon to write. He hadn't the time or peace of mind to think up his own topic so he borrowed from the podcast sermon about actor–observer bias. And he thought of Hank's questions about what qualified as a sin. The first lines he wrote for his sermon were:

'My fellow children in Christ, today I want to remind you that we are not what we do. A person who steals is not a thief. A person who lies is not a liar. When we transgress, it is a mistake, and we do transgress. We are all sinners here. But we are not defined by our sins. We are not defined by our desires. We are defined by our will to supersede them. The Lord asks us: "Are you willing?"'

Brian had to resist the urge to lapse into Gospel lyrics – this was always his problem when writing sermons. Maybe he should have been a Baptist. And it was true, he did like musicals.

CHAPTER 26

'Is THAT JENNY?'

Jenny hadn't recognised the number but she knew the voice.

'Shona, yes, it is, it's me,' she said. 'Hi.'

'Listen, have you sent me any more letters?' She wanted information.

'Well, I sent cookies, did you get them?'

'I did get the cookies,' Shona said. 'I did get the cookies, yes. That's why I'm calling.'

'Good. Good, I'm glad. Uh, how are you?' Jenny was waiting in the school parking lot for Luke and Jesse to come out. She was sitting in her car, door ajar, one foot on the paved ground and one still in the car. She was slowly dragging the keys out of the ignition as they spoke. The car radio beeped at her.

'I am fine,' Shona said. 'I am fine for now.'

Fine? Jenny thought. Didn't sound it.

'Is there anything I can do?' Jenny stuffed moral ballast into her voice.

'Oh, Jenny. Do you know what you're doing? This isn't kindness. This is troublemaking. Please do not send any more of your packages here.'

Jenny pushed the cigarette lighter down and it popped up immediately. She looked at the red-hot coils and blew on them, igniting a little flare of dust.

'Do you hate him?' she asked. She felt heat in her cheeks.

Shona laughed. 'Hate? No. No, I don't.'

'Yeah,' Jenny exhaled with a slight laugh.

'I've known him since I was sixteen.'

Jenny felt relieved at the small warmth erupting between them.

Shona continued: 'I need to get out of here. I have two weeks left. I don't want any trouble that might keep me in here. Do you understand what I'm saying?' Shona's voice was soft. 'You have to stop writing to me, Jenny – do you hear me? All this has to wait.'

'Right, yes. I hear you. I don't want to make things hard for you,' Jenny said.

Shona pushed an exhalation through her teeth. 'I get out in June.'

'What's it like?' Jenny whispered. She pressed her ear to the phone, wanting to close the distance between them.

'This . . . here?' Shona said. There was a pause and Jenny looked at her phone to see if the call was still live. She put it back up to her ear and heard Shona's words: 'This place is like an open wound. With desperate friendships – like . . . like sutures.'

'Desperate friendships,' Jenny repeated. 'Where will you go when you get out?'

'I have a sister in Shaflette.'

'Oh good.'

'But, Jenny, I have to go. Just please. No more messages, okay? No more special messages from anyone.'

'Right,' Jenny said.

'Right. You know that the messages you were supposed to send were special, right?'

'Yes.'

And they hung up. Jenny's ears were hot now too, and her head ached. It was probably the Botox. The muscles were trying so hard to work, to frown, to jump with surprise, but they were paralysed – that's why they ached, Jenny knew, because they were restrained. She wondered if the Botox had affected her mental faculties. Jenny felt horribly claustrophobic; it came as a surge, as though she were trapped inside her face, unable to move it, unable to push emotion through her expressions to the world outside. Her throat tightened. She had a mask now, not a face, and she was locked inside her own surfaces.

Jenny pushed this feeling away when the kids slung their book bags into the car and slid onto their seats. She had to do that – no cross-contamination, she told herself. They expected a snack. They didn't want to answer any questions about their day. She handed a pair of granola bars back to them, and they groaned. They wanted those mini packets of Fruit Loops that Jenny bought at the supermarket.

Jenny said she'd get some for tomorrow. She had given up long ago hoping to find out what had happened at school. In her experience, events would trickle to her many weeks after the fact.

There was something nice about picking the kids up from school. Jenny liked getting a good look at the neighbourhood as she drove along, a sort of maintenance check. The wide streets, the trees in various states of undress, the various emblems that people draped over their properties. There was a smattering of American flags, there was even a Confederate flag over one front door. Some people liked to put their names right on the front of their houses, on neat little plaques: *The Home of the Warners*. Or little axioms like *Home Is Where the Heart Is* – Jenny had seen a few of those; they sold them at Walmart. One house had a wheelbarrow placed slantwise on their lawn, filled with pretty flowers and fake butterflies on sticks. Another house had the fluttering vestiges of a toilet-papering on their tree. There were kids coming home from school, pouncing and ricocheting against one another. They looked into the screens of each other's smartphones, yelping in outrage at whatever image they had seen. Jenny imagined pictures of a teacher's butt (clothed), or some wry-captioned photo of a puppy in a costume. She hoped it was that, but she had heard that some kids at school were caught with pictures on their phones of a person having sex with a horse. Apparently shock-value had some currency.

But ordinary is not a bad thing. Jenny was starting to appreciate the ordinary. The way she saw it, ordinary was becoming a privilege these days, even though everyone, just everyone, seemed to want to be extraordinary. The kids wanted to be rock stars, while adults lurched along a series of nasty milestones – from turning thirty, to turning forty, having kids, to empty nests, peppered with forays into infidelity. And how often did people suspect they or their spouses were going through midlife crises? Was this it? Am I finally having a midlife crisis? These were all bids to escape the ordinary. We want to make a grand gesture that will distinguish us. Buy a sports car, dye your hair. But Jenny now suspected that ordinary was where the magic lay. John had said it; he had once complimented her on being normal. She hadn't liked it, but yes, it was true: being normal was totally unlikely in this day and age. He was right, it was a compliment. When you stray away from ordinary, you are asking for two things: fame or trauma. And everyone knows that fame isn't all it's cracked up to be. Celebrities go off the rails all the time, shaving their heads and overdosing on drugs. Who needs it?

She looked back at the boys, and all she could think was that she was doing them such a disservice. She had managed to get them to the very brink of this moment, but no future second was secure. There would be untold consequences and she wouldn't know about them until it was too late. No one had told her about this either, no one warned her about what it was to be a mother. She had spent years hoping to drum up some sort of career, only to be entirely derailed by the birthing of children. She remembered being pregnant and trying to ignore cravings for bricks and chalk – she wanted to gnaw on the corners of buildings, she dreamed of classroom chalk-sticks. Her Ob-Gyn laughed and said it wasn't uncommon – something to do with the compounds they contain – and he prescribed iron pills, told her to eat more cruciferous vegetables. But now she wondered: was I trying to build a foundation for what was to come? Did I need bricks and mortar just to stay upright and contain my family? It was true, she felt she had to contain her children, to hold them somehow, to let them wash their struggles through her offal and howl into her being, then listen for the soft echo only she could return.

'Boys?' she said.

She felt they were listening.

'Do you think that being normal is a good thing?'

'Yes, it is,' Jesse said.

'Well, you don't want to be abnormal,' said Luke.

Abnormal. There it was, her answer. Normal that strays to mutation was a bad thing.

'You can be normal and special – you don't have to give that up,' said Jesse.

Such clarity, Jenny thought. Extra-ordinary, ordinary with something extra – this was a good thing. Don't be a mutant, but you can be special.

There was a new letter from John in her bag, and she dreaded its contents. She wasn't naive; she was tempted to throw the letter into a public trash can. But she remembered it had her name written on it, so that would be stupid. You have to burn such things, really, she thought. They didn't have a fireplace at home but maybe she would douse it with olive oil and fry it in the microwave. Or bury it in the wood-chips that surrounded the shrubs outside, let the beetles eat it.

WHEN THEY GOT HOME, Luke went straight downstairs, and Jesse flopped into a chair at the dining table to eat a pesto sandwich. Jenny withdrew to the kitchen and slit the letter open with a paring knife. She sniffed it. Fruit Loops again. She could hear banging noises from the basement.

'Jesse, tell your brother to come up from down there,' she yelled.

She opened the envelope: there was a prayer card enclosed – this time a prayer for the meek. *For they shall inherit the earth*, it said. There was no inner envelope; the card itself was orange and fragrant. *For S.* was written at the top, and scrawled at the bottom, in light pencil scratchings, were the words: *Chew me*.

The letter, this time, was short:

Dear Jenny,
Did you see the face in the spoon I sent you? I thought you might like that. It just came out of the wood like that when I was carving it.

Peace out,
John

Jenny went to her jug of kitchen spoons by the cooker and found the spoon. She pushed her thumb along the length of the bowl of the spoon and looked into it. A face. There it was, with a fine mouth line and the cheekbones that John had sanded there. Was that what he looked like? It didn't look like an African American face. The face was a white man's face, and its expression was oblique, mocking her. She sniffed the spoon like she had the first time she held it, and the dark, low smell was still there.

'Are we making cake?'

Jenny looked over at Luke, who was at the sink washing his hands, and she nodded back at him, moving to the trash can and slipping the spoon and the prayer card into it.

'That a broken spoon?' Luke asked. He was suddenly standing by her, the last mouthfuls of his sandwich stuffed into one cheek.

'No, no, it's not broken, it's just contaminated.' She hadn't chosen her words carefully enough.

'Contaminated with what? Smallpox?' Luke asked.

'Smallpox?' She put her hand on his cheek and laughed. 'There's no smallpox anymore, you know that.'

Jenny pulled Luke onto the countertop and started to lay out the ingredients. She gave him a different wooden spoon, one that she had bought in a set at Walmart.

'Did you know these are carved?'

'Nah, Mom, these are made with a machine. Look at it.' He showed her, pointing with the spoon at all the other spoons in the jug too. The uniform shape, the grainless wood. They were cheap spoons. He was probably right.

'But still, it's real wood,' he offered, and looked through the kitchen window at the cedars outside, as if searching for something.

'You could think about a tree as a whole bunch of spoons, just lined up and waiting inside the bark,' he said, pointing the spoon at the trees. And then he turned to her. 'So what was wrong with that spoon again?'

'It was a bad spoon, that's all,' she explained, setting a bag of flour on the surface beside him while reaching behind her into the trash to pull out the sweet, orange prayer card and slip it into her back pocket.

CHAPTER 27

WHEN YOU WALK INTO your own house and your wife is eating soup with your priest, you are going to worry. This is what Hank told himself as he wiped his face with a tissue in the downstairs bathroom. He had just come back from work and there they were, Jenny and Father Brian, sitting in his dining room. Just two days after Hank had been to see the priest himself.

Hank only heard a snippet of their conversation as he entered the house, and it didn't bode well. Jenny was saying something about a pot of gold and Father Brian was laughing. Hank had only told her about that stuff a week ago.

When Hank entered the room, the two reacted with a slight exaggeration, it seemed to Hank. They had stopped laughing, for one thing.

'You're having soup?'

'I made soup.' Jenny said, rising. 'Do you want some? It's the rice soup.'

It was the only soup that Jenny really knew how to make. Even Hank knew how to make it. Chicken stock, rice and whatever vegetables seemed to be approaching their sell-by date in the fridge.

'Chicken soup for the soul – right, Father?' Hank said, sitting down opposite the priest. He turned up his lips into a smile. There was nothing else for it.

Father Brian wiped his lips and adjusted himself: 'How are you, Hank?'

Hank might have been mistaken, but there seemed to be a touch of concern in Father Brian's voice. Was this Jenny's doing? Did she invite the priest here? Hank had just wanted to come home, have a shower and watch some TV. He didn't need to be on his best behaviour right now. He didn't need divine judgement in his dining room.

'Got a lot of work,' he said, and straightened the table mat. The priest had stopped eating and Hank gestured at him to continue. 'Eat your soup now, don't wait . . . Hey, Jen, you getting me some soup?' Hank winked at Father Brian, and instantly realised the priest probably had never winked at a person in his life and might not even know what to do with a wink. You were supposed, at least, to crack a smile in return, but the priest looked a little dumb and abstracted, straightening his own table mat and cutlery.

'I was just in the neighbourhood, and, well, you know, I like to drop in on the flock when the opportunity presents.' Father Brian finally grinned. 'It's a particularly nice home you have here, Hank, really nice.'

'I'll tell you, it's called Arts and Crafts – the style. And that, I am told, means that it's custom. "Bespoke" is the word. Anyway, we like it.'

Jenny was walking in slowly, balancing a bowl of soup towards Hank.

'I only really know how to make one kind of soup,' she said, quickly glancing up at Father Brian. 'And this is it.' She set it down in front of Hank.

Surely she had told him that already, thought Hank. The thing was, Hank wasn't supposed to be home for lunch; he just happened to have some extra time between meetings and figured he'd stop in and take a rest. So they weren't expecting him.

'So, you just dropped by, just like that?' Hank asked.

'Yes, yes, I just knocked on the door in case anyone was home, wanted to see how things were going,' the priest said, his chair squeaking underneath him. 'Jenny's been telling me about your camping trip, and that you went gold-panning?'

Hank felt a confession coming on.

'Yeah.' Hank wiped his lips with a napkin. 'Was funny actually. I got this piece of pyrite and pretended to the boys that it was gold. Popped it in my pan and made like I'd found it. So now they think I'm a real hero . . .'

Father Brian chuckled and the floorboards creaked. Father Brian was heavy, that was true, but Hank hadn't heard the floorboards creak in the house since they moved in a year ago.

'But seriously, there is gold there. Glacial gold.'

Jenny had been quiet, eating soup. Hank turned to her. 'You knew it was a prank, right? I guess I might have forgotten to tell you that.'

Jenny gave a short nod. Now she knew, at least. And better it came out in front of a priest.

'Show me a hero,' Father Brian said, 'and I'll write you a tragedy. That was F. Scott Fitzgerald.'

Hank took it on the chin. It was true, you couldn't really call yourself a hero; someone else had to do that.

'Did my son Luke, by any chance, send you a confession about the gold? I guess he has it in his head that we have to return the gold to the government and that we are breaking the law by keeping it. But, uh, I can't tell him it's fake. Well, because . . . well, it was quite a performance, put it that way.'

The priest looked baffled.

'I mean on your phone, that God-phone,' Hank said, pointing upwards.

'Oh yes, the phone,' said Father Brian. 'The phone gets a lot of messages.' Father Brian was looking down at the skirting boards, then looked up at Hank. Was there a sadness in his eyes?

'You sure everything is okay, Hank?' the priest said in a low voice.

Hank pointed to himself, raised his eyebrows.

'Aw, I'm okay, thanks for asking,' he said. The light overhead was buzzing because the LED lightbulb didn't suit the dimmer mechanism, and Hank got up to adjust it. He had turned off the clapping prompt for the lighting in that room. Jenny was still eating soup, but very slowly.

'You okay, Jenny?' said Hank.

'How's the soup? I'm liking this one,' she said, slightly slurping. It was unusually sloppy eating for her.

'Fine soup,' said the priest, the floorboards under his chair complaining again.

'Comes out different every time,' she said. 'Do you cook, Father?'

Father Brian squared up to the question: 'I do. I do cook. I like to cook coq au vin when I'm particularly inspired. Generally, I'm eating pork chops most days though.' He wasn't slim, Father Brian. Hank could pretty much guess that the priest was not very mindful about what he ate.

Hank got started on his soup. It wasn't very good soup; it was bland and tasted vaguely like damp laundry that had been forgotten in the washing machine. He put down his spoon and took a slug of water. He had the feeling that Jenny and Father Brian were on one side of something, and he was on the other.

'Get many people for marriage counselling, Father?' Hank busied himself with the terrible soup. He wasn't really interested in the answer, but asked something that he felt might show them that he knew what they were up to. But the soup was so bad that Hank couldn't eat it. So, before Father Brian could get started answering his question, Hank butted in:

'We went to see a priest once, just before we got married. I think they made us do it – right, Jen? Anyway, we sat there, and he asked us lots of questions. And when he asked us what was the point of getting married, I had to pass the mic to Jenny because I just couldn't drum up an answer. What is the point of marriage?

Kids? I mean, I'd say monogamy, but let's face it, that isn't usually the case. Am I right? Well, I can't remember what Jenny said, but the priest seemed to think it was good enough. But, all these years, I've been wondering . . . Getting married – it's what we do, right? So we don't have to keep on looking for romantic interaction. Or so we can just get ourselves squared away, placed in a house, with a yard. It's setting up the family structure, right? I just wonder sometimes. You never got married, Father – and that was okay, right?'

He could see Father Brian was almost finished with his soup. The man clearly had blunt taste buds.

'I didn't get married. It did occur to me, and in theory, I still don't rule it out, but priesthood is a pretty extraordinary life choice. You enter a different kind of a structure, and I have a lot of people that I try to take care of. I mean, when you think about it, I get called "Father". It's a family of another kind.'

The priest seemed to be having these thoughts for the first time, as though Hank had given him food for thought. Jenny was staying quiet, letting them talk. She had also eaten most of her soup.

'Yes, some people get called Father, and some people get called Bro.' Hank huffed a laugh.

'I had no idea what I was getting myself into, if I'm frank,' said Jenny, looking into her soup.

She seemed surprised, when she looked up, to see that Father Brian and Hank were listening to her.

'Yeah, that's the truth. When I was young, I thought the whole man–woman problem, I thought it was done. We were equal. I had work, nobody was telling me that I couldn't do stuff. I really had no fucking idea that getting married was, for women, not a good thing.'

She looked back down at her soup and stirred her spoon through it as though looking for something.

CHAPTER 28

JENNY WASN'T SURE IF she was the only one who hated the soup. Hank was talking so much that he wasn't eating, and Father Brian seemed to have eaten the whole serving. The soup was disgusting. A home-cooked crock of crap. She should have loaded it with salt or something, anything to subdue its claggy undertones.

'Some people get called Father, and some people get called Bro,' Hank had said. And some people get called mothers, she thought, and others, motherfuckers.

Jenny didn't listen to Hank trying to smooth things over with Father Brian after she had said the thing about marriage being 'not a good thing'; it was something about how good the soup was. But Jenny was trying to remember what she had said to the priest that interviewed them before they got married. How on earth had she phrased her response? She couldn't remember what she thought marriage was, back then. Hank was right. It was just a placement. Maybe in those days a placement was comforting, the end of looking for one's place. A saddling.

The soup kept rising up her throat, repeating its swampy seeth-ings. Father Brian had just turned up on her doorstep, and it was lunchtime, and all she had was the beginnings of a soup, so that's what she gave him. She didn't really have anything else in the house, apart from cheese strings and pizza pockets for the kids. She should have microwaved a Lean Cuisine from the freezer. But soup. Marriage soup. A soup of stones.

Father Brian was going to talk now. He seemed to have been preparing something to say ever since he stepped in the door. He took in a large breath, let some out and began.

'You know – and I can tell you two this without breaching any-one's privacy – there have been some disturbing messages come into the God-phone.' The floor beneath the priest let out a short whine, and Jenny felt the nerves prickle at her forearms.

'Someone in our community is in some distress, and I would like to help them,' he continued, folding his napkin, tucking it under the edge of his bowl. He was stifling a hiccup of some kind. 'I'm not even entirely sure what the person is struggling with exactly. But I really do know how to help people. We have lots of outreach programmes and access to care – it's kind of like my professional skill, you know, to find people the help they need.'

Hank and Jenny were silent. For a moment, Jenny was swept up in Father Brian's plight. Who in the community could it be? What was the nature of their crisis? But a moment later she returned to her secret knowledge. She knew it was John.

'The thing is, and I wouldn't ordinarily say something like this, but

the person mentioned a wife and a donkey – and I just wondered . . .'
He looked back down at the skirting boards. He seemed interested
in the skirting boards, and Jenny wondered if he had noticed they
weren't flush against the wall. 'I just wondered if you knew anyone,
with a wife or a donkey, that might be in trouble?' He looked at
Hank, then at Jenny. Hank looked at Jenny.

'Jenny?' Hank asked.

A drop of the soup slipped up her throat once again and she
swallowed, cleared her throat and tried to smile.

'Gosh, I wish I did . . .'

She looked guilty, she knew she did. But she didn't know what
messages the priest was receiving – how bad they were. She pushed
it back at him; the priest had to tell them more.

She busied herself with the foul soup and asked, 'What did they
say about the donkey? Are you allowed at least to tell us that?'

'Well, it's hard to say. I really can't say any more. I shouldn't
have even said what I've said.'

'A donkey? Huh. I'm trying to think if there are any farmers in
the parish,' she said.

'Or donkeys,' said Hank.

Father Brian brushed his lap and reseated himself. 'Uh, you see,
I'm not entirely sure. Not everyone comes and introduces themselves
to me, so I don't know everyone's profession.'

Hank was still frowning slightly, and seemed to have paused all his
movements. Jenny took her seat and was struggling with her recently
frozen Botox face but quickly left it to its naive, blank arrangement.

The whole John story would be a pain to explain. And, frankly, she didn't want to – it was none of their business that she had such a long correspondence with an inmate, and she didn't want to relate what kind of exchange had led to her giving him the confession number. It wasn't just that. Jenny wanted to put the whole John thing behind her. She excused herself and went to the kitchen. Her bag was open on the kitchen counter – and John's letter was sitting among a sheaf of bills and receipts. She tore a big piece from the prayer card, and stuffed the letter deep inside her bag.

'I'll think about it and let you know if anything comes up,' she said loudly, popping the bit of orange paper in her mouth before she re-entered the dining room. As she sat down, that orange feeling, the liquid, sweet warmth, surged in her, and her jaw relaxed.

But Father Brian didn't seem to be interested in Jenny. He couldn't take his eyes off Hank. Or at least it seemed to Jenny that the priest was leaning towards her husband, that he was breathing in Hank's direction.

'I wish you could say what the problem was – maybe we could help you.' Jenny was curious now. But Father Brian wasn't even listening to her. He and Hank were exchanging something.

'I'm not sure, Father, that I know what you are referring to,' Hank said in a slow rhythm, straight to Father Brian. Then he severed the trance and stood up. 'Excuse me for a moment, I have to do something.'

Father Brian seemed to shake his head slightly and set his jaw, as Hank left the room. The priest shifted backwards in his chair, and the floor emitted the small sound of straining wood fibres. They heard Hank belch loudly in the next room.

Jenny took in the room: the strange LED lighting that gave the room the appearance of an operating theatre. She had argued with Hank about it, told him that it looked so damn clinical. The light was too blue, she tried to tell him. He told her it was energy saving; the light was not soft, that was true, but you could clearly see the food you were eating, and that was a priority. In that brief and still moment, along with Father Brian, among the vicious photons of that room, Jenny was reminded of a funeral parlour. The photographs on the credenza: Jenny and Hank as bride and groom, all made-up and hairsprayed. White teeth bared. And studio photographs of the children, with their combed heads, trussed up in old-fashioned clothes. The photographs were framed in swirling frosted glass, like ice sculptures. Why had they chosen Whirling White for the wall-paper again? It wasn't stunning, as the roll advertised; it was just weird. A swirling pattern of whites that were possibly supposed to mimic marble, but instead they made the room look like it had been subjected to a series of floods and the marks were the high-tide lines. The wooden floor beneath Father Brian groaned again.

'That floor sounds like it's going to collapse.' Jenny shook her head slightly. 'You're not epileptic, are you?' she asked Father Brian, noticing his plump and loose lower lip for the first time, and the way the top rim of his glasses occluded his meagre eyebrows.

'No, I'm not,' he said.

'It's just that this room . . . It could make you a little dizzy.'

CHAPTER 29

FATHER BRIAN FELT THAT he had been as bold as he dared. He wasn't dizzy from the wallpaper, as Jenny had suggested, but he couldn't keep track of the eye movements around the room. The couple seemed to be accusing each other. And now he was even more confused than before. How he wished that he could just show them the text messages.

Jenny's soup was not the most comforting of soups. He had finished it partly because the snack he had eaten in the car hadn't been enough, and partly because he had needed time to think while Hank was talking about panning for gold. He remembered Hank's confession about visualising pots of gold – none of it was surprising, most people these days were obsessed with getting rich.

The dining room looked like a laboratory. The utensils and bowls were white and clinical. The table was metal. The skirting boards were loose. The floorboards kept groaning underneath him. Brian felt compelled to rock a little in his chair, to repeat the movements, to make a point of the creaking so that they wouldn't think that he was farting. The soup was disgusting. There were angry little cacti on the windowsills. *What sort of family is this?* he asked himself. He realised he didn't really know them beyond some chat at coffee hour.

'Excuse me.' He stood up. 'Can I visit your facilities?'

Jenny pointed towards the bathroom by the back door.

Once inside, Father Brian wondered when it was that he had ceased to be able to see his own penis while urinating. He could just about lean in and see over his round belly, but that screwed up his aim so he never did it. He needed to lose weight. He exhaled as he finished peeing and gave his penis a little shake.

In his trouser pocket, a cellphone buzzed. He pulled up his trousers, buttoning them and reaching into his pocket for the phone. It nearly fell into the toilet but he grasped it and recovered it.

It was the God-phone: **GET ME OUT OF THIS PLACE.**

Father Brian's heart sank and, without giving it much thought, he called the sender's number.

'Hello?' a voice whispered.

'Hank, it's me. It's okay,' said Father Brian.

'Excuse me?'

The voice was very deep and quiet.

'It's me – Father Brian.'

'Father who?'

'Brian,' he said. 'I'm sorry, I thought you were someone else.' Father Brian was whispering now too.

'Why are you calling me?' the deep voice whispered back.

'I'm calling you because . . . because God is here. He is everywhere and He is with you.'

'Oh,' said the voice. 'Thanks.'

Silence.

'I guess you aren't God then.'

'No, I'm sorry about that.'

'Yeah, well, I'm a Buddhist now. It's less judgemental.'

'Oh, I see. Well, I just wanted you to know that God loves you,' said Father Brian, still whispering, but his voice now faltering a little. He was nervous.

'Can I come and see you?' said the priest.

'I guess so. You need to call up Flainton and find out the procedure. I think it's easier for priests.'

The procedure, *the procedure*, thought Father Brian. Maybe the guy is in a hospital. Or a hospice.

'Are you in a care facility?'

'Huh.' The voice laughed. It was a hard voice, a stone-grinding voice. 'You have no idea, do you?' it growled.

'I'm sorry, I don't.'

'John Jones, Flainton Prison. I have to go. Don't call me on this phone.'

The line went dead.

'I'M SORRY, I HAVE to go.' Father Brian emerged from the bathroom and went straight for his coat. 'I do appreciate the soup, but I have something I need to do.' He wrapped a scarf around his neck twice and wrenched it into a small knot.

Jenny walked him to the door. 'Well, then. It was nice to see you.'

Her pupils were tiny, her voice was sing-song, she had flushed and was scratching her arms.

'Are you having an allergic reaction?' he asked.

'Oh, this?' she said, pointing to the arm she was scratching. 'No, no,' she said. 'No . . . no, it's just an itch.' And she gave him a toothy, beatific smile as she opened the front door for him.

'God bless you, Father,' she said, with the rushing voice of an evangelist. And he was a little confused because that was supposed to be his line.

CHAPTER 30

THE PLASTIC-SURGERY CLINIC WAS extending its opening hours. There were a lot of people who needed to come before and after work, and Dr Simmons wanted to cater to that. So, that Monday, Jenny needed to come in early too. The boys would get themselves to the school bus.

But she felt rotten. She'd felt rotten all weekend. She ached, her joints hurt. She felt a crushing sadness and her heart hurt, but instead of crying, she couldn't stop yawning. Plus she had diarrhoea. It must be the flu, she told Hank. But she didn't take a sick day because she remembered that John's prayer card was in her desk there, she'd left it there over the weekend, and she knew that a nibble of it would make her feel okay. After all, it was cold medicine of some kind.

At the clinic, she fumbled with her keys. She might be getting a little arthritis – the doctor said that it was something that could start once you hit your forties. A blast of hot air hit her as she opened the door, and it was so overwhelming that she wondered if she had a fever as well. Or was it a hot flush? Surely she wasn't yet menopausal? That was just too much to think about. The sweat down her back made her long for another shower. She left the door open, pulled her coat open and unbuttoned her cardigan.

The cleaning staff had been there during the night. Everything was pushed around a little. The leaves of the fake tropical plant were shining. The magazines were fanned out on the side table. Jenny huffed, and shook out her hair a little – her headache was tightening its grip. She went to her desk and opened the drawer – but there wasn't anything there. She opened the next one. Nothing there either. Had she left it on top of her desk?

It wasn't anywhere – she shifted papers, she looked under the mousepad.

The cleaners had cleaned it away. A ripped prayer card: it looked like trash and they threw it away. She sat down. The desk was beige and the computer was beige, even the complementary pens were beige. Jenny hated beige. She used to love beige. But now she wanted the world in blues. Greens maybe too. She closed her eyes. There was no one else at the office yet. This flu was really pulling at her core. She needed Tylenol at very least. Then she spotted it – crumpled and torn, and poking out from underneath her computer keyboard. She pulled it out and put it to her mouth – and there it was, the familiar feeling that rushed up in her as the sweet orange taste spread across her tongue. The invisible elastic bands of duty that squeezed her so tightly pinged apart and let her breathe.

That morning, she had asked Mr Salton, standing in the sunny centre of Maple Drive, about a medicine she needed to get for her Aunt Mary. She told him she couldn't remember what it was called but that it was orange and sweet. Did he know a medicine like that? He smoothed his hair from his parting over the side of his head and told her that flavours weren't what defined medicine – that there are a whole lot of orange-flavoured prescriptions. Was it maybe cough syrup? Or cough drops? But Jenny knew it wasn't either of those because the orange concoctions she had bought at his pharmacy had nothing like the same effect as John's prayer cards. They were alright, they could loosen your cough, maybe clear a headache, but they didn't really feel like the orange stuff. They didn't release you. And they didn't get at the flu that kept dogging her. 'Oh well,' she said to Salton, 'I'll have to just ask her what exactly the name of it is. You know, to be more precise.'

'Yes,' he said. 'That would be wise.'

DR SIMMONS'S ASSISTANT, AMY, came in a few minutes later, and Jenny was already feeling a little better. She had turned on the reception computer and was printing the day's appointments.

'No coffee?' Amy said.

'Nah,' said Jenny. She didn't take her eyes off the screen. She was looking at the cursor. Is that what it's called? she wondered. The mouse thing, the little arrow that you move around the screen – which sometimes turns into a vertical line. It was so fickle. It did what you said, but then, just sometimes, it didn't, and you knew you weren't in control of it. It was actually in control of itself, only allowing you to suggest things to it. There was no symbol more distressing than the whirling circle of colour it sometimes became. Jenny dreaded that circle of colour. She shoved the cursor into the lower left corner of the screen. The doghouse of the computer. Stay there, she whispered.

There was a pile of mail to open. She searched for the letter opener. She liked the letter opener. It meant she didn't have to risk a paper cut, and that she could present a clean pile of mail to Dr Simmons. Actually, it was he that insisted upon it, after the last receptionist brutalised his envelopes and delivered them to him in jags and rips.

She slipped the letter opener along the top rim of each envelope, without looking at their contents. She lined the envelopes up along the slitted edges, and slipped an elastic band over them. What else was she supposed to do? Oh, right, turn on the coffee machine. She went to the machine and found that Amy had already switched it on. Right, she thought. Amy. And went back to her desk.

She was so happy that her flu was abating. She could think more clearly now. As a receptionist, her task was to manage the inflow and outflow of the office – papers, humans, telephone calls. She realised the phone was ringing. She hadn't yet taken the voicemail off, so it wasn't ringing audibly, only flashing on the handset.

'Hello, Dr Simmons's clinic, how can I help you?'

'Jen, it's me,' said Hank.

She was confused. He never called her at work.

'The school called me. You're not answering your phone.'

'Oh shoot.' She reached into her bag, found her phone. Seventeen missed calls.

'Luke had to stay at school today with one of the teachers. He didn't have a permission slip for the field trip.'

'The field trip.'

'To the science museum.'

'To the science museum.'

She did not remember that there was a field trip.

'Anyway,' Hank continued, 'they're saying he's pretty upset about it.'

'Oh,' said Jenny. She was sad for her boy. She would have gone to pick him up but she couldn't leave work. He'd get over it though.

'Well, that's a shame,' she said to Hank. And then: 'I'd better go now.'

'Jenny?' she could hear Hank ask as she put down the phone.

She turned in her chair towards Amy, who had a desk behind hers, at the back of the reception area.

'Amy, can you read lips?'

'Read what? . . . Lips?'

'Yeah, I mean, it seems like a weirdly useful skill to have,' Jenny said.

'Yeah, I guess it is,' said Amy.

'I always wanted to learn sign language,' said Jenny, turning back to her computer. She tapped the mouse and the cursor appeared again, wiggled upwards. Again she placed it in the doghouse.

'Oh, I forgot to switch on the phones,' she said to herself.

*

THE FIRST PATIENT OF the day was an earlobe detachment, Mr Talley. He blew in, pushing both doors open and bringing with him a refreshing blast of cool air.

'I'm here,' he announced. 'And ready.'

'You will have very nice earlobes later today, Mr Talley,' said Jenny. She felt today that it was important to reassure patients.

She tried not to look at his earlobes, but as he turned his head after she gestured at the seating area, she caught sight of his ears. They seemed perfectly normal to her. He had pretty small ears. But he wanted the earlobes to dangle separately, instead of curving inwards and attaching to his face. She wanted to tell him that he really did have perfectly nice ears, and that he really might not need the surgery, but she didn't want Amy to hear her. Anyway, she knew better than to do that – especially after the episode with the anorexic girl who came in wanting liposuction.

That was a while ago, but she could still remember the girl clearly. She led the girl through to the doctor's room, feeling that the girl was rocking on her knee joints to walk. Like she might just buckle to the floor. Jenny hoped her own face was neutral, and she racked her brains for something – anything – to say. She didn't say anything, but when the girl came out, frowning and rigid, she told her there was no payment to make. The doctor had messaged Jenny to say that the consultation would be free. And Jenny – she couldn't help it – she simply said, as the girl was turning to go: 'You're beautiful, by the way.'

But ever since then she had regretted it. Because the girl, in the throes of anorexic possession, probably thought she was complimenting her on her thinness. Jenny's comment had probably backfired completely, and she had felt guilty ever since. You never knew how people would contort your best efforts to comfort.

The guy with the earlobes would be fine. He would have new earlobes and he would feel better with them. The only thing Jenny could hope for was that he would be satisfied and not then need any further adjustments to his appendages.

There was the usual smattering of Botox appointments, a few consultations on breast-lifts, one buttock enhancement, and a batwings. Jenny felt for the underside of her arms. She had batwings too, but if she flexed her muscle they seemed to lessen, so she did that, and put her hands back on the keyboard. She looked at her hands, lifted her fingers. The backs of her hands were a record, a record of so many little events. The cat scratch by her thumb that she had had since she was a child. The scar where they had misapplied a cannula during her delivery of Jesse. The nail that snagged her forefinger pad when she climbed out of a window in high school. She had needed a tetanus shot for that. Jeez, was that the last time she had a tetanus shot? There were new little moles that had appeared in the last decade or so. One, two, three, four, five, six, seven, eight. Eight little moles. And some vague shadows that may be nascent age spots. Age spots. And veins that looked like so many sleeping earthworms. All these marks – somehow she had forgotten that these hands had been with her all along. They were her little loyal workers that had grasped thousands of objects, thrown countless things and waved to every degree of the compass.

'Jenny?'

Dr Simmons had been standing over her for some time. She looked up, tucking her fingers under themselves.

'Jenny, I need Mr Talley's file.'

'Oh, right,' she said. 'The earlobe . . . omect . . . omy.' And she used her toes to pull her rolling chair to the filing cabinet.

CHAPTER 31

'I T'S A FUCKING STOP sign, Hank, not a slow-down sign. Fuck. I bet you drive like this when the kids are in the car.' The air in the car was hot and filthy with fury.

'You wanna drive?!'

They were spitting their words.

'You, with your fucking smart house. I hate the house. All that jazzy technology, and it doesn't even protect our kids.' Jenny did jazz hands as she said it.

'The security settings are on,' he said through clenched teeth. 'You don't even understand, do you, that he has gone around the security. It's a *browser*.'

'Yes, I get it, an onion router . . .' She was inspecting her nails with a kind of fervour now, and Hank was snatching glances at her. She didn't seem to notice.

'Fuck.' He gripped the steering wheel and blew air from between his teeth. 'There's something weird about you these days, Jen, I swear. It's been like a few weeks of this weird wife.'

'Shut *up*,' she said. 'You should have dealt with this like I asked you. Back when it was only Japanese cartoons.'

Silence.

Hank tried to look over at her without turning his head. His eyeballs strained to the right.

'But what has he seen?' Jenny lamented towards the world outside. 'What . . . is in that little head now?'

Hank could imagine what he'd seen. The butt-slapping, the orifices, the cum-shots. He wished he could erase it all from the boy's brain, like you erase a hard drive.

THEY DIDN'T SPEAK THE rest of the way home from the school. It was Saturday, the long halls had been empty, but when they entered, Hank could sense the ghost-crowds of kids, the faint smell of juice and rubber soles, the echoes of his own footsteps. The receptionist had met them at the door and led Hank and Jenny to the principal's office.

'Thank you for coming.' The principal stood up and gestured roundly for them to come in as he stepped behind them to close the door. 'Take a seat.'

Guilty. Hank felt guilty immediately.

'I'm going to get straight to the point here, Mr and Mrs Tinkley,' he said. 'We've had some intel that some of our eighth-graders have been accessing the dark web. Uh, and unfortunately, the source, as far as we can make out, is your son Jesse.'

'What?' Hank said. Jenny's mouth fell open.

The principal continued: 'I mean, I don't have information about what searches have been done or anything. But some kids have told their parents, and there's one thing they all agree on, which is that Jesse has access to the dark web . . . and I'm afraid that we all know that the dark web is a toxic place.'

'Are you sure it's Jesse?' Jenny asked. Hank could feel that she felt guilty, and really hoped she wasn't going to blab to the principal about the hentai boobies.

'We're going to have to put him on some kind of probation while we look into this,' the principal said. 'And I need to ask you to talk to him about it, and let me know what you find out.' He picked up some papers from his desk and tapped them to straighten them. It was a false gesture, and Hank knew it.

'Well, this is serious,' Hank said. 'We will get to the bottom of it.' He sat up straight. He was much bigger than the principal.

The principal looked at Jenny. 'Mrs Tinkley, I let this go on as long as I could. I don't know if you got the messages I've been leaving for you?'

'Oh yes, I'm sorry, my cell has been acting up. I didn't . . . I wanted to . . . I have them now.'

The Tinkleys stood up to leave and the principal made to open the door for them. But he stopped short. 'Uh, I had Luke in here the other day – just something I wanted to mention. He said something like, that . . . things haven't been the same ever since you found out you were Vikings? I don't know what that means, but it certainly meant a lot to him. That's when the "trouble began", he said.' And the principal raised his fingers into quotation marks.

'Right.' Hank nodded. 'It's actually true. Yeah, I have Viking DNA, you know; we're descended from the Vikings. That's what he's talking about.' He could tell the principal did not have Viking genes. 'Except for Jenny, of course,' Hank added, with a slight flick of his thumb in her direction.

The principal looked at Hank, and then at Jenny. He didn't smile.

'I did a spit test,' Hank said, standing in front of the principal, who still had his hand on the doorknob.

'My heritage is Anglo-Saxon,' Jenny said, her eyes wandering around the principal and his door.

Hank was looking at the wall behind the principal. There sure were a lot of certificates hanging up there, he thought.

WHEN THEY GOT HOME, Jenny opened her car door before the car had stopped moving. Jesse was out skateboarding with his friends. Luke had spent the morning with the Jamesons, a family on Maple Drive that had a tree house.

'Hey, Home, make coffee,' Hank announced at the kitchen when they got in.

'Coffee,' the smooth female voice of the smart house returned. 'There is no milk in your refrigerator.'

'No milk?' He looked at Jenny. 'No fucking milk. Are you serious?'

'Shut up,' she said to Hank. '*Shut up!*' And then, at the ceiling:

'No coffee! Halt coffee! Stop making the coffee! Give up making coffee!'

Silence. Then the coffee machine began to splutter and gurgle.

'How the fuck do you get it to stop?' Jenny said, sitting at the kitchen table, her face in her hands.

'I'm sorry,' said the voice. 'I'm not sure how to help.'

'Just stop helping, you fool,' Jenny whispered.

Hank chuckled. It was kind of funny. His wife and his house having a fight. He thought he better calm things down though.

'Hey, Home, can you order some milk to be delivered tomorrow, please,' he announced.

'Okay. Delivery booked,' said the house.

JESSE ROLLED RIGHT UP to the back door on his skateboard, earphones in and baseball cap on backwards. He looked happy.

When he walked into the kitchen and saw his parents, he pulled one earphone out.

'What's up?' he asked, flipping his skateboard to vertical and leaning it against the wall.

'You better sit down, son,' said Hank, trying to put an arm on Jesse's shoulder. Jesse shrugged it off and went and sat at the opposite end of the table.

'Mom, what's going on?' he said.

Jenny didn't look at him directly. 'You've been suspended from school for going onto the dark net.'

'Jen!' Hank boomed.

'What?!' Jesse shouted, standing up. 'I don't even know what the . . . What even is the dark net?'

'Wait a minute, buddy.' Hank stood up too.

'I am not even having this conversation. You guys are such *invaders*. Can you just leave me alone?' Jesse shrieked at them, his voice breaking with the strain.

'Now just wait one minute,' Hank said.

'No! No! I can't get *any* privacy in this house. No one can. There's like no privacy anywhere!'

'Would you like to change your privacy settings?' said the voice of the house into the room, and the three of them looked up.

'Shut up, Home,' said Jesse, deflated.

They were quiet for a moment. The house said nothing more.

'But what did you see there?' Jenny lamented in a whisper, eyes closed.

'It's not a place, Mom, there's no *there*,' Jesse said.

'What she means is that we'd like to know what you were looking at,' Hank said. 'So we can help you.'

'Help me? You guys don't know how to skateboard – how can you help me?'

'Jesse, you have secrets, and you have interests, and it's really normal,' Hank was trying to get the right words out. 'Wait . . . skateboarding?'

'You're not the one in charge anyway, so butt out,' Jesse shot at Hank. And, turning quickly to Jenny: 'I just want to be left alone!'

'We left you alone and look what happened,' Jenny said, trying to frown but only managing to wince with her eyes.

'Oh, I get it,' said Jesse. His face turned mean. 'You want to know about secrets? Just go in the basement.' It was a challenge.

'Jesse, honey.'

'No, seriously, go in the basement. Check out what's behind the purple poster. Go on. Then you'll learn. Ever wondered what Luke's been doing down there? How bad he needs to get away from you two?'

Hank and Jenny looked at each other. They sidled towards the basement door, watching Jesse as they moved.

'He wants some privacy too,' Jesse hissed at them.

HANK FELT THE COOL ground rush at him when he opened the basement door. Jenny was behind him and reached forward to switch on the light.

The white neon light meant that nothing sparkled but everything glowed. Bottles of liquid. Marbles. Rocks gleamed at Luke's parents, and they walked around the room like they were in a forbidden chamber. Jesse was right – there was a lot of secret here.

'This is the one part of the house that isn't smart,' said Hank, picking up some kind of dried plant. 'What is this – tumbleweed?'

He looked at the posters. They were the same posters they'd been for a while. Luke was at the Jamesons' house. Now Hank knew that Jesse had just been trying to distract them with a trip to the basement.

'We-ell, we-ell,' he said, and sighed, climbing back up the stairs to talk to his elder son. He needed to make sure Jesse didn't tell Jenny that the TOR browser had been installed in the house already. Hank had installed it a few months back. He was a member of lots of groups that would be the first to find out about any serious government trouble. Area 51 and all that. It was a security measure. But Jenny wouldn't understand that.

CHAPTER 32

'WHAT ARE YOU? BLIND? You didn't even see it,' Jesse said to Hank.

Hank seemed to falter, like he wasn't sure whether to stop and give Jesse a lecture in the kitchen, or go back down and investigate.

'Go!' Jesse said, flinging his arms at Hank.

Hank headed back down to the basement, and Jesse stood at the top of the stairs, watching his parents as they faced the wall where the poster hung.

The lightbulb in the basement threw a vicious vertical light onto his parents. Their hair shimmered with silvers and blacks, like they had flattened porcupines on their heads. Their noses looked big, their foreheads loomed, and Jesse thought they looked more like Neanderthals than he'd ever noticed. Whitish-green faces, rumpled clothes, bad posture. Miserable. They were standing side by side, looking at the wall. Jesse suddenly regretted the shock he was about to give them. Or could they handle it? He hoped they would be able to handle all this. To tell him that everything was going to be okay. To come back together, somehow.

Hank read what was on the poster: *'The present was an egg laid by the past that had the future inside its shell.'* – *Z. N. Hurston.*

'Oh my God,' he heard Jenny say, falling to her knees.

'It's okay, Mom.' Jesse heard Luke's voice, muffled, and he took several steps down to see for himself. There was the sound of paper ripping.

She rushed forward. 'Oh my God! Oh my God!'

This is what beseeching sounds like, Jesse thought.

Hank was right behind her, and Jesse watched as his parents tried to pull Luke from his basement hole.

'You don't have to pull me out,' Luke whined. And he wiggled his way out, dropping onto his feet before them. He was wearing his boiler suit and had white powder and dirt in his hair. He took off his goggles, switched off his flashlight.

Both Hank and Jenny were on their knees, pawing at Luke, holding his arms and hands.

'What have you been doing?' said Jenny. 'What have you been doing? My boy.' She drew him to herself, and Hank tried to get closer too, still holding Luke's elbow.

'Why aren't you at the Jamesons'? . . . My little boy, what have you been doing?'

Jenny was whispering, like she couldn't find her voice, with fat, lone tears dripping and seeping. Jesse could feel tears stinging his eyes too. Luke looked scared now. Hank was shaking his head and licking his top lip. He stood up and took a step to see into the cave.

'Oh my God.'

Luke's clothes were folded neatly in a pile on the floor to the side of the cave.

'I came home early. I was taking a nap,' Luke said, with the shadow of a voice.

'COME UPSTAIRS, EVERYBODY NEEDS water,' Hank said, and Jenny stood up, bringing Luke to her body, heading to the stairs.

'I'm not hurt,' Luke whispered.

When they reached the top of the stairs, Jesse stepped back to let them pass and followed them into the kitchen.

'Home, make ice, please,' Hank told the house loudly, and a crunching sound came from inside the fridge.

Jesse wasn't sure if this was supposed to be a water ritual, with the sipping and the breathing, so he watched his father.

Hank gulped down half the glass and looked around at his family.

'Drink,' he said.

They lifted their glasses. Jenny's teary eyes had been closed; now she was looking up at the ceiling.

'Well, I'm okay,' Hank said. 'You okay?' he asked Jesse.

'I'm okay,' Jesse said. 'Are you okay?' he asked Luke.

'I'm okay,' said Luke. 'But, Mom, are you okay?'

Jenny didn't answer. She was holding her head in her hands.

And then, 'I'm here,' came the rumpled words from beneath her hair.

THEY HADN'T TUCKED THE boys into bed in a long time.

Hank came in first, looking at each of them and trying to decide which one to go to first.

'Luke, my boy.' He sat down on the edge of the bed. 'I'm going to have to put some supports in there, you know . . . so the house doesn't fall down,' he said, smiling, and ruffled Luke's hair. 'Now, get some sleep, everything's going to be okay.'

He stood up slowly and took the three steps over to Jesse's bed.

'Okay, big guy,' he said, straightening the covers. Jesse was lying down already.

Hank leaned in. 'Now, I have one question for you.'

'What?'

'Did you look at sex on the dark net?' he whispered into Jesse's ear.

'No, Dad.'

'What were you looking at then?' Hank asked the question aloud.

'Skateboarding tricks. There's a skateboarding forum, and I want to learn how to do an XYZ.'

'Okay.' Hank adjusted the covers again. 'Okay.' He patted them down.

He sat for a moment, looking out the window.

'I believe you.'

Jesse waited.

'But I'm guessing you used the home computer for these, uh, misdemeanours.'

Jesse nodded.

'Okay, so listen, I don't want the school, or anyone else, to know that we have TOR downloaded on our home computer. Okay, buddy?'

'Okay, Dad.'

'I just had it there so I could keep track of security situations . . . you know, in the world. To keep us safe,' Hank said quietly. 'From terrorism and stuff.'

'Okay, Dad.'

When Jenny came in several minutes later, she went straight to Luke, folding into him in a hug. 'My little boy.' After a time, she lifted up and looked at him. 'It's all going to be okay . . . Okay, sweetie?' She wiped her nose with a sleeve.

Jesse watched from across the room. He hated it when his mom cried. It made him want to cry too, but then it made him angry, really angry.

She came over and leaned down to hug Jesse. He let her but didn't offer his arms, and instead lay motionless.

When she lifted up slightly, to look him in the eyes, his whisper broke and he felt that he might crackle open. 'But, Mom,' he said with an urgent quiet, his face flushing, 'why didn't you ever ask me about the flares?' He looked up at the ceiling, hoping to keep the new tears in his eyes from overflowing.

'The flares,' she said. 'Oh my God, I forgot about the flares.'

'They're for emergencies.'

Jenny looked away, and then closed her eyes. 'I can't keep up with the emergencies.'

CHAPTER 33

LUKE HAD BEEN DIGGING his hole in the basement wall for a few weeks. First, he wanted just to see what was behind the wall, whether there were arrowheads and archaeology there. Then he thought it would be cool to sit in the hole, so he dug a little further, until it was big enough that he could climb into it. He had heard about total darkness in underground tunnels, far beneath the earth's surface, where there was zero per cent light. And, although he had covered the entrance to his cave with an old towel and switched off all the basement lights, he was trying to see if, after a certain time, he could detect any light source. He thought that the door to the basement probably leaked light, and he supposed that if he lay in darkness long enough, any seeping light would become visible to him. He had eaten a lot of carrots in his life.

But there was no light that he could see. He held his hand up to his face, and though he could feel its heat, he could not see it. 'Hand?' he whispered. His eyes rolled and scanned the darkness. 'Earth?' he asked. He realised that you couldn't try harder to see – there was no effort he could make to see better. His eyes just had to do what they could do, and if they didn't see, they didn't see. But the cave was sooty, and bits of earth fell constantly from the top surface, so he closed his eyes.

This was the only real beginning he could visit. The beginning of his home, the foundations of the house. He felt that he was lying amidst invisible roots, and there was the round smell of truth there, in his small cave space.

He'd asked his mother for truths too. She was the one true witness to Luke's own beginning, and he often asked her to recount the story of his birth. She always started by saying that Jesse had screamed when he entered this world. But Luke was totally silent. She looked down at her second-born, the struggling, wincing newborn, cringing at the light. 'Turn down the lights,' she told Hank. 'The light is too bright for him.' Why was he so quiet?

'Why is he so quiet?' she had asked the nurse, who was mopping up Jenny's uterine effluence from the floor around her. The nurse looked up, rubber gloves holding a big wad of paper towel. She peered over. 'He's okay, isn't he?' she said, reassuring Jenny. 'He's just that kind of person.' The nurse bent over again to paw at the floor with her paper towels. 'He's a gentleman, that's all.'

But Jenny always told Luke that, in fact, she had wanted him to scream a little. Just to clear his lungs. It's healthy for babies to clear their lungs after they're born. And she wanted him to let her know that he could really feel this world. She wanted to show him that she could comfort him too. But he blinked and squirmed, and didn't make a sound for days. Jenny told Luke that in those early days she would whisper to him: 'Are you sure you don't want to yell, not even once? . . . Tell us who you are,' she would say.

'Tell us who you are,' Luke repeated in the dark quietude of his own cave.

THE CAVE THAT LUKE and Jesse had found on their camping trip with their dad was different. They still talked about it sometimes — and had never told either parent about those hours when they had been lost in the Endless Mountains. It was an abandoned mine, and it was lined with a wooden frame, propped open with vertical posts. Rain had formed several small puddles, but Jesse and Luke stepped around them and found a log on which to sit. The day had been hot, but it had then started to rain, and they were glad of the shelter. Plus, they were tired of walking and wanted to sit for a while.

'We're not really lost, are we?' Luke asked Jesse.

'Could be,' said Jesse.

Their voices echoed briefly, and then seemed to be absorbed by the mud walls.

'Do you think this is a gold mine?' Luke asked.

They looked into the back of the cave, and they could make out piles of dirt, and parts of machinery, that seemed to form a back wall. Neither ventured any further inside. Every time they glanced at the opening of the mine, they were light-blinded and couldn't see back into the deep interior.

'We should go and look,' Luke said. 'Dad would be so amazed if we found more gold.'

'You dummy, there's no more gold here; they've dug it all out.'

'How do you know?'

'Because they gave up on it – obviously.' Jesse squinted into the darkness. 'No one's been here for years.'

The boys sat in the cold cave and listened to the three sounds of rain outside. Big, plump drops were dripping at the mouth of the cave, plopping into turbulent puddles, messy with little waves. There was a higher shushing of the rain just outside, which was hitting the rock and soil so hard that it hissed. And then the larger roar of the rain in the forest, which was beating at the trees, bashing the pine needles around, shaking the pine cones.

'I'm thirsty,' said Luke, and he stood up and headed out.

Just outside the cave, he looked up, blinking at the spatters of rainwater, and opened his mouth a little, and then wider. So little rain reached his throat that he opened his mouth as wide as he could. It was a bit better, but it was too little water to touch his thirst.

'This is going to take a long time!' He turned his head and smiled at Jesse.

Jesse sat there for a moment longer before getting up to join Luke.

'Oh my God, this is so not helping!' Jesse laughed as he stretched out his tongue and tried to catch raindrops with its tip. He started counting them, shouting out a number after each successful catch. Luke joined in too, and yelped. 'I got two at the same time!'

No one heard the boys counting triumphantly, shouting at the patch of mottled grey sky that was visible between the jagged tops of the pine trees.

Luke hurried to catch up to his brother's number; they swayed like circus performers balancing something on their tongues, this way and that, trying to catch as many drops as they could. 'One hundred!' they shouted in unison, and laughed, looking at each other, both wet, with their hair splayed in strands down their foreheads.

'Should we go back inside?' Luke said.

'I have a surprise,' Jesse said, and waved him inside.

The boys settled back onto the thick wooden beam they had sat on before. They shook their arms, stamped their feet, flicked the drops from their hair. Jesse unzipped the side pocket of his shorts and pulled out two shiny packets containing energy bars.

'What?' said Luke, impressed.

'Yep,' said Jesse, and pulled his arms away as Luke tried to get hold of one.

'We should only eat one,' Jesse said. 'Just in case,' he added, as he slid one back into his shorts pocket and put the other to his mouth to tear off an edge of the wrapper.

'Cashew and goji berry,' he said.

Luke tensed his chin and neck, and the sinews of his neck emerged. It wouldn't be delicious, but it would be sweet, and he was hungry. 'I want a chocolate chip-cookie,' he said.

'Just eat it,' said Jesse, whose half was nearly finished. And he stood up and went to the front of the cave. 'If it wasn't raining we could tell which was was north . . .' He turned back to Luke. 'But as it is, we have no clue. We're going to have to wait it out.'

'Why don't we walk in one direction, and get somewhere in the end?'

'Because some directions would only make us go deeper into the woods, and get more lost than we already are.'

The day wore on, and the boys started to get cold. It wasn't warm at the mouth of the cave, but it wasn't warm deep inside the cave either. The warmest spot seemed to be about two yards from the cave entrance. But the cave floor would pull the warmth right out of your body – whichever body part was touching it – so they dragged the log over to the side and sat on it, side by side, hands around knees, shoulder to shoulder. They were only in long shorts and T-shirts, because the day had started off so hot, and Hank said they would be in the bright sun for gold-panning. But it had turned cold, and they were waiting for the rain to stop.

'Don't worry, Luke, I have protection,' said Jesse.

'You have a gun?' said Luke, looking up at his brother.

'No, stupid,' replied Jesse. 'Well, kind of,' he said, and pulled a small red cylinder from his other side pocket.

Luke was amazed. 'Is that dynamite?'

'No-o-oo – Aw, man, come on.'

Luke tried to take it from Jesse's hand, but Jesse wouldn't let him hold it.

'It's *very* dangerous. For emergencies.'

'But what is it?'

'It shoots fire, so people can find you – but we could also use it if a bear attacked us.'

'It's raining too hard for bears.' Luke waved a hand.

'You kidding? Bears live here. You think they're afraid of the weather?' said Jesse. 'You just leave it to me, I know what I'm doing.'

Luke accepted that.

'Can I just hold it, though?' he asked.

'It could explode in your hand – because you don't know what you're doing.' Jesse's voice hardened.

Luke went quiet again, glancing over at the flare now and then, watching Jesse inspect it, looking for any faults or scratches. Luke looked from the flare, and past it, to the rain outside.

'That thing won't work in the water of the rain. But it would scare a bear, so that's something,' Luke said, looking down, pushing some dirt around with his sneaker. He reached into his pocket and pulled out three red crayons. 'I brought these,' he told his brother.

'What, so we can colour the walls?' Jesse laughed.

'No, stupid. Crayons can work like candles. They will burn for thirty minutes each.'

'Oh,' said Jesse. 'Cool.'

The boys sat holding their crayons and flares, their shadows streaking from them towards the depths of the mine, shaped like acolytes with their votives.

'Cave, turn the heat up,' Luke said, looking up to the ceiling of the cave.

They turned to each other, and laughed.

'Guess it's broken,' Jesse said, still smiling.

The rain had died away, and the boys watched the soaked forest, with its thousands of stray drops sliding from pine needle to pine needle and onto the wet tree litter of the forest floor. The smell inside the cave was dark and grave, but the air that blew in from the forest was urgent with plant messages. Minutes after the rain's end, a fog pushed through the tree trunks, and as the boys stood at the mouth of the cave, the woods began to be erased by a thick white vapour. The dark limbs of the trees faded to grey and then disappeared.

'We are in a cloud,' Luke said, venturing into the edge of the fog.

'Don't go there,' Jesse said, catching the back of Luke's shirt with a pinch.

'Come on, let's go together,' Luke said, and pulled Jesse forward, still holding on to his shirt. They slowly walked into the forest, barely even able to make each other out, such was the density of the moisture around them. A tree loomed up and was suddenly in front of Luke; he stopped short and Jesse bumped into him.

'A tree,' Luke said, and he held on to it for a moment. His fingers were gentle because the bark of the tree was especially rough, and Luke thought he could probably cut himself on it if he grabbed it too hard. They touched it as they walked around it, and continued, with small steps, avoiding the rocks and fallen branches they could feel at their feet. Water dripped onto them but they didn't care; they were still wet anyway.

'It is hard to see, but the sounds are clear,' said Luke. And it was true: the strange thing was that the thick, soupy air was in fact thin for sound – every tiny crackle and breath from the life of the forest was audible.

'Jesse,' Luke said, as something scurried away from them, 'what's a shroud?'

CHAPTER 34

THE CHURCH WAS PACKED that Sunday. Everyone had been attending church since the scandalous text messages had been seen by Mrs Trevear on the God-phone. Some said there was an adulterer in their midst. Others said there was a thief somewhere in Bentonville. Lots of people presumed it was a confession of some kind of sexual perversion. So, as Jenny and Hank prodded their children through the tall doors of the church, past the good-faced parishioners who were handing out programmes and prayer books, they noticed that there was hardly anywhere to sit.

They settled in the penultimate pew, next to a family who were wearing matching green sweaters. Once they had filed in and removed their jackets, Jenny, who was seated on the aisle, looked along at her family in a row. They weren't colour-coordinated but they looked clean. She wished Jesse and Luke would tuck in their shirts, but there were only so many times she could ask them. They were there, that was what mattered. Hank had said this morning that they absolutely had to go to church this Sunday because otherwise it would look suspicious. She looked up the aisle and saw a lot of adjusting going on – mothers smoothing and arranging the hair of their daughters, fathers pulling up the collars on their sons' shirts.

The organ began its wheezing and rushing music, and Father Brian processed up the aisle to the altar with his gaggle of acolytes. Jenny thought the organ sounded like a very large cow. In fact, if you squinted a little, you could see the church as a great big manger. Father Brian was the colourful cockerel, crowing his big hallelujahs at everyone in front of him. The congregation were sparrows mostly, possibly some other kinds of finch too, shifting lightly on their feet with eyes darting about the group, softly tittering to each other. The carved pulpit was a salt lick, and they would all soon make their way up to the altar, the drinking trough, and line up like little piggies. But where – Jenny looked around – was the donkey? The donkey and the wife – these were both beings that belonged to a farm scene. But then, of course, the whole business was called 'animal husbandry'.

Jenny spent most of the service trying to figure out which animals she could see in the faces of the churchgoers, and it passed quickly for her. She spent some time looking up at the huge Jesus suspended on a cross, and then it came to her: he was a shepherd of course. Except there he was, the shepherd, dying, and all the animals were looking at him, suspended in the moment of his death. The liturgy had progressed to the Last Supper: 'On the night that he was betrayed, Jesus . . . said, "Take this and eat of it, for this is my Body, which is given for you. Do this in remembrance of me."' Father Brian held up the large wafer circle and proceeded to break it up in his hands. That wafer is Jesus, and I'm supposed to eat it so that I can remember that his death is being traded for my sins. And the wafer reminded her of John's prayer card – there was sacrifice there, and remembrance too.

HANK WATCHED FATHER BRIAN hold up a giant chalice of wine, and he felt that this gesture justified the water ceremony he had initiated at home. He listened to the words and nodded along: 'Drink ye all of this; for this is my Blood of the New Testament, which is shed for you, and for many, for the remission of sins. Do this, as oft as ye shall drink it, in remembrance of me.' He was right; there was holiness when you drank something as pure as water and, in the olden days, wine.

The fact that it was supposed to represent Jesus's blood didn't faze Hank – it was sacrifice, plain and simple. Hank wondered if Jesus would qualify as a hero. Heroes sacrificed themselves. In fact, Hank could imagine a scenario in which he would sacrifice himself. It was obvious: if he was on a plane and there was a hijacker, he wouldn't just let some asshole crash the plane or fly it to Libya.

The Tinkleys had to wait a while before their row was summoned up to Communion, and when the time came, Jesse sat down and wouldn't move.

'Come on, Jess,' Hank said, and tugged at the shoulder of Jesse's shirt.

'I'm not going,' Jesse whispered.

Jenny and Luke were already walking up the aisle, and looked back to see what Hank and Jesse were doing.

Hank bent down. 'Jesse, you have to come – now come on.'

'Nooo,' Jesse said back.

Hank sat next to him, and he could feel the row behind them focused on his back.

'Why not?' He had his arm around Jesse to protect their conversation from the craning ears in their vicinity.

'Because.'

'Because *what*?'

'Because it's gross.'

'What? Oh, come on,' Hank said. He looked up at the lines of people waiting to reach the altar and knew there was no time for this.

'There are too many germ., I'm not doing it.' Jesse said.

Hank looked around again. 'Look, you can just eat the wafer.'

'I hate the wafer.'

'What's to hate?'

'It gets stuck to the roof of my mouth.'

'Just come up, please, Jesse, just come,' Hank said. They had already drawn attention to themselves enough.

'I'm not going.'

Hank turned and smiled at the faces in the row behind him – a sort of apology. He rolled his eyes. 'Kids,' he whispered at them, and raised his hands like *What are you gonna do?*

But he had to go up; there was no way he was going to stay seated in the pew next to Jesse. Yes, it was an admission of sin to go up and take Communion, but it was an admission of something much darker not to go up at all. Plus he was sure there were people in the congregation who knew about Jesse's misadventures on the dark net. Hank stood, took a large sidestep, like he was stepping into a Warrior yoga pose, and exited the pew. He processed up the central aisle with as much dignity as he could muster, his gaze directed at the altar.

CHAPTER 35

A WEEK HAD PASSED since the revelation of the basement hole, and Jenny tried to keep up with the routines. Get up, get half dressed, try to get the boys up, get a little more dressed, try a little more to get the boys up, put their socks on for them, hurry them downstairs, ask them what they wanted for breakfast, wait for an answer, make them toast anyway, get their book bags together, check for any teachers' notes. She knew the drill, but it seemed like she was having to organise a grand event every time. When they left, she went back to bed, sometimes watched TV. She slept a lot that week, at least she tried to – she managed to sleep more in the daytime than in the night-time. On Friday, she called in sick.

That day, Jesse brought home an electronic baby. There was a programme at school for the eighth-graders that was part of their 'Family and Consumer Science' teaching, and each pupil had to take care of an electronic baby for one weekend. It was called an 'infant simulator', and the device was connected wirelessly to the class teacher, who monitored the pupil's care-taking of the doll. Jesse brought it home in a baby car seat – it came with the doll – and with two diapers and a baby bottle.

'It's making most of the girls actually want to have babies,' he said, plonking the car seat down on the floor by the door. 'They think it's cute,' he said, looking down at it. 'Which is, like, the opposite of the point.'

'You're going to leave it on the floor?' Jenny asked Jesse, and the electronic baby started to cry.

'Here we go again,' he said, and picked the baby up from out of the car seat. He was wearing a wristband he had to touch to the baby's heart area each time it started crying – if he didn't respond to the crying within two minutes, it would be recorded on the baby's internal computer, and the teacher would mark it as neglect. He put the baby on his shoulder and started bouncing it up and down lightly. 'You have to rock it – sometimes that works,' he said.

Jenny found it extremely odd, but her heart soared to see Jesse taking care of something. She hadn't known he had it in him – and she was blindsided by the pride that surged in her. She didn't want to look at him because she knew he would get mad at her curiosity. She knew, now he was thirteen, you couldn't look at him in any direct kind of way. But she glanced back at him, wondering if she should offer advice.

'What are you supposed to do when it cries?'

'Mom, it's like a real baby. You either change the diaper or you feed it a bottle. There are things like these signal patches inside the diapers and the bottle that, like, switch off the baby when you put them in contact.' He rocked more vigorously, but the baby's cries were getting louder. 'Okay, I'm going to try the diaper.'

He lay the baby onto the kitchen table, so gently. 'You have to hold its head,' he said, 'or the teacher will find out and you will get points taken off your score.' And he took off the baby's diaper to replace it with the other one. 'There's, like, sensors in its neck.'

'Those diapers are kind of grey and dirty,' said Jenny.

'Mom, it's not real,' Jesse said, without moving his head from its position above the baby, but looking at her out of the corner of his eye.

'Well, you look like a pro,' she said.

The baby's cries died down once the diaper was changed. 'Come on, baby, you have to coo,' Jesse said. And then to his mother: 'When they coo, it means it's over . . . for now.'

He put the baby back into its baby carrier, and put a blanket over its legs.

'Do you have to keep it warm too? Do they check that?'

'Naw, you only have to feed it and change it.'

'So why'd you put the blanket over it?'

'Well, I figured I would do what *I* would want – like to be a little warmer, like it might have cold feet. I don't know why it doesn't have some, like, baby socks that come with it.'

The baby was quiet, and so Jesse sat at the kitchen table and ate a sandwich Jenny had made for him. While he ate, she went over and looked at the electronic baby. It had the weirdest glassy eyes: kind of realistic, but they looked a little mean too. The baby's skin was a kind of mid-tone – and Jenny figured they were aiming for the most generic colour – something that could ostensibly be both dark white and pass for a light African tone. She leaned down and sniffed the baby, which did actually smell like baby powder.

'Apparently, the hungry cry is different from the dirty-diaper cry – they said you could tell the difference if you really listen,' Jesse said, with a mouth full of bread and cheese.

Jenny touched the baby's foot. It wasn't the cold rubber feeling of a regular doll, but it was dense, room temperature and smooth. Nothing like a real baby, she thought, and she remembered the floppy limbs of warm and soft flesh that found edges at the lines of little bones. She had no desire to pick up this fake baby – it was somehow horrible to her. Almost as though it were a lifeless baby – basically a mother's worst nightmare. If this were a real baby, you would want to call an ambulance.

The baby started to splutter a little, and make some short groaning sounds. The noises were pretty damn realistic, Jenny thought.

'Oh man, I swear they put it on the hard setting,' he said, getting up. He lifted the doll from its seat and cradled it in his arms. 'For some kids, it almost didn't cry at all.'

Jesse took the baby to the living room to watch some TV. Jenny could hear the sounds from the sitcom mixing with the baby's fussing while Jesse talked to it. 'Aw, come on,' Jenny heard him say. 'You're okay, I just changed your diaper.' The baby's crying got worse until Jesse came in and retrieved the little milk bottle from the baby carrier, and took it back into the living room. When Jenny poked her head through the doorway to check on him, he was sitting there, baby tucked into the crook of his arm, and he was holding the bottle to its lips. The baby, amazingly, was making sucking noises.

Jenny sat on the stairs and read the 'Participant Care Card' that came with the baby. Instructions said that the baby would have at least twenty caring episodes in twenty-four hours. It said the baby would require rocking, feeding, changing and burping. If you handled the doll roughly, that got recorded. 'Don't forget to burp it after you feed it, Jess,' she shouted towards the living room.

HANK BROUGHT LUKE HOME from his soccer practice, and after Luke looked in to see what Jesse was doing, he returned to his mother in the kitchen. 'Why is Jesse holding a doll?' And Jenny had to explain to him that they were teaching children how hard it was to take care of babies. 'That's a weird thing to learn,' he answered. 'Do they make them go to offices too, to see how hard that is?'

'No,' she said. 'No, they don't, but they probably should.'

Hank went into the living room and sat next to Jesse, watched a little TV and then looked over at his eldest boy.

'So, you're learning about childcare,' he said.

Jesse said, 'Yeah,' and got up to go into the kitchen.

'Mom, can you hold it while I go to the bathroom?' He gave the doll to Jenny, holding its head until it rested on her arm. But she didn't want to hold it. She stood in the kitchen with the infant simulator draped over her arm. She wasn't cradling it, and she wasn't loving it. She just wanted to put it down, but it was murmuring, so she knew it was on the verge of something, some demand.

'Here you go, Luke, hold a baby,' she said, placing it into Luke's arms. 'Just for a minute, until Jesse is back.'

'This is a weird baby,' Luke said. 'Does it talk?'

'You need to rock it,' Jenny said. 'No, it doesn't.'

Jesse came back in and went straight for Luke. 'Mom! You are not allowed to let children hold it!' He grabbed the baby from Luke, making sure to hold its head, as he placed it up to his shoulder. It was such a bizarre scene for Jenny – her thirteen-year-old son, with a baby on his shoulder, shouting at her, reprimanding her. 'He could have dropped it! You have to pretend it's a real baby! What were you thinking . . . ?' And he cradled the robot-baby as he left the room to go upstairs. The baby was wailing now, and Jesse went to his room and closed the door.

Luke gave Jenny a look as if to say *Well, this is unusual*, and Jenny smiled.

AFTER SEVERAL HOURS OF having the baby in the house, Jenny's nerves were shredded. The baby had constant needs and now Jesse was getting flustered. 'I don't know what it wants,' he wailed at her, after Luke had gone to bed. Jesse was going to sleep in the living room so the baby didn't wake Luke in the night. But he couldn't go to bed because the baby kept making noises. So far that evening, he had changed the diaper twice and fed it twice, burped it. 'When is it supposed to go to sleep?' he asked her.

'Having a baby is not easy,' she told him. She was pretending to Jesse that she could take all this in her stride, that she was experienced and unfazed. But the crying was so realistic – the brochure said that it was a recording of a real baby crying, and Jenny knew that she still hadn't outgrown the visceral clenching she felt when she heard a baby cry. The urge was to pick up that baby and hold it to her chest, to warm it with her enfolding. But this baby repulsed her, so she felt pulled and pushed, and it was relentless.

After Hank had warned Jenny and Jesse not to walk around in the dining room in case the floor was unsafe because of Luke's hole, everyone went to bed. 'The house might be compromised,' Hank said to Jenny before turning over, falling asleep and snoring within minutes. Jenny could hear the baby crying – even when it wasn't crying. She received every whisper of the house, every noise from the street, with the kind of urgency you feel when you are the parent of a newborn. And just when she thought that the robot infant had finally turned itself off, it would start again. She wondered if she should put her headphones on, but that idea made her nervous – what if she didn't hear something important? Did the doll have a sensor that would tell the teacher if Jesse rolled onto it in the night and smothered it? Jenny couldn't sleep these days anyway. She got up and sat on the floor, leaning her back against the side of the bed, hands resting on her propped-up knees. The headphones lay in her lap.

At about one o'clock in the morning, Jenny heard the electronic whining become louder and louder as Jesse mounted the stairs and appeared in the doorway of her bedroom.

'I don't know what it wants,' he said. Jesse was exhausted and pale, and tears were spilling from his eyes. 'I did the diaper, I did the drinking, and I've been rocking it for a long time. Mom, you have to help me. What do babies want?'

Jenny stood up. 'Give it to me,' she said.

'Are you mad at me?' Jesse said.

'No, I am not,' she said, and put a hand on his shoulder to turn him around. 'Go to your own bed. I will deal with this.' And she walked him down the hallway landing to his room, letting go as he went in.

'Mom, it just won't stop crying, I can't stand it,' he whispered, still crying. 'I just don't know what I'm doing wrong.'

'You're not doing anything wrong,' Jenny said to him, pointing at his bed. 'Let's not wake up Luke,' she said, and closed his door with the hand that wasn't holding the wailing doll. She wrapped the doll inside her bathrobe and padded down the stairs, all the way to the basement, where she stripped the doll of its onesie, turned it over, and unscrewed the panel to remove its batteries. In the silence of the cold basement, Jenny felt her heart, heavy like a fishing weight, dragging her down to the rounded hard bottom of her life, her house, her town, her country, the world. Like she'd been pulled down some long stony slide by this infant simulator and, now she had stopped sliding, there was a cold place to rest, like a grave-womb – and if she reached out, there was no texture her fingers could find to grasp. There was smoothness on every side, and smooth gravities, she knew, only made you slip like a cockroach trying to climb out of a stainless-steel pot.

'WHERE IS THE SPOON, where is the spoon?' Jenny was whispering to herself. She was in the kitchen but hadn't turned on the lights. She grabbed all the spoons from the jug that held her kitchen utensils by the stove and laid them out on the counter. 'Not that one, not that one, not that one . . .' She sorted through them. 'Shoot!' She scooped them all up and shoved them in the bag by her feet. Next, she scrabbled through the kitchen drawers looking for a flashlight, and then she opened the fridge and took a package of cheese, stuffing it all into her bag. She looked at her hands: her fingers were stretched out, shaking. She gripped them together to still them.

The house was quiet, and every noise she made was dangerous. 'Just don't let the house hear,' she hissed to herself. 'For God's sake, don't let the house hear me.' She stopped herself and looked up at the grille from which the house's voice came. Would the house know where she was going?

You can't read my mind, she mouthed at the grille. It occurred to her that the house couldn't really read her expressions either, now that she'd had Botox, and this was gratifying.

She wondered what, in fact, the house could see right now. Jesse in his room, all wound up in his covers, with limbs thrown around the bed like a rag doll. But the house didn't know that he had nightmares. Jenny knew that. She knew that he had always had nightmares, and that they were fantastical. Objects morphed, people transformed into animals, flat surfaces vibrated like spider webs in weather. Jenny often thought that the reason for these wild unstable dreamscapes was the mobile she had above his cot as a baby. It was a swirling infinite loop called a Möbius mobile, and it had one surface and no boundaries. Must have been confusing to a new little eye. But the house wouldn't know that either.

Luke had different dreams – he never dreamed outside the realms of reality. Jenny, in fact, had only just found this out recently, when she was helping him to make up a story for school and she suggested he told the story of a dream he'd had. 'Like where a horse turns into a unicorn,' she said.

'That never happens in my dreams,' he said. 'I only dream true things, Mom.'

She was sort of impressed, and then immediately worried – why didn't his mind explore the strange psychologies that most people dream? Did he, after all, have some peculiar architecture to his brain? He told her that he dreamed about getting to school, about cracking eggs, about walking through gigantic factories. She would forever worry about that child. But meanwhile, she thought, directing a spiteful eye at the house speaker, you don't give a shit. They're not your kids, they're mine.

The house could also probably see that Hank was snoring. Or at least it could hear it. He was spread all over the bed, the comforter grabbed over to his side so that it enveloped him, its excess draping onto the floor at his side of the bed. May you sleep, my husband, she thought. He's not your husband. She pointed at the ceiling.

She sat at the table to write a note to Hank. She would empty her brain of everything she had stored there for the next twenty-four hours. She would just leave him with a bunch of questions and problems.

The house is a mess. Programme it to clean up?

Is there enough butter to make toast tomorrow?

Need to have a talk with Luke about the value of money and
    why not all kids need pocket money.

Did I put the laundry in the dryer?

Is it too late to register Jesse for hockey sessions that are nine
    months away?

Are they caught up on their tetanus shots?

Do we need more hand soap?

I should do a spring clean someday soon.

The sheets need to be changed.

Where is Jesse's piano music?

Need to call the exterminator before the ants come back.

Iron the shirts for Sunday church.

I hope I bought the right shower gel for the kids and not one
    that makes them itch.

When was the last time I watered the cacti?

We have run out of chocolate.

Check Jesse's feet aren't peeling again. Make sure the kids
    wear fresh socks.

Forget about the fake baby – it is a stupid assignment. I'll talk
    to the teacher.

She took the spoons out of the bag again and lay them out on the counter. Dammit, she didn't know which one was John's spoon. She clenched her fists, held them both up to her neck, looking down at them. Would Shona remember her? She shoved the spoons back in her bag. John said she was a medical person. Maybe she was just a drug-head. I need someone who knows about orange stuff.

Inside the car, outside, Jenny winced as she turned on the ignition. It sounded like the awakening of a growling monster in the sleepy hush of Maple Drive, and she rolled away without looking back at the house. But at the side, in her peripheral vision, she saw a figure at the window of the Saltons' house. 'You don't know where I'm going,' she said into the dark car.

CHAPTER 36

FATHER BRIAN DIDN'T REALISE that, even as a priest, you were forced to undergo body searches when you visit a prison.

He waited in line for three hours of the morning, along with about twenty other people, mostly women. He looked for Jenny's face among them but it wasn't there. Where could she be? Hank had called Brian in the hopes that he'd know where she might be. She had disappeared in the night a few days ago. 'Can you check your God-phone?' Hank had asked, and though it was against the whole principle of the thing, Brian had checked it. But there was nothing there of any relevance, only a bunch of lies, some desperation and a few pranks.

Father Brian and the other visitors stood along a hallway, and there were seven chairs pushed at intervals against the wall. The ladies seemed to know the system well, and Brian noticed they took turns on the chairs, silently signalling to each other to offer a seat when one person's time was up. Many of them knew each other too. Brian listened to their hushed conversations.

'Someone got burned with an iron a few weeks ago.'

'Shit, I hope it wasn't mine.'

'Yours got long to go?'

'Seven months.'

'Nice for you. Seven years here.'

A CORRECTIONAL OFFICER PASSED by the front of the line and they fell silent.

'Excuse me,' someone said loudly, and the CO stopped in their tracks.

'Oh, shut up,' a woman said from the side of her mouth, pretending to wipe her lips with her forearm.

'Excuse me, but can you tell me how much longer we have to wait?' said a man.

The CO was looking down the line at the man, head tilted, a deep frown. 'You want to lose your visit?'

'Just shut up,' someone else said to the man in the line.

The CO walked on down the hall and out of sight.

'You don't talk here.' The woman in front of the rookie visitor turned to him.

'You're not allowed to ask a question? They can take away your right to visit?'

'Yes.' She didn't turn around this time.

'Just be quiet – that's how it works,' someone else said.

No one had anything to do – you had to leave your cellphone and personal belongings in a locker. You only had your ID and visiting card. Father Brian wondered if, by some heinous administrative mistake, they were all being taken into custody. The guards treated them like criminals.

He rubbed at the stamp on his hand – it was some round symbol, in invisible ink. He wasn't sure when they would check for it but he figured it was still there, even if he couldn't see it. He hoped so.

He could hear loud buzzes and the clanging of metal from distant corridors. He felt a little claustrophobic.

'Father,' he heard from behind him.

There was a little girl behind him, and she had touched his elbow. When he turned, she stepped backwards, and her mother pulled at her pigtails. 'Hush. Don't talk here. You be quiet,' the lady said to the girl, without looking at Father Brian.

Father Brian gave the girl a smile and shrugged sympathetically, and the girl smiled back.

THERE WAS A RIPPLE of reactions from the front of the line, some intakes of breath, a shuffling of shoes.

A CO had appeared, walking energetically along the line with a dog. The dog was jumping up and sniffing underneath people. The pair were concentrating. Brian wasn't afraid of dogs, but everyone else seemed to be, pulling up and away as the dog worked vigorously at searching the visitors. The little girl behind Brian started to cry, and as the dog worked on Brian, sniffing his shoes, his crotch, his shirt buttons, the girl cried harder. When the dog moved on to her, she screamed and grabbed her mother. The dog persisted, sniffing up her legs. In her panic, the girl swatted at the dog. 'Get away!'

The handler shouted, 'Hey!'

The girl's mother pulled her closer. 'She's afraid of the dog!'

He wasn't having it. 'If you don't make her stand still for the search, you will be asked to leave.'

The mother prised the girl from her and held her out in front of her body. The girl was pulling back, but the mother squeezed her arms and held her there, arms shaking with the effort.

The little girl was pale with fright, and stood there, held, as the dog sniffed around her feet. The dog was going to move on but the CO turned the dog in a circle and put it back on to the girl. It pushed its nose up one leg, jumped up slightly and moved on to the mother. The CO let out a half-laugh of contempt and followed the dog down the line.

Father Brian had kind of hoped that people would behave better. His priest's collar often had that effect. People in stores would be more polite to each other when he was around, and he moved through shopping malls as though he emitted some kind of force field that made people behave their best. But he was having no effect here. The CO took no notice of Brian's ecumenical clothing. It was strange, and unsettling. Brian didn't like it at all. His force field didn't work here. Maybe they didn't believe he was a priest.

The group was eventually moved along the corridor and through a gate, and again their IDs were checked and they were patted down. They took their shoes off for a metal detector, and the officers confiscated any belts that people had been wearing, including Brian's. At the last inspection, Brian was asked to sit down in front of a CO, to remove his shoes again, and this time also his socks.

'Lift up your pant legs,' said the officer, and Brian pulled up one trouser leg to mid-calf.

'As far as they can go,' said the officer.

Brian struggled and pulled up his pant leg a little further – it didn't go very high at all, wouldn't turn the corner of his knee. His pale leg with its shin dents and stray long hairs. He looked up at the man. 'That's about as far as I can get it to go.'

'Other one,' the man said, not looking Father Brian in the eyes but focused still on his lower legs.

'Now, pockets,' the man said, and Brian pulled out the linty linings of his pockets, pulling at them like he was trying to tease a puppet from the wrinkled cotton.

'Step forward.' And the CO started to run his fingers along Father Brian's waistband, and up the back of his shirt to his collar.

'That will have to come off.' The CO stepped back and pointed to Brian's priest collar.

Brian was sweating, and lifted his arms, exposing the damp patches at his armpits, and reached back to unpin the collar from its stud. He pulled it through the black sheath and held it out to the man, bent like a boomerang. The man took it and pushed a thumb along the inside of the folded collar.

'Never seen one of these before,' he said, and handed it back to Brian.

FINALLY HE WAS LET into the visitors' waiting area. Brian noticed that the most practised among them went straight for the vending machines and bought up several items at once. He joined them and bought a Snickers bar, hoping that John would like it. His trousers kept riding low and he wondered if he was going to have to hold on to them for the whole visit. Would they give him back his belt?

There were no windows and the clattery din of the place was tiring. Brian sat down on a plastic chair. He realised that he didn't know what John looked like. He presumed John was tall and big, given the man's very low voice, but he wouldn't recognise him. Hopefully, John would see his ecumenical clothes and approach him instead.

The walls of the room were painted in a shiny wipeable beige paint, and there were banks of plastic seating in rows. A sign on the door in the corner read *Non-contact visits*. Brian had managed to sit down, and the seats were now all taken. He was tempted to offer his seat to someone, but no one would catch his eye. He patted his pocket, checking for a cellphone, or wallet. It was really strange to be without these things. He barely knew what to do with this waiting time. He looked up and smiled at a few people whose gaze he intercepted – but they didn't really smile back. Most pretended not to see him. A lot of people were inspecting their fingernails. Some had closed their eyes. Brian realised he was still holding his collar in his hand and so he threaded it into his shirt collar and started to button the studs. This seemed very interesting to the other visitors and many were now staring at him, which only made his fingers clumsy, and he thought that they would probably think he wasn't a real priest. A real priest would button his collar effortlessly. Father Brian's fingers had never been adept at small-scale fiddling.

When the corner door opened, everyone looked up.

'Jones,' the officer shouted. Brian was confused. Was that the name of the prisoner or the visitor? Everyone looked at each other to see whose visit was being announced.

'Jones!' The officer was angry.

Father Brian got to his feet and made his way to the officer.

'I'm here to see Jones.'

'What the fuck were you waiting for, trumpets?' And the man moved through the doorway, holding the door for Brian.

THROUGH TWO MORE DOORS that the officer opened with codes, and Brian was led to the last of a row of booths with glass screens. He sat there and waited. The smell was colder here, and metallic. Brian did not like that he was alone here. No one told you anything of what to expect.

John turned the corner, led by a correctional officer who walked him to the booth and removed John's handcuffs. He was short, skinny and pale, with a thinly traced beard that ended in a tight little braid at his chin.

John sat down without smiling and picked up the phone. Father Brian smiled at him and said hello, but John just gestured at him that he had to pick up the phone. *Of course, of course*, Brian mouthed, and picked up the phone, looked at the voice receiver and put it to his ear.

'You don't look an awful lot like God,' John said, his face unmoving. His voice was even deeper than Brian remembered it.

Brian huffed a little laugh, and immediately dropped his smile, shaking his head. 'That was inappropriate. I – I'm sorry, I just wanted to keep the God-phone, um, somehow, pure.' He closed his eyes and briefly shook his head. 'But how are you?'

'I kind of get the feeling we should be talking about how you are.'

'Oh, me? I'm fine. I just, well, you see, I didn't know who was sending me messages. In fact, I thought it was someone else entirely . . . It was . . . it was . . . There's a guy with a wife named Jenny.'

'Oh, I know the Jenny you're talking about,' said John with assurance.

'You do?' Brian peered up with something like a hopeful feeling. 'I was hoping you did.'

'Yes, I do. She is the one who gave me my . . . connection to God.' He smiled.

'Oh. Right. I see.'

'She's intense. And smart. And frustrated,' John said.

'Oh?' Brian said. 'I'm sorry to hear that.'

Other visitors were being led into the room and placed into the other cubicles. Prisoners walked behind John to their own booths, and Brian saw that they were all black. And they were all young. The noises from this side of the glass, from the visitors, were colourful: there were tears, there was joy, some of the noises were angry and aggressive. Father Brian couldn't see them because there were panels either side of him, but the sounds were sharp, and the air was electric. These timed moments were precious.

'The thing is, John, that Jenny has disappeared and I was wondering if you knew where she was,' Brian said.

John tipped his head; it was a gesture of questioning, and consideration. He knew something.

'She ran away?' he asked.

'We don't know.'

'She wasn't that happy,' John said.

'Yes, perhaps,' Brian said. 'She left a note that said she would be back in a few days, and that was a couple days ago . . . Her husband is pretty worried.'

Guards were walking around, listening and watching the conversations. Brian presumed that they were also listening to the phone exchange. He wondered what John would be telling him if it weren't for these horrible guards and their vicious persecution. Brian frowned at one that was standing behind him for longer than usual.

'I wonder, John, if you have any idea where she might be,' Brian said. 'Even if it's just an inkling.'

'Sorry, Brian, I don't know anything,' said John, and then more clearly: 'I would've called but cellphones aren't allowed in jail. You know? They're not allowed at all.'

Brian was silent.

'Anyway, she stopped writing to me after I sent her a wooden spoon I made. Not sure why.' John pulled at his beard-braid, smoothing it, lengthening it. 'That was about a month ago.'

The guard had moved on. Brian noticed that John had draped the fingers of his right hand over his left arm – it was an artificial, awkward-looking pose. And when John saw that Brian saw his fingers, he raised three of them, then raised two of them, then raised four of them.

'What's the weather out there like then?' John asked Brian.

Brian was slow to answer. John's knuckles were knotty and large, his fingernails clean and short, except the fingernail on his little finger that was long and a little yellow. Brian had always wondered why some people had long pinkie nails – did they use it to play guitar? He knew there was something it was supposed to signify.

'It's good, it's fine,' he said. The fingers were repeating 3-2-4, with a pause between the series of the numbers.

Brian's heartbeat quickened; he sprang a sweat, took a deep breath. He then put his fingers on his shirtsleeve and copied John: three fingers, two fingers, four fingers.

John nodded. 'And how *is* your congregation? I hear you got all kind of digital hoo-ha going on?'

'Yes, yes, I am really trying to keep up with the rest of the world – you know, to make Christianity a part of our technological advances . . .' Brian faltered. John's fingers had changed their rhythms. Now it was 2-5-5. So Brian did that back to him, and he was pleased to see that John's eyes were smiling. Brian was keeping up, receiving some kind of important message. Maybe he would understand later how to decode it. But it was also making him extremely nervous. He didn't want trouble.

'Well, I'm just thinking that by the time I get out of here, I won't know how the world works anymore. All those people with all those apps. And I still don't get what memes are.' Now it was 3-3-1-2. 3-3-1-2. John repeated the series several times, and Brian copied him.

'You're doing a good job, Father,' John said, and Brian exhaled. He felt that he had never been given such a compliment, never been made to feel so congratulated, man to man.

'Your messages worried me,' said Father Brian. 'How much longer do you have here?' Brian spoke in a lower voice, a voice with more peace and confidence to it.

'I have three more years. I've done eighteen months.' John looked down. He slowly moved his fingers to show the numbers again, this time in a long series: 324-255-3312. 324-255-3312. 324-255-3312. He pretended that he was rubbing his fingers, lifting two or three at a time and rubbing their underside with his thumb. For the number five, he stretched out his palm, as though needing to alleviate some kind of pain.

'Do you have arthritis, Father?' John asked. 'Because I do. Just started. Then I asked around, and I guess it's normal to start getting arthritis in your forties. I didn't know that.' And then quieter: 'I did not know that.'

The long series of numbers were intimidating Brian, and he didn't copy them immediately. He couldn't talk and think of digits at the same time. But John continued, calmly and patiently, speaking and extending his fingers. 324-255-3312.

It was a phone number. Brian put his fingers to his lips as though considering something carefully. He placed three fingers at his lip, pulled one down and released it upwards again. That was 3-2-4.

'I wonder . . .'

2-5-5 was easier. He touched two fingers to wipe the sweat off his forehead and smoothed his hair twice with an open palm. 'I wonder . . .' Then he simply tapped 3-3-1-2 onto the table as though he was biding his time, drumming his fingers for a moment.

'I just wonder what this is all for,' Brian said. He was slow and righteous in his speech now, relieved the number recital was over. 'I never believed that prison was a place for punishment.' He looked up into the corner of the booth. 'I don't think this works.' And he shook his head a little.

Brian couldn't really connect the man who wrote the desperate texts with the man in front of him. Am I not good enough for you? Where are you? Get me out of this place. These were desperate words, and yet the man in front of him looked strong and rooted.

'Are you suffering, John?' Father Brian had to ask. He had to give the guy a chance to be administered to.

'Everyone suffers,' John replied. 'It's the way of things.'

And then John leaned in towards the glass, looking Brian right in the eye. 'The problem is,' he said, with a gravity that had Brian locked into his gaze. 'The problem is that I am claustrophobic.' John held him with his eyes. There was no movement in the man's face, and his wrinkles were still, as though carved into wood. Brian could see that John had an impressive spread of crow's feet.

'Ah, now that's . . . inconvenient,' said Brian, his head bobbing like some kind of toy.

John laughed and sat back. It was the first time Brian had seen play on the man's face, and it was a relief, even if Brian was sure he was being mocked somehow.

'No, it's true,' John said, now more relaxed. 'I can feel it when an attack is coming on and I have ways I can try to deal with it, but that is the one thing I wish I didn't have.'

'Is there some kind of medication they can give you?' Brian asked.

'Heh, yeah, but not any kind that they let you have in here,' said John.

Brian was embarrassed; yet again he was being naive. But still, he pressed the point. 'I mean, medical medicine – you know, prescribed by the prison doctor.'

'Father, they just don't care that much about us.' His words were slow and sharp.

'Yes, I can see that,' Father Brian said. 'I really can.' And he was sorry; sorry for the man before him, and sorry for all of them. The sounds in the visiting booths had mellowed, and they were quieter than they had started – but Brian was sure that they were sadder too. He looked down at the back of his hand – he hoped the invisible ink was still there, because that was what they needed to see – their official symbol under the black light – in order to let him out of there.

CHAPTER 37

H ANK TOLD THE BOYS that Mom was visiting Aunt Mary for a
few days. They accepted that, with a little hesitation – probably
wondering why she hadn't told them she was leaving. She had never
left like that, in the middle of the night. And she had removed the
batteries from the electronic baby, and left it, in the basement, opened
up, with its batteries scattered, as if abandoned on an operating table.

'Aunt Mary drives Mom nuts,' Jesse said, as he brushed off his
feet before getting into bed.

'Yeah, Aunt Mary is nuts,' said Luke, already in bed.

They were remembering all the trips to visit their great-aunt, who
lived in an assisted-living facility in upstate New York. Aunt Mary
talked ceaselessly. She was a self-described 'hoot' with an exercise
bike in her front room, which she demonstrated at the slightest
encouragement. She always wore bright pink sports clothes, and a
vivid shade of some kind of lipstick. Hank wondered if all old ladies
got as much lipstick on their teeth as Aunt Mary. Over the years, she

must have ingested gallons of whale blubber, or whatever it was that they made lipstick from.

Hank was very respectful of old people though, and when the Tinkleys visited Aunt Mary, he sat on her peach velour sofa and asked about all her appliances – were they working? How were her electrics in general? But she wasn't the helpless type, and batted away his efforts with a swat of her arthritic, manicured hand.

'Oh, everything is in good shape. The handymen take care of the place real good,' she would say, offering them the sugared cookies that they sold in the community centre in her facility. 'So, how's ma-a-a-ariage?' she would ask Hank and Jenny mockingly. Aunt Mary thought it was a stupid institution.

'Aunt Mary is getting older and she needs people to visit her.' Hank was folding the boys clothes, assessing them for a second day's wear. *Of course I can do these things*, he answered Jenny in his mind. He had given them lentil casserole, he had made them shower, he had looked at the bumps on Luke's knee. 'I think they're warts,' he said. He'd have to ask Mr Salton what you put on kids' warts – there was some kind of ointment, he remembered.

WHEN THEY WERE ASLEEP, Hank sat in the living room. If she hadn't left a note, he would have been really worried, like that she'd been kidnapped or murdered. But the note he'd found in the morning, sealed in an envelope on the table at his side of the bed was clear. *I don't want you to come look for me*, it said. *I will be back in a few days.*

She didn't say where she'd gone, and he thought it must be that she was having an affair, or completing an affair, maybe even becoming a lesbian. The note didn't say. It said: *Don't let Luke dig. And don't let Jesse online.* She signed off with: *If you have any burning questions, just ask the house – it knows everything.*

On the kitchen counter, he found a list in Jenny's handwriting, which he figured she had made for herself. He scanned the words and noted that she was planning on doing some spring cleaning. The house was a mess, it said; *Programme it to clean up?* Jenny hated the house, he knew that. She'd asked him so many times to disable the house. To turn it into a regular house 'with all those lovely inconveniences', she said.

He switched on the television and selected the smart-house footage from the menu. It kept only ten days' worth of footage – just enough to find out what had happened if, say, there had been an incident.

He started at the beginning and watched the kitchen, thinking that he would see the most relevant activities there. He couldn't watch it in real time – that would take ten days – so he put it on 50X FAST FORWARD and watched his family buzz around the kitchen, like frantic insects, busy as all hell. He wanted to get to the parts where Jenny was alone – for these would be the more informative moments. As the shadows skittered around the screen, Hank wondered at how often his wife opened the refrigerator – if he could count that fast, it would probably be about seventy-five times a day. That was quite a waste of electricity.

He could see her actions, though, at this vicious speed, and something else was clear – the frequency with which she did some things. She sourced, prepared and offered; sourced, prepared and offered. The food was taken away. Then she prepared something again, and she took things elsewhere. The preparation of things was relentless. He saw she paid bills at the kitchen counter, she sealed envelopes, cleared things away. It tired Hank just to watch it.

Then he saw images of himself, entering the kitchen after work, stopping at the kitchen island, exchanging a few words with his wife, taking a plate of something and walking out. She made some kind of gesture after he left the room, and he had to rewind it several times to make it out. At first he thought she might be swatting at a fly or some other flying bug. She threw up her arms in his direction – and because it was in black and white, and because the camera was overhead, he found it hard to interpret the movement. He paused it, dropped the remote and stood up to make the motion himself: he threw up his arms, unfurling them as they dropped back down, his open, upturned palms arriving at his thighs just as he had seen her do. It was a motion of supplication. *Oh, come on*, it said. Exasperation maybe. But her torso crumpled forward as she did it. Desperation?

He scanned through the footage to find other instances in the last ten days of his presence and her reaction to it – what did she do when he left the room? He found that same motion three more times, often ending with her turning away, or leaning her elbows on the counter, her head down. If he slowed these scenes, he saw that she remained that way for several minutes, until someone came in, whereupon she roused herself and responded to another request.

Upstairs, on the landing, the footage showed her zooming back and forth carrying clothes and laundry baskets, the children also entering and exiting bedrooms and the bathroom. Hank thought he saw the boys go into the bathroom together for a significant time, and that seemed strange, but there was no camera in the bathroom so he couldn't check what they were up to. At one point – the time imprint read 11:34 a.m. – Jenny was alone in the house, and as she walked along the upstairs hallway, she suddenly sat down, setting the laundry basket down beside her. She stayed there for twenty-eight minutes, apparently doing nothing, just leaning against the wall, knees up, her head lifting and dipping, which in fast forward looked seriously demented, but when he slowed it down, it just showed a woman thinking. Why would you sit there like that?

CHAPTER 38

S HE WASN'T SURE IF she'd find Shona Brendon in Shaflette
— but thank God that gas stations still had yellow phonebooks.
'Almost never get asked for it, but here you are, it exists,' said the
man at the cash register, handing her the big, floppy book. He was
old and curious, and Jenny wasn't in the mood to explain anything,
she didn't want this nosey fellow to know who she was looking for,
so she pulled the book away from the counter and turned to flick
through it. Flip, flip, flip, bingo — she was lucky: there were four
addresses for Brendons in Shaflette. She took a picture of the page
with her smartphone and gave the book back to the man.

'Found your person?' he asked.

'Maybe.' She shrugged. He would be just the kind of person that
would merrily tell the police about her, make a note of her licence
plate, describe her car, tell them that her hair was all frizzy, that he
hadn't expected a person like her to come and get gas in the middle of
a Saturday night — that he knew there was something fishy going on.

Jenny had kept the rest of the prayer card in her wallet, and she only took small pieces from it when she really needed it, when her symptoms returned and the hollowing agonies became too much. She was trying to hold off, just a few more hours, just until morning. She thought maybe her immune system would kick in soon. It was 5 a.m., and Jenny parked the car under a tree, next to a row of houses that indicated resident children — the tricycles, the plastic shovels, flower pinwheels stuck into the lawn. She tried to get comfortable in the car; the seat reclined, but the steering wheel hampered the arrangement of her legs. She wasn't going to get much sleep — but she was used to that now; she never had any decent sleep anymore.

She cracked the window open; the air inside the car was becoming clammy, and she was catching vague whiffs of the salty odour of day-old clothes. She wanted to eat a little more orange paper. This time she understood what she needed from it. It made the ground feel solid once again. Like she was sure-footed, finally. Jenny hadn't felt truly safe since she'd had children. But with the orange paper, she felt connected, like some gentle electricity had been turned on again after a protracted power outage.

The street lamp had several bugs looping in its flickering yellow light. They came bouncing against the lamp and fell away, then regained themselves and went back for more. Jenny watched, from her reclined position, as the branches shimmied with leaf shadows overhead.

*

IN THE MORNING, WHEN the sun was up, she tried the first address listed, under the name *A. Brendon*. It was a little white house, with green shutters, and a dry lawn in front of it. There were no signs of life in that house – no cars in the parking space, and the curtains at every window were shut.

The second address was nearby, and as Jenny rolled up, she saw one downstairs window was open, and there was a corner of curtain flapping against the wall just outside the frame. Jenny killed the engine and absorbed the sounds of the neighbourhood. There was laughing somewhere, shouting somewhere else. A young voice was chanting, 'Mama!' A baby was fussing. There was a buzzing from the crickets in the brush behind the houses. There were little eruptions from several televisions in the houses nearby. People were at home with their families on a Sunday morning.

'UH, HELLO, I'M LOOKING for Shona?' Jenny was smoothing her hair but there was no point, it kept bouncing back after her fingers had passed. She was holding a bunch of wooden spoons in her lowered hand.

The lady who answered the door was not friendly. Her hair was up, she was wearing slippers, she had just finished chewing something.

'No one here called that.' She spoke through the screen door, looked down at the spoons.

'My name is Jenny.' Jenny was nervous but not ready to give up. The woman's suspicion didn't surprise her. A strange face at the door was almost never a good thing.

'So what?' the lady said.

'Oh . . . well,' Jenny said. 'Thanks anyway. I was just looking for a friend,' she added.

'Sorry about that,' the lady said. 'Good luck to you,' she added in quiet tones, taking another bite of the bread-like thing in her hand as she started closing her front door. Jenny turned back to the car.

The car was warm and Jenny was tired. But she was too anxious to relax. She didn't want to eat the prayer card yet, not until the shaking and the sweating came back. She sat in her car and looked at the last two addresses where Brendons lived – or used to live, at least. She wondered if she ought to look up the local hospital in case she started to feel really bad. She leaned her head on the steering wheel.

'Jenny.' There was a rap on the passenger-side window.

Jenny looked up, and there was a woman standing there, a different person to the one who had answered the door. She was beautiful and slender, and dressed in slacks and a blouse. Jenny lowered the window.

'Hello?' Jenny said. She felt she might throw up.

'Is that you, Jenny, who writes letters to John? What are you doing here?' Shona said, having bent down and leaned in the window a little. It was such a gentle question that Jenny thought she might cry.

'It's you.' Jenny was almost whispering. She hadn't expected Shona to look so poised and so healthy. She had envisioned missing teeth and lurching gestures. But this woman in front of her was a clear-eyed and equable person, certainly not the kind of person you expected to have been in prison. Was it really her? Jenny had been right, she was African American, but she had been wrong too; she wasn't the tattooed jailbird convict of her imagination.

'May I?' Shona said, taking hold of the door handle.

'Please, please, yes.' Jenny pressed the UNLOCK button and took her purse off the passenger seat, brushing the seat with a quick swipe of her hand.

Shona got inside, leaving the door open.

'I saw John. He explained everything,' she said. 'I don't know what he thought he was doing. But I just wanted to thank you for not sending anything.'

Jenny nodded, and then stopped. 'Wait . . . thank me?'

The women looked at each other, puzzled.

'Wait, you're not here to give me that stuff, are you?'

'No,' Jenny said. 'I'm here—'

'Because I don't need it.'

'You don't?'

'No, I'm not a user,' Shona said, almost like scolding, like *Didn't you know?*

Jenny wiped the sweat from her forehead. They sat for a moment quietly.

'A user?' Jenny said.

Shona frowned, looking at Jenny, inspecting her face and clothes for the first time.

'Are you okay?'

'Oh yes, I'm fine.'

Jenny was taken aback by this grounded woman, with her open

and round voice, so resonant in the car compared to Jenny's flat words. The woman exuded energy, breathing herself into the car in a way that Jenny could never have done. Shona had the lucid countenance of a professor or a scientist. Jenny tugged at her shirt and wiped her lips. She was sure she had sleep dust in the corners of her eyes and that Shona probably thought she was trashy. Shona had rings on her fingers, gold and swirly. She was shifting her feet, and looked into the passenger footwell.

'Oh yes, the spoons.' Jenny lurched down by Shona's feet and grabbed at the spoons scattered there. She brought them up and sifted through them, from hand to hand. 'One of these is from John, it's from John, he sent it to me and I think it was for you. I mean, that's why I came, to give you a spoon.' But she couldn't find the one that had the face on it. 'It's weird, none of them has a face,' she said, holding them in front of her like a hand of cards.

Shona interrupted. 'A spoon?'

Jenny continued shuffling the spoons, but Shona was already getting out of the car.

'Oh . . . you don't have to do that. I don't, I don't need a spoon.' Shona was out of the car and looking back at the house. She bent down and said firmly into the open door, 'Honey, I don't need a spoon.'

Jenny looked up from her spoons. 'I'm sorry.'

'Listen, Jenny, it was nice to meet you but I better go now.' Shona brought the door to a close with a slow sweep, and patted the car.

Jenny couldn't move – she felt her one chance at knowing some-thing was slipping through her fingers. She was trying to think of something she could say to bring Shona back into the car. Shona turned, squeezed a hand into a small wave and walked away. 'Keep well.'

Jenny put a hand up and let it stay there a while. She watched Shona make her way up the path to the house, her long legs, her black leather sandals with their little heels, the stripe of light skin where her sole met the shoe. She placed her feet one in front of the other, and it looked like a solemn dance up the gentle gradient to the front door.

Jenny had to take a piece of prayer card – it was no longer possible to wait – and she fished the little dirty patch of paper from the bills pocket of her wallet and put a tiny fragment on her tongue. It tasted like pewter and pond scum, the orange flavour only coming afterwards, like something bitter now, not sweet – like orange peel that had been run over by a car. She had made a fool of herself. *I came to give you a spoon?* She mouthed the words as she looked out of her window at the tarmac and its interruptions of white lines.

She moved the car a little ways up the street, parked outside someone's house – no one she knew – and she felt vulnerable, out of place. She couldn't stay there. Some husband would come out all angry and ask her who the hell she was. Tell her to move on. Imagine that happening in Maple Drive, she thought. So she put the car into gear and moved on.

As she drove around she saw that there were lots of drive-thrus in Shaflette too. She visited several of them, bought herself coffee and some food, through the concertina windows, from the people with microphones bending around from their ears to their cheeks. 'Enjoy,' they said. She couldn't eat though, and the food stayed in its paper bag on the passenger seat until she couldn't stand the smell and she threw it out. She sat in the parking lot of Taco Bell for a few hours, then moved to a different parking lot in front of Linens Etc, then to Dunkin' Donuts. She did not want to drive back to Bentonville.

She went to the CVS and bought a pad of paper and a pack of envelopes to write to John. Maybe he could help her. And she sat in the car with a bottle of cherry-flavoured water and leaned the pad on the steering wheel.

Dear John,

I did get the spoon. Thank you for that. I put it in with my other spoons and now it's almost like it joined ranks, like it wanted to be like all the other spoons. The reason I say this is because now I can't find the spoon with the face on it. The face, I think, disappeared. Is that something that can happen to wood? Maybe it aged? Maybe it turned? Should I wait for another face to appear? I'll keep the spoons and see what happens. My son told me that most of the spoons were made by machine so I guess they have less living wood. Wasn't that what you called it – living wood?

I'm sitting in the parking lot of a drive-thru bank and the weird thing is that you can't actually enter the bank, it is only for drive-thru customers. I guess the parking lot is so you can sort out your paperwork before you drive through? Well,

I'm writing a letter instead because I don't have any business with this bank. But I'm also wondering if you could just live in a car. I mean, there is heating when you want it and the seat goes back for sleeping and there is a coffee-cup holder. Plus when you need to get around, you just turn it on. It has a radio, and your phone can hook up to the sound system. I think some cars even have wifi now. I guess the only thing you need to find would be bathrooms – but you could always go to a gym for that.

Anyway, I'm really writing because I wanted to tell you that I met Shona and she's really pretty and neat and smart. You're a lucky guy. And well, we just said hello really, but I was trying to give her the spoon but then I couldn't find it. So, anyway, we met and it was nice.

From,

Jenny

BY THE LATE AFTERNOON, she made her way back to Shona's house. When she rang the bell, that other woman answered it again.

'Huh? You again?' she said. She was dressed now.

'Look, just ask Shona for me – what was that orange stuff? I'm a mom, I have a family, and I need to know what that orange stuff was that John sent for her, that I was supposed to send—'

The woman didn't let her finish. 'Shon! . . . Shon!' And she opened the door wider to show Shona. 'She's here again. The spoons.'

'What?' Shona came from behind the front door. Again the screen door remained closed. 'Is everything okay?'

'I'm not here to bother you, I'm sorry I'm still here,' Jenny rushed to say, hand on her chest.

'Alright . . .'

'I took the stuff that John sent you. I mean I *took* it. Like, I ate it.'

'Oka-ay . . .' Shona had not understood.

'What was it?' Jenny said. 'I need to understand what it was. You have to tell me. It was meant for you.'

Shona opened her mouth, and then smiled. 'Oh no, you didn't!' She looked concerned. 'Oh, you better come in.' She pushed the screen door out and open, and flapped her fingers downwards to say *Come inside*.

'Thank you,' Jenny said. 'Thank you, I really appreciate it. Thank you.' She tried again to smooth down her hair, and wiped her shoes on the coir mat outside the door. The mat just inside the door said: *Don't Step on Me*. Jenny wasn't sure whether she was or wasn't supposed to step on it, so she made a large step and placed her foot on the wood floor beyond it. Shona watched Jenny's strange footsteps.

'Thank you,' Jenny said, following Shona into their kitchen.

'Kool-Aid,' said Shona, pouring Jenny a glass of purple juice. She looked at Jenny. 'I was wondering why you were so different from the person called Jenny that John talked about.'

'Yeah.' Jenny rifled through her purse and pulled out her driver's licence. 'I usually look more like this,' she said. Shona held it and gave it back to Jenny with a flash of serious in her eyes.

Jenny was glad to have the Kool-Aid, not just because she was thirsty, but because she hadn't tasted Kool-Aid since the summers of her childhood. She remembered those hard plastic pitchers that poured the Kool-Aid, with the white lids that you turned to let the juice come out.

CHAPTER 39

'WE SHOULD MAKE A time capsule,' said Luke. He and Jesse were helping their dad to fill up the basement cave.

'That is a great idea,' Hank said, his head inside the hole, arranging the rocks they were using as filling. 'More small rocks,' he said, reaching a hand back.

Jesse passed him a couple of rocks the size of oranges.

'I just need to fill this little space here,' Hank said with effort.

He pulled his torso from the hole and wiped his face with a sleeve.

'Luke, why don't you go ahead and get things together for that time capsule – that's just along your line of work, right?' Hank said. 'Thanks for helping me, Jess,' he added.

Luke felt kind of proud; they were having such a nice time filling up that hole – it felt like they were a team. It was like exactly what you would want to do with your dad. Jesse was enjoying it too. Luke was glad his dugout had done something good like this. Now they understood about his cave. Except Mom. She got scared by it, and then went to visit Aunt Mary.

Upstairs, he went to the kitchen. What, in this room, looked old-fashioned? The wooden spoons, for one. Where were they? And the can opener; Luke didn't think people would be eating from cans in a hundred years. People of the future would probably laugh that people cooked at all. But he would be glad to put a spoon in the capsule if he could find them – because, as a matter of fact, a spoon is a pretty perfect shape, and you really can't beat it for stirring and lifting liquids. They might need to be reminded of that.

A Tupperware box. They wouldn't use polycarbonate plastics anymore. A drinking straw. Those would definitely stop existing. What was the point of a straw anyway – just to bring water from a cup to your lips? Your arm and hand could do that.

Luke opened the lid of the trash just to see. Trash was always archaeological, he knew that. He picked out a Dazzlebucks coffee cup, turned it around. That would be a good idea, he thought, as he rinsed it at the faucet. People drink a lot of coffee these days.

You needed something like a newspaper for time capsules. They had done one at school, which is how Luke knew about them. But the Tinkleys didn't ever read newspapers. Luke's dad and mom got news on their phones. You couldn't put a phone in a capsule. His class put an empty soda can in their time capsule – but the Tinkleys didn't really drink soda because Hank said it was unhealthy. There was club soda though, so Luke got a mini can and poured the fizzing water into the sink, shaking the last drops out. He regretted it instantly and wished he'd poured it into a cup so that Hank could have drunk it, or Jesse. That was wasteful.

He opened the kitchen drawer that his mother called the 'catch-all' because it was full of all the odds and ends that didn't have their own place. He scrabbled his fingers through it and found a crumpled dollar. Almost nothing cost a dollar anymore, so these would soon be so old-fashioned that they wouldn't exist. It was a dirty dollar, with a pen mark across it, and he looked to see if he could find the pyramid with the eye on it. Some kids at school said that if you looked at it just right, the eye would wink at you, and you might possibly get some kind of magical power or message. Some dollar bills were special, he knew that.

There was this one time at school when Mr Saffe brought in a package of Roman coins and each of them was allowed to hold one for a short time. The other kids asked if they were gold or silver. Luke didn't remember the answer; maybe the teacher had said they were bronze, or was it brass? All Luke could remember was that he had been holding a coin that had been held by real Romans, and that maybe, just maybe, there would be dirt on it from some Roman gladiator's hand, a little particle of dirt from where the gladiator had been holding his horse's reins, and there had been dust and it had rained and his hands were dirty, but he had paid for passage into a city-state and the coin, dirtied by his hand, had passed into the hands of the guards. Had the guard dropped it? How did it get buried in the ground? He had raised his hand and asked, 'How did the coin get buried? Like, did someone bury it, or did someone lose it?'

Mr Saffe looked like he was thinking. 'Well, let's see . . .' He had a very friendly face, and was really trying to get an answer for Luke. 'I would say that probably it was kept by someone, and, let's say, it was kept so long, in an earthenware pot, and eventually it wasn't the right currency anymore, so it just became a . . . forgotten thing.'

'Well, where was this actual coin actually found?'

'Oh, I see, well, that I don't know.'

As usual, Luke thought. How can people know so little all the time?

The teacher decided to move on to the story of Romulus and Remus. They were studying ancient Greece. Luke had desperately wanted to slip the coin into his pocket – he needed it way more than anyone else in his class. It was true treasure. And it told him that the stories they were learning in school were actually real. This was metal with a story. Not just some kind of ore that you dig up.

The person who opened the time capsule would maybe think the same thing: who were the Tinkleys and what did they use this stuff for? Mr Saffe didn't know about the coin, but Luke could help those that found the capsule. It might matter to someone. Luke got out a piece of paper. His handwriting wasn't very good but you could read it.

We are the Tinkley family. Our names are Jenifer, Henry, Luke and Jesse. We like water but we can't put that in a time capsule because that would make no sens. We found gold in the Suskwahana one time but we gave it back to the goverment so you can't have that eether. We never had any pets or I'd give you a peece of its fer. Our house can make coffee and switch on music because it is smart. Our hous looks old but it was made in 2008. That is new for us since it's only 2015 now. Which won't be new for you.

He thought about whether he should tell them about the Viking DNA. It might explain something. And he went to the desk in the living room to find the print-out that detailed Hank's genetic make-up. On the desk were piles of fat envelopes, half opened. Luke swiped his hand down them, knocking some onto the floor, and found the green envelope he needed. There were two. One showed the name Henry, but the other had Jenny's name on it. *Jennifer Harrison*. It wasn't yet opened.

'WHAT'S THIS?' LUKE LIFTED the envelope as he got to the bottom of the basement stairs.

Hank was arranging rocks on the floor into sizes.

'It has Mom's name on it,' Luke said.

'Oh, right,' Hank said with a delighted tone. 'That's Mom's DNA profile, we forgot to open it.'

'Let's open it now,' Jesse said, standing at the side.

'Are we allowed to? Isn't that *her* information?'

Hank straightened up. 'Well, yes, we could do that. She won't mind. It's your DNA too. If you think about it, she already shared it with you.'

'She will be so surprised to know who she is,' Luke said with a smile.

They sat on the basement steps, under the dangling light bulb that illuminated strands of cobweb towards the ceiling. Hank sat on the third step, Luke below him and Jesse looking over his shoulder.

'She's seven per cent North African . . .' Hank scanned the pages.

'She's twelve per cent Jewish,' Jesse said.

'Three per cent Native American,' Hank said. 'That's cool.'

'How!' Luke said in a low voice, holding up his palm to the basement's darkness.

'That's possibly the coolest thing I have heard this year,' said Jesse.

'We have to send this fact into the future,' Luke said.

He was relieved that she had no Viking blood at all.

CHAPTER 40

H ANK BROUGHT THE COFFEES to the table, but the names on the paper cups were all wrong. *Hanc* and *Brain* they said.

'Well, someone's dyslexic,' Hank said as he gave Father Brian his latte, nodding at the scrawl on the cup.

'Oh, oh, thank you,' Brian said, taking the cup with both hands.

Hank lowered a wooden stirrer into his cappuccino, but then noticed a pattern in the foam. It looked like a flower. It looked like a vulva with extra lips. It seemed a little improper to sip at a vagina in front of a priest, but Hank figured Father Brian wouldn't recognise the shape.

WHEN BRIAN HAD INVITED Hank to meet at Dazzlebucks, he had reminded Hank that Jenny had taken part in the prisoner correspondence scheme. He said he would explain why that was relevant when they met.

'So, Jenny wrote to prisoners and this is something we need to discuss?' Hank got straight to it.

'Yes, right, yes.' Brian had taken a sip, and there was the finest line of foam on his top lip that he licked off. 'Jenny was writing to a man named John. I just visited him. He's at Flainton.'

'Oh, okay.' Hank was nodding, took a drink of his cappuccino.

'Anyway, so he gave me a number at which you can reach Jenny,' Father Brian said.

'Oh, I know where she is,' Hank said. He puffed out his chest, seeming to need a stretch. 'She's at her Aunt Mary's.'

Then he relaxed, then looked at Brian, who wasn't answering. 'Wait, does John know Aunt Mary? Because that would be weird.'

'No.' Brian shook his head. 'No, no, it's not that.' He didn't know about this Aunt Mary, and hoped that it wasn't some code word for marijuana. He was slightly in over his head here.

'John said . . . Well, so it seems Jenny is with John's wife.'

'What?'

'With his wife.'

'I knew it,' Hank said.

'You knew it,' Brian said, resigned.

Hank looked away.

The priest went on. 'We often refuse to acknowledge what we know deep down.'

'Did you know she was going to turn into a lesbian?' Hank said, vaguely attacking the priest.

'Who's a lesbian?' said Brian. He couldn't pretend to know everything.

'Jenny.'

'She is?'

'Well, that's what you're telling me, right?'

Brian scratched the back of his head vigorously and pulled his hand back over the pate of his head, over his forehead, wiping the sweat from his temple before dropping his hand back to his cup.

'No, not at all.'

Hank leaned in. 'Look, Father, I'm going to tell you something,' he said. 'I know why she left. I know it because I thought about it and now I know.' He leaned back and then lowered his voice. 'I mean, she was walking around the house at night, eating little pieces of paper. Picking things up, putting them away. Getting things out, and getting things ready. Sometimes she had so much on her mind –' he leaned forward again – 'that she would be unable to enter a room like a normal person. She would stop at the door . . . and, like, jump back and forth. At the threshold.'

Brian's big blue eyes felt like watering, he felt hot, and the feet in his shoes were sweaty. What was happening here?

'The house is a disaster without her,' Hank said. 'I don't know where anything is.' He whispered the last six words because some feeling was getting caught in his throat. Hank exhaled and rubbed his forehead hard.

'I have a number you can call to talk to her,' Brian said.

'She doesn't want me to call,' Hank said, waving a hand.

Brian had to rise up a little to reach into his trouser pocket. He slid a small piece of paper across the table to Hank. 'In case you get worried,' he said. 'In case you need to call.'

Brian was tempted to signal the numbers with his fingers at Hank – somehow to get across the urgency that John had conveyed to him with those same gestures. 324-255-3312. 324-255-3312. He could still remember it by heart.

'Three-two-four, two-five-five, three-three-one-two,' he said to Hank.

The man before Father Brian looked like a child, with that mixture of wonder and alarm that children sometimes have. Hank took out his phone and typed into it.

'The wife of a guy, a guy in prison, a guy that Jenny was writing to. His wife,' Hank said, as though to himself, and pushed his coffee cup away just a little bit. 'I better go,' he said, and stood up. 'Thanks, Father.'

Father Brian watched Hank walk away, and the phone in his pocket vibrated. It was the God-phone, and a message had just come through. It was from Hank and it said: 'I want things the way they were before.' Father Brian's first thought was of Barbra Streisand's song 'The Way We Were', and he knew he would be damned to hear the song all day long, running through his head.

CHAPTER 41

'W HY'D HE SEND THE prayer cards to you then?' Jenny still didn't understand.

'It counts like money in prison, it's like money . . .' Shona trailed off. 'The problem was that they were raiding the cells every week, and it was the kind of thing that could get you a long extension to your sentence.'

'Oh,' Jenny managed to say, through her dizziness.

'Are you alright?' Shona asked.

'Well, it's just that . . .' Jenny couldn't find the right words.

Shona was shaking her head. 'I'm sorry, I can't help it.' Jenny watched Shona heave a breath and lick her top lip. 'It's like *Alice in Wonderland*, but with Box . . .' Was Shona going to laugh at her?

'Yeah,' said Jenny. And then: 'Wait, what box?'

Shona looked Jenny in the face, raised her eyebrows: 'Box. Suboxone. It's the stuff they give you to get you off drugs. It's like methadone.'

'Oh,' Jenny said. She felt sick.

'They soak paper in it, and pass it around that way.'

Jenny looked up at Shona. The lights inside weren't on, but there was a warm light coming through the window from the setting sun; it was like a candle without the flickering, Jenny thought.

'So, he was trying to ... It wasn't for you.' And tears came to Jenny's eyes. She could hear the jagged sounds of a true-crime programme coming through to the kitchen from another part in the house. A deep voice was telling a sinister story.

'No, it wasn't. And I was so mad at him. What was he thinking?' Shona sent breath through pursed lips. 'Then, you see, I visited him,' she said.

Jenny looked into Shona's eyes with a kind of thirst, wondering if she could somehow suck the images from them, to see what Shona had seen when she had visited John in jail.

'And you know, he was so worried about me, he knows how much you need points in jail. I told him, "You underestimate me, John. You underestimate me," I told him. I mean, I was about to get out.' She placed her wrist onto the edge of the table, with the hand in a loose fist. 'We didn't have contact for eighteen months, because, you know, you aren't allowed to. But, well, I guess once he had you on the line, he thought he could get something through to me. He says he did it because he wanted to say sorry, to help me, you know.'

'Yeah, that's what he told me too.'

'He told you that?'

Jenny's ears turned hot. 'He asked me ... he asked me what I thought a wife would want to hear. And that was a question I just . . . I just couldn't answer.' She wiped at her forehead. 'I didn't know who you were.'

'Yes, I suppose I can see that.'

'Actually –' Jenny had recovered now somewhat – 'I sort of thought you would be more like a person who was in jail. You know, like a little rough around the edges. Not . . . like you are.' And Jenny offered an open palm to Shona, as though she were giving her something.

'He told me about you too,' Shona said.

'Oh yeah?' Jenny said in a small voice, though she wasn't sure she wanted to hear the answer.

'He said you were smart. And funny. And a little paranoid. And that you were lonely.'

Jenny closed her eyes and took a breath, and at the edge of that breath she felt a rising of heartache, which she she pushed away with an exhale. The kitchen smelled like something delicious had been cooked there, and though Jenny wasn't hungry, she felt it was just the right smell for a kitchen. And there were notes of perfume, and the air was warm. And she realised that there was just air and smell and warmth. She looked at the walls: there were no button pads or speakers. And there was a kind of silence.

'Do you think that, like, we don't realise it, but our bodies can feel invisible electrical signals?'

Shona frowned. 'You're Christian, right?'

'Yeah – well, no. We go to church. So there's that.' Jenny looked up at Shona. 'Are you religious?'

'I guess you could say so,' Shona said. And she looked away, through the door into another room. 'Until the thing that happened. Now it's a little different.'

Jenny didn't know what to say. *The thing that happened*: was she supposed to know about that? 'I heard about your . . . incident,' she said. 'It sounds like some kind of very terrible mistake.'

'Hmm,' Shona agreed. 'That it was.'

Jenny thought that she had maybe never seen a face look so grave in all of her life. But the silence made her nervous, so she spoke. 'I still don't understand why you had to go to jail too.'

Shona's answer was loose and easy. 'Well, you see, I tried CPR on him. And I was the one who pushed him off John first . . . And we told them that. We told them everything. We told them that it was an accident. We told them that he had mental-health problems.'

'And they didn't believe you,' Jenny said.

'No CCTV, no neighbours, no nothing,' Shona replied.

Jenny rested her head on her palm and started rubbing her temples in small circles with her fingertips. Her stomach was grinding at something, bubbling with pockets of hollow distress.

'You're not well,' said Shona, standing up. 'Here,' she said. 'You can go and lie down in my mother's room. She's not here. I mean, she's not here anymore.' They walked to the back of the kitchen, where there was a little room with a single bed and a nightstand. 'She passed last year, and the room is empty.'

Jenny sat down, and Shona left, closing the door behind her and saying, 'Stay here.' Jenny wasn't sure whether to lie down in all her dirty clothes. She took off her shoes and socks, and sat there. The room was quiet and cool. A small crucifix hung in the corner on a wall, next to a cream-coloured vanity table. There was a red glass vase with a solitary flower in it. Jenny closed her eyes.

She could hear voices in the other room, beyond the kitchen. Shona and her sister were arguing, and Jenny couldn't hear all their words but she felt she knew the why.

'Spoons?' The sister's voice rose. And Jenny could hear the word 'dirty' repeated in among muffled syllables. 'We don't know her,' the sister said with a deep and emphatic voice. Jenny heard the sister say something about business, and Shona replied in deep, muted tones. A door closed, and the conversation was reduced to ascending tones and grumbles. Moments later, the sister was laughing. Jenny lay back on the bed and breathed in and out, trying to smooth out the catches in her lungs, and she smiled. They could laugh. It was funny. Jenny, the pen-pal low-grade addict. She was glad they found it funny – because it meant that they didn't hate her.

The conversation ended and the house went quiet; Jenny wondered whether they'd all gone out and left her there alone.

'OKAY, JENNY, HERE'S THE thing . . .' Shona was speaking quietly as she opened the door to the room without knocking.

'I – I'm just wondering if you've ever tried any of the box stuff?' Jenny interrupted, sitting up suddenly. 'I just – it's like, a very particular feeling.' Jenny held her hand to her mouth.

Shona had her hands on her hips now and was looking at Jenny with hard eyes.

'Now, listen to me,' she said. 'I do not have any Box and I have never put it to my lips.'

Shona looked so strong and powerful, with her long, slim fingers wrapped around a slim hip. She was now wearing a maroon velour jumpsuit, and she smelled of gardenia and lily of the valley.

Jenny sat on the edge of the bed and tensed her legs to stop them jiggling, but it didn't help – the jiggling was trapped inside, like something was plucking at her bones. She looked to the end of the bed at the small crucified Jesus and said:

'A life for a life. When I was little, I asked my mother – I don't know where I got the idea – but I asked her, "Momma, if you and me were dangling above the fires of hell, and the devil said to you that you had to choose whether you would fall into the fires or I would – who would you choose?" And my mother . . . Well, I guess it wasn't a question she was expecting, so she only looked deep into my eyes. She never answered the question – you know, if she would sacrifice herself for me. Die for me, I mean. I'm sure she would have said yes if she had understood that I was really asking for an answer. I know I would do that for my kids. I would just let go and burn if you could promise me that my death meant that they would live.'

She looked up at Shona, who said to her, 'Is there somewhere you can go, Jenny?'

'Just tell me what to do,' Jenny said, her voice low. Her heart was beating rapidly.

'I cannot believe you took that Box.'

Shona went off, and came back some time later with a plastic bag, from which she pulled a large bottle of ibuprofen, a pack of Imodium, some small cans of ginger ale and a sleeve of Saltine crackers. She locked the door to the backyard and put the key in her pocket.

'You can stay tonight. After that you're going to need a few weeks in rehab. Now you probably need to take a bath,' she said, and released a pair of grey pyjamas from her arm onto the bed. 'We wear indoor clothes here, so you can go ahead and change out of your outdoor clothes.' And she placed a small bag of Epsom salts onto the bed next to Jenny. 'You know you are going to need to taper whatever you have left, and get done with it,' Shona said. '*Tay-per*,' she repeated, like she was spelling it out for a puppet on *Sesame Street*.

CHAPTER 42

THEY NEEDED TO FIX the lawnmower, which had been left unused in the garden shed for a few years now. The boy that mowed all the lawns on Maple Drive had been taking care of theirs too, but now Hank wanted to mow his own lawn, and show the boys how you could get nice straight lines if you did it carefully. But the mower wouldn't start, so they took it to the garage to see if the mechanic could get it going.

'There are usually three things that go wrong with them,' the car mechanic said. 'Air, water and gas.' He hung his thumb on his thick and grimy forefinger: 'Either the carburettor needs to be replaced.' Middle finger: 'Or the fuel is old and needs to be siphoned off.' Pinkie finger: 'Or it's rusted and needs oil.'

Luke was impressed. 'Like the four elements,' he said to the guy, who didn't seem to understand. 'Earth, Wind, Fire, Water.' Luke showed the man his own four fingers.

'Right.' The man smiled at Luke. 'Smart kid,' he said, looking at Hank, sending a thumb in Luke's direction.

The garage was warm, and to Luke it smelled like earth. You just couldn't call a place like this dirty. The black smears on the walls, and the brown patches on the cement floor, they weren't dirt. They were more like paint, or medicine. This was a car hospital after all.

'So leave it with me and I'll take care of it for you by tomorrow,' the mechanic said.

Luke had walked a few steps over to a Cadillac that was propped on metal joists. He had never seen underneath a car before. He was careful not to stand directly underneath it because he guessed it could fall down. But he wanted to see the hard black guts of the engine.

Hank followed him over.

'Pretty cool.'

Luke was still looking, wondering if he could figure out any of the parts he could see.

'Yeah,' he said.

Hank put his hands on Luke's shoulders.

'You know, Dad . . .' Luke looked back up into his father's smiling face. 'These cars, they are running on fire . . . from ignition.'

'Right.'

'And that fire happens because dead beings are . . . they are flammable.'

'Dead beings?' Hank frowned, focusing his eyes hard on the boy looking up at him.

Luke's voice rose as he turned around to reassure him. 'Carbon. You know? It gets on fire. It's dead matter.'

He took his father's hand and held on to three fingers.

'All the cars, and all the planes, and all the electricity in all the houses,' he went on. 'It's all the burning of old lives. Old lives, giving their spark. To us. For our engines.'

'Right, okay, I see where you're . . . going with this. Carbon. Everything's carbon, right?'

'Yeah, but carbon – carbon is rotted-down and packed-down leaves and animals,' Luke said. 'From a very long time ago. Dried out.' He was making motions with his hands to explain the rotting, the packing down.

'You know, I'm not really sure, Luke,' Hank said with a slow voice, crouching down a little. 'I guess I could try to learn what gasoline, and car oil, and petroleum . . . how they're different. We could, I don't know, go to a library maybe. To find out about carbon.'

The mechanic laughed in the background, rubbing a wrench with a rag.

Luke put his hands in his pockets and his shoulders fell into place. 'That would be good.'

He pulled his father down. 'That guy probably doesn't know either,' he whispered. And they smiled at each other.

'Maybe we should come and tell him once we know,' Hank whispered back.

HANK AND LUKE WERE walking back to their car, and Hank opened the passenger door for Luke.

'Only Mom knows where the library card is.'

'She'll be back soon to tell us,' Hank said. 'Everything will be alright.' And Hank closed Luke's door for him. That was Luke's favourite thing to hear his parents say – that everything was going to be okay. He loved it because it made him feel safe, and guided.

In the car, on the way home, Luke showed Hank all the dead things he could see.

'There's those leaves . . . And that fallen branch . . . Don't forget that dirt is all dead matter – and that's everywhere. Soil here, soil over there.' Luke swiped his finger over his side of the dashboard. 'Dust. That's dead stuff. Cells, mostly.'

Hank was nodding. 'Yep, dead stuff,' he said.

'Actually, even our cells are always dying. Ever bite your fingernail? That's death too.'

'Yup.'

'So, it's everywhere,' Luke said happily, looking up at the sky.

'Heaven?' Hank said.

'Naw, just looking for, I don't know . . . vultures?'

Luke cackled, and Hank laughed too.

They drove on in silence. Luke could have told his father about more things that were dead. The electricity posts: dead trees. The tarmac: carbon-based. Slate roofing: from sediments of more dead matter. There were few cars on the streets, and Hank was driving with a slow gentleness. They rolled to a stop sign and Hank paused for a time.

'I mean, this car, it is fired with the remains of the dead, and they are giving us their fire – you see?'

NATASHA RANDALL

Hank looked at Luke, and smiled.

'It's a gift. To the living. So we can live.' Luke said.

'Right I can see that.' He pressed the gas pedal with gentle pressure and moved across the intersection. 'I had a yoga teacher once who talked about the circle of life. I know what you're saying.'

'It's like our ancestors left themselves to us,' Luke said, looking through his window.

332

CHAPTER 43

JENNY HADN'T BEEN TAKEN care of by a woman for a very long time. Shona made her eat graham crackers and drink ginger ale. Jenny followed her instructions.

'You're a nurse,' Jenny said to Shona, newly bathed but still sweating, sitting at the kitchen table late in the evening.

'I'm a medical technician,' said Shona. 'I administer mammograms. Or I used to.' Shona was at the sink, rinsing a glass. Jenny's mind skipped from a mammogram room to a prison cell and back to the kitchen where they were now having a snack. Rooms, rooms and rooms. Jenny was clean, but still wretched.

'I work in healthcare – or at least, it's kind of like healthcare,' Jenny said. 'It's plastic surgery. I guess that doesn't count.' She looked down at the fluffy slippers on her feet that Shona had lent her. How did they have new, spare clothes for Jenny to wear? Everything was so clean in this house.

Shona lifted another dripping glass out of the sink and put it on the drying rack. 'Right, John told me that, yes . . .' she said.

Jenny put a hand to her forehead and felt for wrinkles, rubbed her head. She wanted a sign from Shona that she liked her, that she didn't hate Jenny for being such a lowlife. Shona was so decent, but Jenny really didn't know her, standing there, rinsing glass after glass.

'The girls in Penn used to slip tiny strips of Box into pages of the Bible and let it melt, and then they just used to cram the whole page into their mouths. Eating up the word . . . They said Suboxone feels like love,' Shona said, her voice mixing with the rushing sound of the water coming from the faucet.

Jenny looked up, her hand falling from her brow to her cheek. 'Yes. Yes, it does.'

Love. The first tastes of the envelope glue had given Jenny the sensation of the rushing beginnings of romance. It was a feeling she hadn't experienced in some time, a feeling that had subsided with the drip-dripping of little offences over months and years of familiarity with Hank.

'But familiarity breeds contempt,' Jenny said, though she wasn't sure that Shona had heard her over the sound of the flowing faucet.

Shona told Jenny how everyone shared out the ibuprofen and the Imodium on Shona's cell block in jail. Jenny remembered that Shona had described jail as full of 'desperate friendships', and as she looked at Shona's lithe figure leaning towards the sink, Jenny thought she maybe understood the phrase better than she had before. She wanted to tell Shona how warming it was to be taken care of by a woman – but she wasn't sure if that would sound too intimate, or even, to her private horror, patronising.

'Orange love,' Jenny said, poking a finger at the ice cubes in her drink.

'The thing about pain pills is that they take away pain. Any kind of pain. It gets so that people can't even get out of bed for the pain that life becomes . . . compared to the high.' The water swished around the sink. 'And it takes away their anger. Makes a bad life seem okay.'

Jenny inhaled widely, and her ribs expanded so she could feel aching pinches along her sides. If you're lucky, Jenny thought, after the romantic love wears off, you admire each other, there is respect. And your lives have knitted together in such a way that there are shared goals.

'But it switches fast, and pretty soon a drug is taking you, you're not taking it.' Shona turned to her. 'It makes you into its carrier . . . Its, well, you know . . . bitch.'

For a while they were quiet. Jenny definitely felt like something's bitch.

'I wish I belonged to a tribe.' As soon as she said it, Jenny regretted it. Shona didn't react, she was still at the sink, tossing handfuls of water around the basin to clean it. The word 'tribe' sounded racist. What word should she have used, dammit?

'I mean, not *tribe*, but that we're all alone all the time, each woman,' Jenny muttered.

'No, I'm guessing you really did mean tribe,' Shona said, and turned around, drying her hands. Her face was open, she was offering a new sympathy to Jenny.

'Yes. Okay. Maybe I meant tribe.'

Shona was putting away the glasses. 'Look at me. All I have is a sister and a husband. And barely that.'

Jenny gulped her ginger ale and wiped her mouth.

'No tribe,' said Shona. 'No job, no tribe, a husband in jail, and a life on my conscience.'

'I don't want to stay too long. I'm just . . . I'm sorry.'

Shona didn't say anything right away but took the large ginger ale bottle from the counter and poured more into Jenny's glass. 'I just have this terrible feeling that something bad is going to happen,' Shona said, sitting down, resting the bottle on the table but not letting it go. 'There has to be a big payback when you take someone's life, accident or not.'

'But it wasn't your fault.'

'People always say that. But that . . . doesn't end up mattering. There's a festering on you and nothing heals it. Not even time in jail.'

Jenny took up the glass. 'Is John really a carpenter?'

'Yes.' Shona looked up at Jenny. 'He is a carpenter.'

The women nodded at each other. Jenny remembered Hank and all his bluster. She couldn't help remembering that the house was supposed to order milk.

'He once told me he was a good man who made bad choices,' Jenny said.

'Yeah.' Shona sounded unconvinced. Her elbows were propped on the table. She folded her long fingers into each other; her knuckles were sharp and pointy, her nails were so clean. 'But I don't know what is a choice anymore and what is not.'

*

THE NEXT MORNING, JENNY'S skin was crawling, and the only thing distracting her from it was the stomach pains. The house was quiet and she could hear kids playing outside, already on summer vacation. A small child wailed and a car beeped.

When Shona made her come to the kitchen, she winced, and walked bent over to the table.

'My stomach really hurts.'

'Yes. That happens. Drink the ginger ale.'

Jenny sat down and waited for Shona to tell her what to do. Jenny's cellphone pinged in the next room.

'I'm not answering those,' she told Shona. 'Because I don't know what to tell them.'

Shona was in front of her and holding her own phone.

'Well, you're going to rehab, so you could tell them that.'

'No, no, I can't tell them that. They don't know about the orange stuff.'

Shona put the phone to her ear.

'Yes, hello, I'm calling about placing a friend into your rehabilitation centre . . . Yes, she is experiencing addiction . . . Suboxone . . . Yes, I'm aware of the cost . . . Yes, I'll hold . . . You don't? . . . Yes, I'm aware of the cost . . . Yes, that does sound expensive . . . Yes, she is able to pay the cost.'

Shona put her hand to the phone. 'They want to be paid upfront – is that okay?'

'Yes,' said Jenny. She would use the money she got when her dad died last year.

'Yes, that does sound expensive . . . Ma'am, I know the cost, and, yes, she can pay it – are you telling me there is availability? . . . I see . . . Yes, I understand.'

She hung up. Jenny couldn't tell what the look on Shona's face meant.

'Apparently, they don't have any room,' she said, 'but I'm guessing that's based on the sound of my voice.'

Shona put her elbow on the table and fingers to the side of her head. 'I should have put you on the line . . .'

Jenny sipped the ginger ale, trying to work out what she could do. Her vision was throbbing, and Shona's face was pulsing with a fuzzy halo.

'Sorry for making you do all this,' she said.

'I know. I'll get you an appointment with a pain doctor. They can advise you on recovery,' Shona said, and picked up the phone again.

'I know you didn't ask for this.' Jenny cleared her voice. She was squirming, if only to feel the clothes against her skin, a kind of mild scratching that didn't quell the itch but made her feel as though she were doing something.

CHAPTER 44

Hank hadn't slept well since Jenny had left. He had programmed the house to say goodnight to him, but it hadn't really settled him down. 'Goodnight, Home,' he said to her before he turned off his bedside light. But it wasn't helping, and he lay there, the blanket up to his waist, his hands by his side. Maybe she would come back tomorrow. The yellow light from the street lamp came through the curtains and rested against the parallel ridges of his legs.

'Where are you?' he said. He reached for his phone by the lamp.

Where are you? Hank typed to Jenny. He scrolled through his emojis but couldn't find any that he wanted to use.

He held the screen in front of him and waited until the blue light on the screen went black. The darkness, tinged with yellow again, settled onto him, and into him.

During the night, there were only rustlings from Maple Drive, the business of raccoons conducted among gutters and trash cans.

A lost car made it to the end of the drive and swept its headlights across the houses as it turned around and headed back. A squeal of cats ripped the quiet, once.

Hank was asleep but he could hear some of these noises, and slowly he began to hear other noises. There were words. People were talking. There was a TV on somewhere. Or a radio. The chatter was pulling him up from sleep, and he awoke.

'*Fuck you*,' he heard, and the sound of light gunfire. The house panel was illuminated and the recording was coming from its speakers.

'Home, be quiet,' Hank said, and stood up. He could hear it down the hall too.

He stepped out into the hall and could see light flickering from the boys' room. He went to turn it off. He thought it must be a YouTube video or something that the boys had left playing by accident, but when he pushed the door open, he saw Jesse at the computer, headphones on, jerking around, playing Battlesite.

'Jesse,' Hank said, coming towards him.

'*Fucking die, bitch*,' he heard another voice say from the computer.

Jesse pushed back on his chair and said, 'Man, Dad, you scared me.'

Hank looked over at Luke, who was still asleep, and then back at Jesse.

'You're not supposed to be playing this – what the hell are you doing?'

'Uh, sorry,' Jesse said, but he was still thumbing rapidly at the controls in his hands.

'Put it down,' Hank said.

'Okay, wait, just a sec,' Jesse said, his eyes fixed on the screen.

Hank stepped forward and grabbed the handset. 'What's wrong with you?'

Jesse watched his avatar stumble and get killed. His eyes were shiny and bloodshot.

'Fuck, Dad, what did you just do?'

Hank wasn't angry, he was surprised. 'What's wrong with you? Why are you doing this?'

'Why are *you* doing this? You're supposed to be asleep,' Jesse hissed.

'And you have been banned from the internet.'

Hank got down and tugged on the wires at the back of the computer; he was considering carrying the whole screen out of the room.

'It's the middle of the fucking night, Jesse,' and he sounded plaintive. 'Why are you doing this?'

Jesse slammed his fist on the desk.

Luke sat up in bed. 'What?'

'Go to sleep, Luke,' snapped Jesse. 'You can't take it away,' he said to Hank.

'*What the fuck is going on, bro?*' A voice came from the computer.

Hank grabbed the headphones. 'Who the hell is this?' he said into the mouthpiece.

'*Whoa, Jesse dude, what the fuck – are you getting robbed or something?*' said the voice.

Jesse tried to grab the headset from Hank, but Hank wouldn't let go. He shouted towards the microphone: 'Dude, it's my old man!'

'*Oh fuck, dude. Okay, good luck.*'

'Who the hell is that?!' Hank asked Jesse.

'No one.'

'You are supposed to be sleeping.' Hank was confused. 'You look like a rabid animal.'

'All I wanted to do was build fast and go for a high kill. That's all I wanted! . . . You don't understand, Dad. This is like . . . You can't cut me off.'

The game was still swirling on the computer screen. Armoured figures were running through colourful lands, leaping and bounding over sheds.

Hank switched off the screen and the room went dark.

'Go to bed now.'

'I hate you,' Jesse seethed from his half of the room. '*You* are taking away the most important thing in my life.'

By the tiny green light at the back of the computer, Hank could see the wall socket and he unplugged the extension lead. The wires were too tangled to separate. He took the headphones and disconnected them, wrapped them in their own wires and kept them.

Hank sat on the computer chair and swivelled around to face the boys in the dark.

'Used to be that people had to survive, they had to fight to live. Hunt. Gather. And to fend off enemies. That was what we did. But we don't have to do that anymore . . .' he said, as if to the darkness itself.

The boys were quiet. Jesse had pulled the covers over himself and turned to face the wall. But Hank knew they were listening.

'Now, it's different. And you might not understand this, but those guys on Battlesite, the ones that are mowing each other down with bullets, it might not be real. But they are the ones we have to protect against now.'

'They're not real,' Jesse said from his corner. 'It's not real.'

'Jesse, it doesn't matter what's real and what's imaginary anymore. This stuff is . . . a game that isn't a game anymore.'

Walking down the hall, he wondered how the house had managed to pipe the sounds from Jesse's computer into her speakers. He was grateful to her though – it was like he had his very own Lassie, wordlessly alerting him that his son was in danger. He lay back down and put his hand, still holding Jesse's controls, onto Jenny's side of the bed.

CHAPTER 45

'D3 TO E-5!'

There was a booming chess game going on, and John was listening. Guys had money on this game so lots of them were shouting interference.

'Nf3 to Nc6!'

'C4? Should be Nf6!'

John heard someone call out 'Bitch-fool!' and he smiled. It was a bad move, and John knew it too, because everyone on the block was following it, recreating it with makeshift pieces in their own cells. The figures of John's chess set were made from the cardboard cylinders of toilet rolls that were wetted and moulded into various shapes. The rook was particularly beautiful, as majestic as a tiny sandcastle, and it leaned slightly to the side, as though it had some seismic history.

John knew the sounds of prison now. He could pick out the voices of the players. Other times though, when there wasn't a game on, he could only follow the consonants and vowels of the cell block. Most words ended in the sound of *uh*. All the words sounded angry.

'Bi-foo!' was what 'Bitch-fool' sounded like.

And there were other outbursts:

'Peesh-a. Wa-a. Munufuh!'

'Sua-fuh!'

'Boom-bbat-bimbun! *Mo'fuh*.'

There was plenty of mocking laughter ringing along the metallic grids of the cell block, punctuated by thumps and bangs. Doors slammed with a clamp and clip.

JOHN LAY DOWN ON his bunk. The walls of his cell were whitish, patchy – one patch was shaped like a stout cow, and another looked like a sack of fighting cats. He could watch them like they were TV if he was chilled enough. Not today though. The game was too hot and the yelling was too loud.

His cellmate, Sergei, didn't know how to play chess and John had offered to explain it, but the boy was too depressed to take an interest. He had only been in jail a month, and never before, so he was focused on getting out. He sat on his bunk, scrawling notes and letters to his lawyers for hours a day, ripping up paper, rewriting the letters; he was looking for ways to appeal his sentence of assault and robbery. Did John think that he had a chance? He wanted stories of successful appeals. John had none. He told him to wait it out. The guy was lucky to have landed in a cell with John. Other cellies would have him whooped by now.

John was lucky too though; Sergei was clean, picked up after himself and had routine. He'd been less lucky previously with the grumpy old arsonist who farted and slung racial slurs around the place from morning to night. And the crackhead with DTs who vomited and shat all over the place the first few days. Then there was the Chinese fellow who didn't speak any words of English except 'cunt-fuck' (which applied to people he didn't like) and 'crapola' (which he used to refer to any food or drink that came into the cell). In the three years he'd been held there, John hadn't managed to get a single cell – they were reserved for the psychotic or the bed-wetters. A lot of guys tried to act psychotic starting fights and freaking out, in order to get a single cell, but John couldn't pull off the performance. Some really were psychotic too, and the true test of a good cellie was whether you could actually go to sleep at night. Sometimes you just didn't dare, and slept with your ears pricked, your fists over your face.

John had earned some perks by being well behaved, including admittance to the wood-shop. He made spoons there, wooden spoons, that were sold in prison gift shops, and other places, too. In actual fact he wasn't sure where they went, but they were functional spoons and he hoped, every time he finished one, that someone, somewhere, would be soon stirring up some soup with his spoon.

The wood was still green when he worked it. It was fresh and wet. In that way, it was still living wood when he started in on it. He could feel the life in the wood – it was life from outside and it smelled like growth. It shifted and swelled as he whittled. He had learned: you have to carve with the grain. But grain direction is not obvious right away. If you carve against the grain, you will get splintering, or tear-off. You have to release the spoon from the wood. He often thought that what he was actually making was mountains of little wood-chips. And then after a time he would look into his hands, and he was holding a spoon. If you got carried away, you could whittle until it was a slip of a spoon, and no good to anyone; too fragile, it will snap at the neck.

The spoons kept him going. He would hold a spoon blank, and sense a future there, a new suggestion of a spoon. The blank is a flat block, a spoon-ish shape, which you could never use because all the soup would just slip right off it. It's a spoon with no use. A pretend spoon. A fetal spoon. It was really just a block of wood until you put a knife to it. He was telling Sergei about it, trying to coax the guy into understanding that you had to make something of your life in prison while you were there or it would just eat away at you. You never know what spoon you're going to get, he told him, until the chips start to fall. Shapes appear in the lines of fibre. Like those clouds that form and re-form the soft gestures of extinct animals. Sometimes a spoon will tell you a story, a wood-smile will turn to a wood-frown, or something in the wood winks at you. He never found out what Jenny saw in the face of the spoon he sent her. When he made it, it was a kind face, just appeared like that, a soft profile smiling at the side. It had eased out from its spoon blank like a cartoon. A cheekbone and a high brow.

The shapes emerge gently from a spoon but the beginning is brutal. First you gouge twice and pull out a piece of wood that looks like an eye, an almond. Then you widen and deepen, in turns. You can ruin a spoon if you go too far, he explained, although Sergei didn't appear to care. Sometimes John would gather up a handful of wood-chip eyes and bring them back to the cell; he would put them in his pillowcase because the smell of wood took him away from the banging world of the jail. He offered some to Sergei, who took them silently up to his top bunk.

The spoon for Jenny had smiled at him, but it was an enigmatic smile, half formed, and he wasn't sure if she'd liked it. She hadn't said. In fact, their correspondence had dwindled after his efforts to apologise hadn't worked. He had written twice to tell her that mothers certainly would defend their babies to the death, and that he understood that. And he said he was sorry for telling her about prison wives. She had replied to that but her note was short: 'You could have called them "slaves" or even "dogs" but you call those violently violated and debased men in your prison "wives". Why do you think that is so? –Jenny.'

He had given Shona a spoon too, when she had come to visit him after getting out. Shona understood the spoon better than Jenny, for she had seen many of his carvings before. Where they were now, all the little figurines of waves and dolphins he had made, nobody knew their belongings had been removed from their apartment when they were arrested, and the landlord said he didn't know who was responsible. Which can't have been true, but he wouldn't return their calls.

Shona had held the spoon so carefully when he gave it to her. She knew to look into the wood; she smiled. 'I'm glad you're getting to do this,' she said to him. And he put his hand up to the glass of the visiting booth, wanting so much to touch her, to feel her. She matched his fingers with her own and told him that he was going to be okay. 'You should get your GED while you're in there, Jayj.' She called him Jayj because his initials were J. J. and she had shortened it to Jayj over the years. 'Learn a new skill,' she said.

He knew that Jenny had stayed a night with Shona, that she had taken the Box he had given her to pass on. And he felt guilty about that. But also, he hadn't expected her to be so hapless. What on earth possessed her to lick that envelope? He had so carefully thought through his plan – Jenny only used a PO box and he thought she would be smart enough to just forward his prayer cards. He thought of her as 'sensible Jenny', but she turned out to be as wacky as a jester from a fairytale. Shona said that Jenny had called her husband and made him promise to turn the high-tech talking house off – those were her conditions for returning home. That was a strange bargain, but John knew about bargains. He had been bargaining with the fates ever since he had caused his neighbour to die. Father Brian told him that in the Bible, if you accidentally killed someone, you would be allowed to go and live in one of the 'cities of refuge' for accidental killers, so that they could escape the 'blood vengeance' that the law allowed outside these cities. The cities of refuge were places of sanctuary, and their residents could be released only in the unhappy event of the death of the high priest – an event of extreme atonement, said Father Brian. But that didn't matter, Father Brian said; what mattered was that it was very hard to live among people when you had caused a death. He understood John, and he understood it when John told him that he wouldn't ever be able to shake the ominous feeling that dogged him.

Prison was supposed to be a place of atonement – but it was no city of refuge, it was just a gathering of catastrophic lives. John didn't feel lonely at his roots, because he had Shona. And they had done this thing together, so they had some kind of shared karma. She would wait for him, three more years.

He showed her the tattoo he had with her name on it, turning slightly so she could make it out through the thick prison fibreglass.

'I didn't risk trying to get a picture of you,' he told her, pulling up a sleeve, cradling the telephone in his neck. 'Because the skill is minimal,' he said. The tattoos in jail are never as clean as the ones you can get in a parlour. The needles are blunt – they're not needles at all really, but the sharpened tip of the plastic sheath of a Bic biro pen. The tattoo is drawn in blood and then inked straight away, but the lines bleed and the skin cells aren't split nicely, so the lines are thick and fuzzy.

But there it was: SHONA, written in swirly, curly letters. He let her see it, and then put his hand over it and looked down at his hand. 'I'm glad I did it,' he said into the telephone receiver. His deep voice was soft, like he was singing her a song.

CHAPTER 46

SOMEONE WAS WEARING VERY strong perfume. It smelled like lemony roses dipped in brandy. Father Brian had such a sensitive nose that a strong perfume could make him sneeze. He had a hankie, but Communion that day would be testing. You cannot sneeze while administering the sacrament.

As he moved along the kneeling line of parishioners, past the various smells they had applied to themselves, Father Brian breathed through loose lips. His nose just wasn't up to it.

He was glad to see the Tinkley family lined up at his altar rail. He came first to the boy Jesse, all elbows and limbs and spiky hair angles, who was trying to remain aloof at the same time as being on his knees.

'The body of Christ,' said the priest, and Jesse answered 'Uh-huh', letting Father Brian place the round wafer in his hand. The priest pressed it down into the boy's palm gently with his thumb.

Young Luke was still soft and edgeless, and his body moved with the innocence of an animal. His hands were small and held aloft, open and flat. As Father Brian leaned down towards him, Luke switched hands, left on top of right, then right on top of left. He looked up at Father Brian with the question about hand hierarchy in his eyes, but the priest just held the wafer in two fingers over the boy's head and curled his remaining fingers over Luke's neat haircut. 'The blessings of the Father . . .'

Next was Hank, his back as straight as a pillar, big hands cupped in a gesture of surety, like he was going to catch water from a faucet. Kids' hands could so easily open to flat, but adults' hands were always furled. We grasp and grasp, Brian thought, and our hands become claws.

'The body of Christ,' he said, looking into the man's face. He knew it was hard for men to supplicate, and he could see the look on Hank's face. It said: 'Let's not make a big deal of this.' Hank dropped a sharp 'Amen' and Father Brian moved on.

That was three males in a row. Father Brian had been keeping count. Father Adam had asked him if the numbers of men and women were equal in his services, and Brian had assured him that they were. But he began to have doubts once he started trying to count heads. He had never actually managed to get through a service and do a full sample – he had too many words to speak, and sounds to sing, to keep track of the bobbing heads – but the counting he had managed told him that there were many more women in his pews than men. Well, more mothers, anyway.

Father Brian shuffled to the right, and stood before Jenny.

'Jenny,' he said. 'The body of Christ.'

She looked tired. She was wearing make-up, and her face was tinted chalky amber with it. It was the first time he'd seen her since she came back from her time away. She had been helping John's wife to get back on her feet after prison. When Brian had called them, Jenny explained that Shona was having difficulties, and that there was no one else that could help.

She took the sacrament and placed it on her tongue. 'M-mm,' she said, looking forward at the folds of his cassock and red vestments.

He had smiled when he first noticed Jenny that Sunday during his sermon. Her gaze was fixed on him, and it had been slightly unnerving. Vaguely flattering too. Most other people looked around, looked down, or whispered things to their kids. The sermon that day had been about Mary the mother of God. She was a vessel, he told them. She was the Holy Mother. She came to Jesus when he was on the cross. In fact, there were three Marys there that day, he told them. There was Mary, the mother, and another lady called Mary who was her sister-in-law, and then there was Mary Magdalene. Mary was a very popular name in Biblical times. Something like thirty per cent of women would have been called Mary, he said. Or in fact, Mariam, which was the Jewish version of the name. Because Mary was Jewish, like Jesus was Jewish, he reminded them.

He reached up and put a finger into the side of his collar, hoping to loosen it a little without the congregation noticing.

Jenny was still looking at him intently, and in the glimpses he took of her, he saw an expression he couldn't read – was it pain?

'Mary . . . is the fusion of opposites, of God and humanity, of body and spirit. We hear about this in the Magnificat, where we learn that the humble are lifted up and the proud are dismissed, and that hunger can lead to satisfaction.'

At this point, he looked into the rest of his congregation to see if he was losing them. Not that he could have done much of anything about it – he had to read his sermons word for word. He had tried sometimes to improvise, but then his enthusiasm for the digressions were so bouncing that he struggled to return to the theme of his sermon. Today he could feel the heat and the bodily mass of the congregation. They were one large, shining, breathing beast that he was trying to corral towards the cross. Sometimes he could enthral them if he paused between statements:

'Through Mary, we are given the future, a coming together of the divine and the human.'

But the light in his pulpit made him sweat. Sometimes he remembered to switch it off before he climbed the small swirl of stairs. Today he forgot, and the heat was making him feel slightly defeated.

'Mary is only reported speaking on four occasions in the Bible, but her presence shows us humility, obedience, compassion,' he said. 'She is the mother to all of us.'

Father Brian smiled at the parishioners, and tried the only other oratory trick he knew, which was to vary the register of his voice, as if singing a psalm.

'She brings to us, in her earthly womb . . .' his voice rose. He looked up, and saw Jenny was still transfixed . . . 'the awesome expanse of heaven.' He brought his closing words down like the baritone in an opera.

AFTER THE SERVICE, THE Tinkleys were headed in the car to the sushi restaurant, but on the way there Jenny asked Hank to stop at the drugstore.

'You feeling okay?' Hank asked her.

'Yeah, I'm okay, I just need something. I'll go inside.'

'Like what?' he asked.

'Just something for ladies,' she said, slipping out of the car.

The boys stirred in their seats. 'Mom, get us some candy!' Jesse called to her.

AT THE PHARMACY COUNTER, Jenny passed her prescription to Mr Salton.

'Well, hello there, neighbour,' he said, taking the slip from her hand.

'Hi, hello,' she said.

'Now, let me see,' he said, looking at the paper. He quickly assumed the gravitas of pharmacists that Jenny knew. 'I think we have some of this,' he said, rubbing his chin and turning to the storeroom. 'Give me just a moment.'

The pain consultant that Shona had found for Jenny assured her that Suboxone was kept in most pharmacies these days. And it wasn't like methadone, you didn't have to take each dose in front of the pharmacist. She said to him that she had been given Suboxone by a friend to help with terrible migraines. He nodded, wrote her a prescription and told that the last two milligrams were the hardest to kick. 'Some people find Suboxone withdrawal to be worse than with heroin,' he said, tearing the sheet off his pad and passing it to her.

'ARE YOU TAKING THIS for——?' Mr Salton was asking.

'I have pain,' Jenny interrupted, scratching her arm while pointing to a leg.

'I see,' he replied. 'Well, a few questions then.' He held the boxes in his right hand.

'Are you pregnant?'

'No.'

'Have to ask that . . .' And then: 'Side effects are nausea, rashes, sleep disturbances,' he said, looking at the packets.

'Yes, I know,' said Jenny.

'And finally, some advice on taking it,' he said. 'Now, you'll want to moisten your mouth first, so that the film strip can dissolve.'

'Okay,' Jenny said.

'You hold the small, square strip between your thumb and fore-finger – by the edges. Make sure your hands are clean and dry so they don't stick to it. Then place it under your tongue to the side of your frenulum.' Mr Salton put a finger and thumb up to his mouth and shifted his lower jaw to the side in an effort to show her what he meant. 'It's a sublingual strip. Takes about a minute to start dissolving. Don't chew or swallow anything until the strip has fully dissolved. Just stay quiet.'

'Alright.'

'Alright then.'

Mr Salton slipped the neat pile of slim boxes into a white paper bag and folded the top edge. He held up the bag at its ends with both hands and placed it into her waiting palms.

'For you,' he said, his fingers still releasing the edge of the bag. 'Take as prescribed. One film, once a day.'

Jenny held the package.

'Tastes like orange,' he said, his clean hands folded loosely on the counter, a frown lightly forming on his brow.

Jenny bowed her head, and was about to turn and leave when she remembered she had to pay for the medicine he was dispensing to her. It wasn't a gift – it cost two hundred and fifty-nine dollars – it was just a little deliverance from a neighbour.

ACKNOWLEDGEMENTS

I would like to thank many people for many things— for both practical and intangible support: my family, Gemma Reeves, Jane Saotome, Gerard Woodward, Tessa Hadley, Tim Liardet, Fay Weldon, Lily Dunn, Wylie O'Sullivan, Pom Lampson, Lucy Kelaart, Malika McCosh, Jasmine Palmer, Seren Adams, Caroline Dawnay, Charlotte Nation, Emma Giffard, Luke Palmer, Karla Neblett, Jemma Hillenbrand, Henry Rothwell, Ana Iberi and Sophie Morgan. Some have offered a casual comment that had immeasurable beneficial effect. Many of these people worked hard in support of this book, reading drafts and helping me to find the peaks and troughs. My gratitude, in particular, goes to my editor, Jon Riley, and my agent, Anna Webber. Thank you also to all the good people in my midst.

A NOTE ON THE TYPE

In 1924, Monotype based this face on types cut by Pierre Simon Fournier c. 1742. These types were some of the most influential designs of the eighteenth century, being among the earliest of the transitional style of typeface, and were a stepping stone to the more severe modern style made popular by Bodoni later in the century. They had more vertical stress than the old style types, greater contrast between thick and thin strokes and little or no bracketing on the serifs.